William Shakespeare, William J. Rolfe

Shakespeare's History of the Life and Death of King John

William Shakespeare, William J. Rolfe

Shakespeare's History of the Life and Death of King John

ISBN/EAN: 9783337388263

Printed in Europe, USA, Canada, Australia, Japan

Cover: Foto ©Andreas Hilbeck / pixelio.de

More available books at **www.hansebooks.com**

SHAKESPEARE'S

HISTORY OF

THE LIFE AND DEATH

OF

KING JOHN.

EDITED, WITH NOTES,

BY

WILLIAM J. ROLFE, A.M.,

FORMERLY HEAD MASTER OF THE HIGH SCHOOL, CAMBRIDGE, MASS.

WITH ENGRAVINGS.

NEW YORK:

HARPER & BROTHERS, PUBLISHERS.

FRANKLIN SQUARE.

1887.

ENGLISH CLASSICS.

EDITED BY WM. J. ROLFE, A.M.

Illustrated.   16mo, Cloth, 56 cents per volume; Paper, 40 cents per volume.

SHAKESPEARE'S WORKS.

The Merchant of Venice.
Othello.
Julius Cæsar.
A Midsummer-Night's Dream.
Macbeth.
Hamlet.
Much Ado about Nothing.
Romeo and Juliet.
As You Like It.
The Tempest.
Twelfth Night.
The Winter's Tale.
King John.
Richard II.
Henry IV.   Part I.
Henry IV.   Part II.
Henry V.
Richard III.
Henry VIII.
King Lear.

The Taming of the Shrew.
All 's Well that Ends Well.
Coriolanus.
The Comedy of Errors.
Cymbeline.
Antony and Cleopatra.
Measure for Measure.
Merry Wives of Windsor.
Love's Labour 's Lost.
Two Gentlemen of Verona.
Timon of Athens.
Troilus and Cressida.
Henry VI.   Part I.
Henry VI.   Part II.
Henry VI.   Part III.
Pericles, Prince of Tyre.
The Two Noble Kinsmen.
Venus and Adonis, Lucrece, etc.
Sonnets.
Titus Andronicus.

GOLDSMITH'S SELECT POEMS.
GRAY'S SELECT POEMS.

PUBLISHED BY HARPER & BROTHERS, NEW YORK.

☞ *Any of the above works will be sent by mail, postage prepaid, to any part of the United States, on receipt of the price.*

CONTENTS

KING JOHN.

INTRODUCTION

TO

THE LIFE AND DEATH OF KING JOHN.

I. THE HISTORY OF THE PLAY.

King John was first printed in the folio of 1623, where it is entitled " The life and death of King Iohn," and occupies pages 1–22 in the division of " Histories." It is the only one of the undoubted works of Shakespeare which is not entered in the Registers of the Stationers' Company. Internal evidence shows pretty clearly that it was written at about the same time as *Richard II.*; and it is probable that it

followed rather than preceded that play.   We cannot be far
wrong if, with Furnivall, we assign it to the year 1595.   Dowden (*Shaks. Primer*, p. 90) also says : "The chief point of
difference with respect to form is that *Richard II.* contains
a much larger proportion of rhymed verse, and on the whole
we shall not perhaps err in regarding *Richard II.* as the earlier of the two."   Prof. Ward (*Eng. Dram. Lit.* vol. i. p. 368)
remarks that "the play evidently belongs to the same period of Shakspere's productivity as *Richard II.*, and may be
dated about the same time ; probably before the body of
those in which he mainly followed Holinshed."   Fleay makes
the date 1596, seeing in i. 2. 66–75, as certain other critics
have done, an allusion to the fleet sent against Spain in that
year.   He believes also that " the laments of Constance for
Arthur's death (iii. 4) were inspired by Shakespeare's sorrow
for his heir and only son, Hamnet, whom he lost August 12,
1596."   As it is included in Meres's list in his *Palladis
Tamia* (see *M. N. D.* p. 9), it must have been put upon the
stage before the publication of that book in September, 1598.

II. THE SOURCES OF THE PLOT.

King John varies from the facts of history more than any
other of the "Histories," being founded upon an earlier play
published in 1591 with the following title-page, of which
Halliwell gives a fac-simile :

THE | Troublesome Raigne | of *Iohn* King of *England,*
with the dis- | *couerie of King* Richard Cordelions | Base
sonne (vulgarly named, The Ba- | stard Fawconbridge): *also
the* | death of King *Iohn* at *Swinstead* | *Abbey.* | *As it was
(sundry times) publikely acted by the* | *Queenes Maiesties Play-
ers, in the ho-* | *nourable Citie of* | London.   Imprinted at
London for *Sampson Clarke,* | *and are to be solde at his shop,
on the backe-* | side of the *Royall Exchange.* | 1591.

In the year 1611 this play was reprinted "by Valentine
Simmes for John Helme," with "Written by W. Sh." added

to the title-page ; and in a third edition, printed " by Aug :
Mathewes for Thomas Dewe," and brought out in 1622, it
was ascribed to " W. Shakespeare." This was doubtless a
mere trick of the publishers to help the sale of the book, as
the style proves conclusively that Shakespeare had no part
in its authorship.

While the poet follows this old play in the outlines of his
plot, and occasionally borrows its language, his real indebt-
edness to it is comparatively slight. " The main incidents
are the same, but Shakspere elevates and almost re-creates
the characters ; for the most eloquent and poetical passages
no original is to be found in the old play. The character
of the king grows more darkly treacherous in Shakspere's
hands : barely a hint of the earlier author suggested the
scene, so powerful and so subtle, in which John insinuates
to Hubert his murderous desires ; the boyish innocence of
Arthur, and the pathos of his life, become real and living as
they are dealt with by the imagination of Shakspere ; Constance is no longer a fierce and ambitious virago, but a passionate sorrowing mother ; Faulconbridge is ennobled by a
manly tenderness and a purer patriotism. Shakspere depicts,
with true English spirit, the ambition, the political greed, the
faithlessness, the sophistry, of the court of Rome ; but he
wholly omits a ribald scene of the old play, in which the
licentiousness of monasteries is exposed to ridicule " (Dowden).

Gervinus, after remarking that " Shakespeare entirely followed this older work in the historical matter," goes on to
say : " Artistically considered, he took in the outward design
of the piece, blended both parts into one, adhered to the
leading features of the characters, and finished them with
finer touches. . . . The older *King John* is a rough but not
a bad piece, from which the poet could have borrowed many
happy poetical and historical features. It possesses the old
stiffness, and is intermingled with Latin passages according

to the earlier custom, yet it is freer from the extravagances
of the old school, from which these historical subjects in a
great measure rescued us.   The diffuseness in the second
part is heavy, and here Shakespeare with excellent tact has
remedied the evil by abridgment.   The characters are de-
signed in a manner suitable for our poet's use, but they are
far less sustained than his.   For the mere sake of speaking,
speeches are put into the mouth of Faulconbridge which are
inconsistent with his nature.   Arthur, who once speaks in
the childish tone of his age, loses it again, and in the pathetic scene with Hubert is a precocious disputant.   How far
Shakespeare excelled his best contemporary poets in fine
feeling is evinced by his revised work as compared with this
older play.   Shakespeare delineates his Faulconbridge (and
himself in him) rigidly and bitterly enough as a good Protestant in the base treatment of Popish arrogance.   In suitable passages he gives full vent to the indignation of the
English at Popish rule and intrigue, encroachment and oppression, which at that time was readily listened to in London.   But he did not go so far as to make a farce of Faulconbridge's extortions from the clergy ; . . . to our poet's
impartial mind the dignity of the clergy, nay, even the con-
templativeness of cloister-life, was a matter too sacred for
him to introduce it in a ridiculous form into the seriousness
of history.   There are many similar crudenesses in the old
piece, which Shakespeare has likewise effaced.   At the marriage treaty between Lewis and Blanche, the poor Constance
is present ; at the indelicate discussion (i. 1) between the
brothers Faulconbridge, their mother is introduced ; the illegitimate son subsequently threatens his own mother with
death if she does not confess the truth to him : this lack of
tenderness does not occur in Shakespeare.   In another respect also the accurate comparison of the two works is of
the greatest interest, if we would watch Shakespeare's depth
in the treatment of his poetry, as it were, in the work and in

the creation itself. In many passages of the old play, where motives, delineation of character and actions, lay before him in ample prolixity, he has gathered the contents of whole scenes compactly into a single sentence or a single insinuation ; he disdains superabundant perspicuity, and leaves to the actor, the spectator, and the reader something for his own mind to find out and to add."

III. CRITICAL COMMENTS ON THE PLAY.

[*From Mrs. Jameson's " Characteristics of Women." *]

Constance of Bretagne was the only daughter and heiress of Conan IV., Duke of Bretagne ; her mother was Margaret of Scotland, the eldest daughter of Malcolm IV. But little mention is made of this princess in the old histories ; but she appears to have inherited some portion of the talent and spirit of her father, and to have transmitted them to her daughter. The misfortunes of Constance may be said to have commenced before her birth, and took their rise in the misconduct of one of her female ancestors. Her great-grandmother Matilda, the wife of Conan III., was distinguished by her beauty and imperious temper, and not less by her gallantries. Her husband, not thinking proper to repudiate her during his lifetime, contented himself with disinheriting her son Hoel, whom he declared illegitimate ; and bequeathed his dukedom to his daughter Bertha, and her husband Allan the Black, Earl of Richmond, who were proclaimed and acknowledged Duke and Duchess of Bretagne.

Prince Hoel, so far from acquiescing in his father's will, immediately levied an army to maintain his rights, and a civil war ensued between the brother and sister, which lasted for twelve or fourteen years. Bertha, whose reputation was not much fairer than that of her mother Matilda, was succeeded by her son Conan IV. He was young, and of a feeble, vacillating temper, and after struggling for a few years

* American ed. (Boston, 1857), p. 358 fol.

against the increasing power of his uncle Hoel, and his own rebellious barons, he called in the aid of that politic and ambitious monarch, Henry II. of England. This fatal step decided the fate of his crown and his posterity; from the moment the English set foot in Bretagne, that miserable country became a scene of horrors and crimes—oppression and perfidy on the one hand, unavailing struggles on the other. Ten years of civil discord ensued, during which the greatest part of Bretagne was desolated, and nearly a third of the population carried off by famine and pestilence. In the end, Conan was secured in the possession of his throne by the assistance of the English king, who, equally subtle and ambitious, contrived in the course of this warfare to strip Conan of most of his provinces by successive treaties, alienate the Breton nobles from their lawful sovereign, and at length render the Duke himself the mere vassal of his power.

In the midst of these scenes of turbulence and bloodshed was Constance born, in the year 1164. The English king consummated his perfidious scheme of policy, by seizing on the person of the infant princess, before she was three years old, as a hostage for her father. Afterwards, by contracting her in marriage to his third son, Geoffrey Plantagenet, he ensured, as he thought, the possession of the duchy of Bretagne to his own posterity.

From this time we hear no more of the weak, unhappy Conan, who, retiring from a fruitless contest, hid himself in some obscure retreat; even the date of his death is unknown. Meanwhile Henry openly claimed the duchy in behalf of his son Geoffrey and the Lady Constance; and their claims not being immediately acknowledged, he invaded Bretagne with a large army, laid waste the country, bribed or forced some of the barons into submission, murdered or imprisoned others, and, by the most treacherous and barbarous policy, contrived to keep possession of the country he had thus seized. However, in order to satisfy the Bretons, who were attached to the race of their ancient sovereigns, and to give some colour to his usurpation, he caused Geoffrey and Constance to be solemnly crowned at Rennes as Duke and Duchess of Bretagne. This was in the year 1169, when Constance was five and Prince Geoffrey about eight years old. His father, Henry, continued to rule, or rather to ravage and oppress, the country in their name for about fourteen years, during which period we do not hear of Constance. She appears to have been kept in a species of constraint as a hostage rather than a sovereign; while her husband Geoffrey, as he grew up to manhood, was too much engaged in keeping the Bretons in order, and disputing his rights with his father, to think about the completion of his union with Constance, although his sole title to the dukedom was properly and legally in right of his wife. At length, in 1182, the nuptials were formally celebrated, Constance being then in her nineteenth year. At the same time, she was recognized as Duchess of Bretagne *de son chef* (that is, in her own right) by two acts of legislation, which are still preserved among the records of Bretagne, and bear her own seal and signature.

Those domestic feuds which embittered the whole life of Henry II., and at length broke his heart, are well known. Of all his sons, who were in continual rebellion against him, Geoffrey was the most undutiful and the most formidable: he had all the pride of the Plantagenets, all the warlike accomplishments of his two elder brothers, Henry and Richard; and was the only one who could compete with his father in talent, eloquence, and dissimulation. No sooner was he the husband of Constance, and in possession of the throne of Bretagne, than he openly opposed his father; in other words, he maintained the honour and interests of his wife and her unhappy country against the cruelties and oppression of the English plunderers.* About three years

* *Vide* Daru, *Histoire de Bretagne.*

after his marriage, he was invited to Paris for the purpose of concluding a league, offensive and defensive, with the French king; in this journey he was accompanied by the Duchess Constance, and they were received and entertained with royal magnificence. Geoffrey, who excelled in all chivalrous accomplishments, distinguished himself in the tournaments which were celebrated on the occasion; but unfortunately, after an encounter with a French knight celebrated for his prowess, he was accidentally flung from his horse, and trampled to death in the lists before he could be extricated.

Constance, being now left a widow, returned to Bretagne, where her barons rallied round her, and acknowledged her as their sovereign. The Salique law did not prevail in Bretagne, and it appears that in those times the power of a female to possess and transmit the rights of sovereignty had been recognized in several instances; but Constance is the first woman who exercised those rights in her own person. She had one daughter, Elinor, born in the second year of her marriage, and a few months after her husband's death she gave birth to a son. The States of Bretagne were filled with exultation; they required that the infant prince should not bear the name of his father—a name which Constance, in fond remembrance of her husband, would have bestowed on him—still less that of his grandfather Henry; but that of Arthur, the redoubted hero of their country, whose memory was worshipped by the populace. Though the Arthur of romantic and fairy legends—the Arthur of the Round Table, had been dead for six centuries, they still looked for his second appearance among them, according to the prophecy of Merlin; and now, with fond and short-sighted enthusiasm, fixed their hopes on the young Arthur as one destined to redeem the glory and independence of their oppressed and miserable country. But in the very midst of the rejoicings which succeeded the birth of the prince, his grandfather,

Henry II., demanded to have the possession and guardianship of his person; and on the spirited refusal of Constance to yield her son into his power, he invaded Bretagne with a large army, plundering, burning, devastating the country as he advanced. He seized Rennes, the capital, and having by the basest treachery obtained possession of the persons both of the young duchess and her children, he married Constance forcibly to one of his own favorite adherents, Randal de Blondeville, Earl of Chester, and conferred on him the duchy of Bretagne, to be held as a fief of the English crown.

The Earl of Chester, though a brave knight, and one of the greatest barons of England, had no pretensions to so high an alliance; nor did he possess any qualities or personal accomplishments which might have reconciled Constance to him as a husband. He was a man of diminutive stature and mean appearance, but of haughty and ferocious manners and unbounded ambition.* In a conference between this Earl of Chester and the Earl of Perche, in Lincoln Cathedral, the latter taunted Randal with his insignificant person, and called him contemptuously "*Dwarf.*" "Sayst thou so!" replied Randal; "I vow to God and our Lady, whose church this is, that ere long I will seem to thee high as that steeple!" He was as good as his word, when, on ascending the throne of Brittany, the Earl of Perche became his vassal.

We cannot know what measures were used to force this degradation on the reluctant and high-spirited Constance; it is only certain that she never considered her marriage in the light of a sacred obligation, and that she took the first opportunity of legally breaking from a chain which could scarcely be considered as legally binding. For about a year she was obliged to allow this detested husband the title of Duke of Bretagne, and he administered the government with-

* *Vide* Sir Peter Leycester's *Antiquities of Chester.*

B

out the slightest reference to her will, even in form, till 1189,
when Henry II. died, execrating himself and his undutiful
children.   Whatever great and good qualities this monarch
may have possessed, his conduct in Bretagne was uniformly
detestable.   Even the unfilial behaviour of his sons may be
extenuated; for while he spent his life, and sacrificed his
peace, and violated every principle of honour and humanity
to compass their political aggrandizement, he was guilty of
atrocious injustice towards them, and set them a bad example in his own person.

The tidings of Henry's death had no sooner reached Bretagne than the barons of that country rose with one accord
against his government, banished or massacred his officers,
and, sanctioned by the Duchess Constance, drove Randal de
Blondeville and his followers from Bretagne; he retired to
his earldom of Chester, there to brood over his injuries and
meditate vengeance.

In the meantime, Richard I. ascended the English throne.
Soon afterwards he embarked on his celebrated expedition
to the Holy Land, having previously declared Prince Arthur,
the only son of Constance, heir to all his dominions.*

His absence, and that of many of her own turbulent barons
and encroaching neighbours, left to Constance and her har-
assed dominions a short interval of profound peace.   The
historians of that period, occupied by the warlike exploits of
the French and English kings in Palestine, make but little
mention of the domestic events of Europe during their absence; but it is no slight encomium on the character of
Constance that Bretagne flourished under her government,
and began to recover from the effects of twenty years of
desolating war.   The seven years during which she ruled as
an independent sovereign were not marked by any events
of importance; but in the year 1196 she caused her son Arthur, then nine years of age, to be acknowledged Duke of

* By the treaty of Messina, 1190.

Bretagne by the States, and associated him with herself in all the acts of government.

There was more of maternal fondness than policy in this measure, and it cost her dear. Richard, that royal firebrand, had now returned to England. By the intrigues and representations of Earl Randal, his attention was turned to Bretagne. He expressed extreme indignation that Constance should have proclaimed her son Duke of Bretagne, and her partner in power, without his consent, he being the feudal lord and natural guardian of the young prince. After some excuses and representations on the part of Constance, he affected to be pacified, and a friendly interview was appointed at Pontorson, on the frontiers of Normandy.

We can hardly reconcile the cruel and perfidious scenes which follow with those romantic and chivalrous associations which illustrate the memory of Cœur-de-Lion, the friend of Blondel and the antagonist of Saladin. Constance, perfectly unsuspicious of the meditated treason, accepted the invitation of her brother-in-law, and set out from Rennes with a small but magnificent retinue to join him at Pontorson. On the road, and within sight of the town, the Earl of Chester was posted with a troop of Richard's soldiery, and while the duchess prepared to enter the gates, where she expected to be received with honour and welcome, he suddenly rushed from his ambuscade, fell upon her and her suite, put the latter to flight, and carried off Constance to the strong Castle of St. Jaques de Beuvron, where he detained her a prisoner for eighteen months. The chronicle does not tell us how Randal treated his unfortunate wife during this long imprisonment. She was absolutely in his power; none of her own people were suffered to approach her, and whatever might have been his behaviour towards her, one thing alone is certain, that so far from softening her feelings towards *him*, it seems to have added tenfold bitterness to her abhorrence and her scorn.

The barons of Bretagne sent the Bishop of Rennes to complain of this violation of faith and justice, and to demand the restitution of the duchess. Richard meanly evaded and temporized : he engaged to restore Constance to liberty on certain conditions ; but this was merely to gain time. When the stipulated terms were complied with, and the hostages delivered, the Bretons sent a herald to the English king to require him to fulfil his part of the treaty and restore their beloved Constance. Richard replied with insolent defiance, refused to deliver up either the hostages or Constance, and marched his army into the heart of the country.

All that Bretagne had suffered previously was as nothing compared to this terrible invasion ; and all that the humane and peaceful government of Constance had effected during seven years was at once annihilated. The English barons and their savage and mercenary followers spread themselves through the country, which they wasted with fire and sword. The castles of those who ventured to defend themselves were razed to the ground ; the towns and villages plundered and burned, and the wretched inhabitants fled to the caves and forests ; but not even there could they find an asylum ; by the orders and in the presence of Richard, the woods were set on fire, and hundreds either perished in the flames or were suffocated in the smoke.

Constance, meanwhile, could only weep in her captivity over the miseries of her country, and tremble with all a mother's fears for the safety of her son. She had placed Arthur under the care of William Desroches, the seneschal of her palace, a man of mature age, of approved valour, and devotedly attached to her family. This faithful servant threw himself, with his young charge, into the fortress of Brest, where he for some time defied the power of the English king.

But notwithstanding the brave resistance of the nobles

and people of Bretagne, they were obliged to submit to the conditions imposed by Richard. By a treaty concluded in 1198, of which the terms are not exactly known, Constance was delivered from her captivity, though not from her husband; but in the following year, when the death of Richard had restored her to some degree of independence, the first use she made of it was to *divorce herself* from Randal. She took this step with her usual precipitancy, not waiting for the sanction of the Pope, as was the custom in those days; and soon afterwards she gave her hand to Guy, Count de Thouars, a man of courage and integrity, who for some time maintained the cause of his wife and her son against the power of England. Arthur was now fourteen, and the legitimate heir of all the dominions of his uncle Richard. Constance placed him under the guardianship of the King of France, who knighted the young prince with his own hand, and solemnly swore to defend his rights against his usurping uncle John.

It is at this moment that the play of *King John* opens; and history is followed as closely as the dramatic form would allow, to the death of John. The real fate of poor Arthur, after he had been abandoned by the French, and had fallen into the hands of his uncle, is now ascertained; but according to the chronicle from which Shakspeare drew his materials, he was killed in attempting to escape from the Castle of Falaise. Constance did not live to witness this consummation of her calamities. Within a few months after Arthur was taken prisoner, in 1201, she died suddenly, before she had attained her thirty-ninth year; but the cause of her death is not specified.

Her eldest daughter, Elinor, the legitimate heiress of England, Normandy, and Bretagne, died in captivity, having been kept a prisoner in Bristol Castle from the age of fifteen. She was at that time so beautiful that she was called proverbially " La belle Bretonne," and by the English the " Fair

Maid of Brittany." She, like her brother Arthur, was sacrificed to the ambition of her uncles.

Of the two daughters of Constance by Guy de Thouars, the eldest, Alice, became Duchess of Bretagne, and married the Count de Dreux, of the royal blood of France. The sovereignty of Bretagne was transmitted through her descendants in an uninterrupted line till, by the marriage of the celebrated Anne de Bretagne with Charles VIII. of France, her dominions were forever united with the French monarchy.

In considering the real history of Constance, three things must strike us as chiefly remarkable.

First, that she is not accused of any vice or any act of injustice or violence; and this praise, though poor and negative, should have its due weight, considering the scanty records that remain of her troubled life, and the period at which she lived—a period in which crimes of the darkest dye were familiar occurrences. Her father, Conan, was considered as a gentle and amiable prince—"gentle even to feebleness;" yet we are told that on one occasion he acted over again the tragedy of Ugolino and Ruggiero, when he shut up the Count de Dol, with his two sons and his nephew, in a dungeon, and deliberately starved them to death; an event recorded without any particular comment by the old chroniclers of Bretagne. It also appears that, during those intervals when Constance administered the government of her states with some degree of independence, the country prospered under her sway, and that she possessed at all times the love of her people and the respect of her nobles.

Secondly, no imputation whatever has been cast on the honour of Constance as a wife and as a woman. The old historians, who have treated in a very unceremonious style the levities of her great-grandmother Matilda, her grandmother Bertha, her godmother Constance, and her mother-in-law Elinor, treat the name and memory of *our* Lady Constance with uniform respect,

Her third marriage, with Guy de Thouars, has been censured as impolitic, but has also been defended ; it can hardly, considering her age, and the circumstances in which she was placed, be a just subject of reproach. During her hated union with Randal de Blondeville, and the years passed in a species of widowhood, she conducted herself with propriety; at least I can find no reason to judge otherwise.

Lastly, we are struck by the fearless, determined spirit, amounting at times to rashness, which Constance displayed on several occasions when left to the free exercise of her own power and will ; yet we see how frequently, with all this resolution and pride of temper, she became a mere instrument in the hands of others, and a victim to the superior craft or power of her enemies. The inference is unavoidable ; there must have existed in the mind of Constance, with all her noble and amiable qualities, a deficiency somewhere, a want of firmness, a want of judgment or wariness, and a total want of self-control. . . .

Whenever we think of Constance, it is in her maternal character. All the interest which she excites in the drama turns upon her situation as the mother of Arthur. Every circumstance in which she is placed, every sentiment she utters, has a reference to him ; and she is represented through the whole of the scenes in which she is engaged as alternately pleading for the rights and trembling for the existence of her son. . . .

But, while we contemplate the character of Constance, she assumes before us an individuality perfectly distinct from the circumstances around her. The action calls forth her maternal feelings, and places them in the most prominent point of view ; but with Constance, as with a real human being, the maternal affections are a powerful instinct, modified by other faculties, sentiments, and impulses, making up the individual character. We think of her as a mother, because, as a mother distracted for the loss of her son, she is immediately presented before us, and calls forth our sympathy and our tears; but we infer the rest of her character from what we see, as certainly and as completely as if we had known her whole course of life.

That which strikes us as the principal attribute of Constance is *power*—power of imagination, of will, of passion, of affection, of pride. The moral energy, that faculty which is principally exercised in self-control, and gives consistency to the rest, is deficient; or, rather, to speak more correctly, the extraordinary development of sensibility and imagination, which lends to the character its rich poetical colouring, leaves the other qualities comparatively subordinate. Hence it is that the whole complexion of the character, notwithstanding its amazing grandeur, is so exquisitely feminine. The weakness of the woman, who by the very consciousness of that weakness is worked up to desperation and defiance, the fluctuations of temper and the bursts of sublime passion, the terrors, the impatience, and the tears, are all most true to feminine nature. The energy of Constance not being based upon strength of character, rises and falls with the tide of passion. Her haughty spirit swells against resistance, and is excited into frenzy by sorrow and disappointment; while neither from her towering pride nor her strength of intellect can she borrow patience to submit, or fortitude to endure. It is, therefore, with perfect truth of nature that Constance is first introduced as pleading for peace:

> "Stay for an answer to your embassy,
> Lest unadvis'd you stain your swords with blood:
> My Lord Chatillon may from England bring
> That right in peace which here we urge in war;
> And then we shall repent each drop of blood
> That hot, rash haste so indirectly shed."

And that the same woman, when all her passions are roused by the sense of injury, should afterwards exclaim,

> War, war! no peace! peace is to me a war!—

that she should be ambitious for her son, proud of his high
birth and royal rights, and violent in defending them—is most
natural; but I cannot agree with those who think that in the
mind of Constance *ambition*—that is, the love of dominion
for its own sake—is either a strong motive or a strong feeling; it could hardly be so where the natural impulses and
the ideal power predominate in so high a degree. The vehemence with which she asserts the just and legal rights of
her son is that of a fond mother and a proud-spirited woman,
stung with the sense of injury, and herself a reigning sovereign—by birth and right, if not in fact; yet when bereaved
of her son, grief not only "fills the room up of her absent
child," but seems to absorb every other faculty and feeling,
even pride and anger. It is true that she exults over him
as one whom nature and fortune had destined to be *great*,
but in her distraction for his loss she thinks of him only as
her "Pretty Arthur."

> "O lord! my boy, my Arthur, my fair son!
> My life, my joy, my food, my all the world!
> My widow-comfort, and my sorrow's cure!"

No other feeling can be traced through the whole of her
frantic scene; it is grief only—a mother's heart-rending,
soul-absorbing grief—and nothing else. Not even indignation or the desire of revenge interferes with its soleness and
intensity. An ambitious woman would hardly have thus addressed the cold, wily Cardinal [iii. 4. 76–89]:

> "And, Father Cardinal, I have heard you say,
> That we shall see and know our friends in heaven," etc.

The bewildered pathos and poetry of this address could
be natural in no woman who did not unite, like Constance,
the most passionate sensibility with the most vivid imagination.

It is true that Queen Elinor calls her on one occasion
"ambitious Constance;" but the epithet is rather the natu-

ral expression of Elinor's own fear and hatred than really applicable.* Elinor, in whom age had subdued all passions but ambition, dreaded the mother of Arthur as her rival in power, and for that reason only opposed the claims of the son ; but I conceive that in a woman yet in the prime of life, and endued with the peculiar disposition of Constance, the mere love of power would be too much modified by fancy and feeling to be called a *passion*.

In fact, it is not pride, nor temper, nor ambition, nor even maternal affection which in Constance gives the prevailing tone to the whole character ; it is the predominance of imagination. I do not mean in the conception of the dramatic portrait, but in the temperament of the woman herself. In the poetical, fanciful, excitable cast of her mind, in the *excess* of the ideal power, tinging all her affections, exalting all her sentiments and thoughts, and animating the expression of both, Constance can only be compared to Juliet.

In the first place, it is through the power of imagination that when under the influence of excited temper Constance is not a mere incensed woman ; nor does she, in the style of Volumnia, "lament in anger, Juno-like," but rather like a sibyl in a fury. Her sarcasms come down like thunderbolts. In her famous address to Austria [iii. 1. 114-129]:

"O Lymoges ! O Austria ! thou dost shame
That bloody spoil ! thou slave ! thou wretch ! thou coward !" etc.

it is as if she had concentrated the burning spirit of scorn and dashed it in his face ; every word seems to blister where it falls. In the scolding scene between her and Queen Elinor [ii. 1. 120 fol.], the laconic insolence of the latter is completely overborne by the torrent of bitter contumely which bursts from the lips of Constance, clothed in the most energetic, and often in the most figurative expressions.

* "Queen Elinor saw that if he were king, how his mother, Constance, would look to bear the most rule in the realm of England till her son should come of a lawful age to govern of himself."—HOLINSHED.

And in a very opposite mood, when struggling with the consciousness of her own helpless situation, the same susceptible and excitable fancy still predominates [iii. 1. 11–24].

It is the power of imagination which gives so peculiar a tinge to the maternal tenderness of Constance ; she not only loves her son with the fond instinct of a mother's affection, but she loves him with her poetical imagination, exults in his beauty and his royal birth, hangs over him with idolatry, and sees his infant brow already encircled with the diadem. Her proud spirit, her ardent enthusiastic fancy, and her energetic self-will, all combine with her maternal love to give it that tone and character which belongs to her only: hence that most beautiful address to her son [iii. 1. 43 fol.: "If thou, that bidd'st me be content," etc.], which, coming from the lips of Constance, is as full of nature and truth as of pathos and poetry, and which we could hardly sympathize with in any other.

It is this exceeding vivacity of imagination which in the end turns sorrow to frenzy. Constance is not only a bereaved and doting mother, but a generous woman, betrayed by her own rash confidence ; in whose mind the sense of injury mingling with the sense of grief, and her impetuous temper conflicting with her pride, combine to overset her reason. Yet she is not mad : and how admirably, how forcibly, she herself draws the distinction between the frantic violence of uncontrolled feeling and actual madness !—

> "Thou art not holy to belie me so ;
> I am not mad : this hair I tear is mine ;
> My name is Constance ; I was Geffrey's wife ;
> Young Arthur is my son, and he is lost :
> I am not mad ; I would to heaven I were !
> For then, 't is like I should forget myself :
> O, if I could, what grief should I forget !"

On the whole, it may be said that pride and maternal affection form the basis of the character of Constance as it is

exhibited to us ; but that these passions, in an equal degree
common to many human beings, assume their peculiar and
individual tinge from an extraordinary development of intellect and fancy.   It is the energy of passion which lends the
character its concentrated power, as it is the prevalence
of imagination throughout which dilates it into magnificence.

The sole deviation from history which may be considered
as essentially interfering with the truth of the situation is
the entire omission of the character of Guy de Thouars, so
that Constance is incorrectly represented as in a state of
widowhood, at a period when, in point of fact, she was married.   It may be observed that her marriage took place just
at the period of the opening of the drama ; that Guy de
Thouars played no conspicuous part in the affairs of Bretagne
till after the death of Constance ; and that the mere presence
of this personage, altogether superfluous in the action, would
have completely destroyed the dramatic interest of the situation.   And what a situation !   One more magnificent was
never placed before the mind's eye than that of Constance,
when [iii. 1], deserted and betrayed, she stands alone in her
despair, amid her false friends and her ruthless enemies !
The image of the mother-eagle, wounded and bleeding to
death, yet stretched over her young in an attitude of defiance, while all the baser birds of prey are clamouring around
her eyrie, gives but a faint idea of the moral sublimity of this
scene.   Considered merely as a poetical or dramatic picture,
the grouping is wonderfully fine : on one side, the vulture
ambition of that mean-souled tyrant, John ; on the other, the
selfish, calculating policy of Philip : between them, balancing
their passions in his hand, the cold, subtle, heartless Legate ;
the fiery, reckless Falconbridge ; the princely Louis ; the still
unconquered spirit of that wrangling queen, old Elinor ; the
bridal loveliness and modesty of Blanche ; the boyish grace
and innocence of young Arthur ; and Constance in the midst

of them, in all the state of her great grief, a grand impersonation of pride and passion, helpless at once and desperate—form an assemblage of figures, each perfect in its kind, and, taken all together, not surpassed for the variety, force, and splendour of the dramatic and picturesque effect.

Elinor of Guienne and Blanche of Castile, who form part of the group around Constance, are sketches merely, but they are strictly historical portraits, and full of truth and spirit.

At the period when Shakspeare has brought these three women on the scene together, Elinor of Guienne (the daughter of the last Duke of Guienne and Aquitaine, and, like Constance, the heiress of a sovereign duchy) was near the close of her long various, and unquiet life—she was nearly seventy : and, as in early youth, her violent passions had overborne both principle and policy, so in her old age we see the same character, only modified by time ; her strong intellect and love of power, unbridled by conscience or principle, surviving when other passions were extinguished, and rendered more dangerous by a degree of subtlety and self-command to which her youth had been a stranger. Her personal and avowed hatred for Constance, together with its motives, are mentioned by the old historians. Holinshed expressly says that Queen Elinor was mightily set against her grandson Arthur, rather moved thereto by envy conceived against his mother than by any fault of the young prince, for that she knew and dreaded the high spirit of the Lady Constance.

Queen Elinor preserved to the end of her life her influence over her children, and appears to have merited their respect. While intrusted with the government, during the absence of Richard I., she ruled with a steady hand, and made herself exceedingly popular ; and as long as she lived to direct the counsels of her son John, his affairs prospered. For that intemperate jealousy which converted her into a domestic firebrand, there was at least much cause, though little excuse. Elinor had hated and wronged the husband of her youth,* and she had afterwards to endure the negligence and innumerable infidelities of the husband whom she passionately loved;† "and so the whirligig of time brought in his revenges." Elinor died in 1203, a few months after Constance, and before the murder of Arthur—a crime which, had she lived, would probably never have been consummated; for the nature of Elinor, though violent, had no tincture of the baseness and cruelty of her son.

Blanche of Castile was the daughter of Alphonso IX. of Castile, and the granddaughter of Elinor. At the time that she is introduced into the drama she was about fifteen, and her marriage with Louis VIII., then Dauphin, took place in the abrupt manner here represented. It is not often that political marriages have the same happy result. We are told by the historians of that time that from the moment Louis and Blanche met they were inspired by a mutual passion, and that during a union of more than twenty-six years they were never known to differ, nor even spent more than a single day asunder.

In her exceeding beauty and blameless reputation; her love for her husband, and strong domestic affections; her pride of birth and rank; her feminine gentleness of deportment; her firmness of temper; her religious bigotry; her love of absolute power, and her upright and conscientious administration of it, Blanche greatly resembled Maria Theresa of Austria. She was, however, of a more cold and calculating nature; and in proportion as she was less amiable as a woman did she rule more happily for herself and others.

---

* Louis VII. of France, whom she was accustomed to call, in contempt, *the monk.* Elinor's adventures in Syria, whither she accompanied Louis on the second Crusade, would form a romance.

† Henry II. of England. It is scarcely necessary to observe that the story of Fair Rosamond, as far as Elinor is concerned, is a mere invention of some ballad-maker of later times.

There cannot be a greater contrast than between the acute understanding, the steady temper, and the cool, intriguing policy of Blanche, by which she succeeded in disuniting and defeating the powers arrayed against her and her infant son, and the rash confiding temper and susceptible imagination of Constance, which rendered herself and her son easy victims to the fraud or ambition of others. Blanche, during forty years, held in her hands the destinies of the greater part of Europe, and is one of the most celebrated names recorded in history—but in what does she survive to us except in a name? Nor history, nor fame, though "trumpet-tongued," could do for *her* what Shakspeare and poetry have done for Constance. The earthly reign of Blanche is over, her sceptre broken, and her power departed. When will the reign of Constance cease? when will *her* power depart? Not while this world is a world, and there exist in it human souls to kindle at the touch of genius, and human hearts to throb with human sympathies.

[*From Dowden's "Shakspere."* *]

Setting aside *Henry VIII.*, a play written probably for some special occasion, or upon some special occasion handed over to the dramatist Fletcher to complete ; setting aside also the somewhat slight sketch of Edward IV. which appears in 3 *Henry VI.* and in the opening scenes of *Richard III.*, six full-length portraits of kings of England have been left by Shakspere. These six fall into two groups of three each—one group consisting of studies of kingly weakness, the other group of studies of kingly strength. In the one group stand King John, King Richard II., and King Henry VI. ; in the other King Henry IV., King Henry V., and King Richard III. John is the royal criminal, weak in his criminality ; Henry VI. is the royal saint, weak in his saint-

---

* *Shakspere: a Critical Study of his Mind and Art*, by Edward Dowden (2d ed. London, 1876), p. 168 fol.

liness. The feebleness of Richard II. cannot be characterized in a word; he is a graceful, sentimental monarch.
Richard III., in the other group, is a royal criminal, strong
in his crime. Henry IV., the usurping Bolingbroke, is strong
by a fine craft in dealing with events, by resolution and policy, by equal caution and daring. The strength of Henry V.
is that of plain heroic magnitude, thoroughly sound and sub-
stantial, founded upon the eternal verities. Here, then, we
may recognize the one dominant subject of the histories;
namely, how a man may fail, and how a man may succeed in
attaining a practical mastery of the world. These plays are,
as Schlegel has named them, a "mirror for kings;" and the
characters of these plays all lead up to Henry V., the man
framed for the most noble and joyous mastery of things.

In *King John* the hour of utmost ebb in the national life
of England is investigated by the imagination of the poet.
The king reigns neither by warrant of a just title, nor, like
Bolingbroke, by warrant of the right of the strongest. He
knows that his house is founded upon the sand; he knows
that he has no justice of God and no virtue of man on which
to rely. Therefore he assumes an air of authority and regal
grandeur; but within all is rottenness and shame. Unlike
the bold usurper Richard, John endeavours to turn away his
eyes from facts of which he is yet aware; he dare not gaze
into his own wretched and cowardly soul. When threatened
by France with war, and now alone with his mother, John
exclaims, making an effort to fortify his heart, "Our strong
possession and our right for us." But Elinor, with a woman's
courage and directness, forbids the unavailing self-deceit:

> "Your strong possession much more than your right,
>   Or else it must go wrong with you and me."

King Richard, when he would make away with the young
princes, summons Tyrrel to his presence, and inquires with
cynical indifference to human sentiment, "Dar'st thou resolve

to kill a friend of mine?" and when Tyrrel accepts the commission, Richard, in a moment of undisguised exultation, breaks forth with "Thou sing'st sweet music!" John would inspire Hubert with his murderous purpose rather like some vague influence than a personal will, obscurely as some pale mist works which creeps across the fields, and leaves blight behind it in the sunshine. He trembles lest he should have said too much; he trembles lest he should not have said enough; at last the nearer fear prevails, and the words "death," "a grave," form themselves upon his lips. Having touched a spring which will produce assassination, he furtively withdraws himself from the mechanism of crime. It suits the king's interest afterwards that Arthur should be living, and John adds to his crime the baseness of a miserable attempt by chicanery and timorous sophisms to transfer the responsibility of murder from himself to his instrument and accomplice. He would fain darken the eyes of his conscience and of his understanding.

The show of kingly strength and dignity in which John is clothed in the earlier scenes of the play must therefore be recognized (although Shakspere does not obtrude the fact) as no more than a poor pretence of true regal strength and honour. The fact, only hinted in these earlier scenes, becomes afterwards all the more impressive, when the time comes to show this dastard king, who had been so great in the barter of territory, in the sale of cities, in the sacrifice of love and marriage-truth to policy; now changing from pale to red in the presence of his own nobles, now vainly trying to tread back the path of crime, now incapable of enduring the physical suffering of the hour of death. Sensible that he is a king with no inward strength of justice or of virtue, John endeavours to buttress up his power with external supports; against the advice of his nobles he celebrates a second coronation, only forthwith to remove the crown from his head and place it in the hands of an Italian priest. Pandulph, "of

C

fair Millaine cardinal," who possesses the astuteness and skill to direct the various conflicting forces of the time to his own advantage, Pandulph is the *de facto* master of England, and as he pleases makes peace or announces war.

The country, as in periods of doubt and danger, was " possessed with rumours, full of idle dreams." Peter of Pomfret had announced that before Ascension-day at noon the King should deliver up his crown. John submits to the degradation demanded of him, and has the incredible baseness to be pleased that he has done so of his own free will :

> "Is this Ascension-day? did not the prophet
> Say that before Ascension-day at noon
> My crown I should give off? Even so I have.
> I did suppose it should be on constraint;
> But, heaven be thank'd! it is but voluntary."

After this we are not surprised that when the Bastard endeavours to rouse him to manliness and resolution—

> "Away, and glister like the god of war
> When he intendeth to become the field "—

John is not ashamed to announce the " happy peace " which he has made with the Papal legate, on whom he relies for protection against the invaders of England. Faulconbridge still urges the duty of an effort at self-defence, for the sake of honour and of safety, and the King, incapable of accepting his own responsibilities and privileges, hands over the care of England to his illegitimate nephew—" Have thou the ordering of this present time."

There is little in the play of *King John* which strengthens or gladdens the heart. In the tug of selfish power, hither and thither, amid the struggle of kingly greeds and priestly pride, amid the sales of cities, the loveless marriage of princes, the rumours and confusion of the people, a pathetic beauty illumines the boyish figure of Arthur, so gracious, so passive, untouched by the rapacities and crimes of the others :

> "Good my mother, peace!
> I would that I were low laid in my grave;
> I am not worth this coil that 's made for me."

The voice of maternal passion, a woman's voice impotent and shrill, among the unheeding male forces, goes up also from the play. There is the pity of stern, armed men for the ruin of a child's life. These, and the boisterous but genuine and hearty patriotism of Faulconbridge, are the only presences of human virtue or beauty which are to be perceived in the degenerate world depicted by Shakspere. And the end, like what preceded it, is miserable. The king lies poisoned, overmastered by mere physical agony, agony which leaves little room for any pangs of conscience, were the palsied moral nature of the criminal capable of such nobler suffering:

> "I am a scribbled form, drawn with a pen
> Upon a parchment, and against this fire
> Do I shrink up."

[From Mr. F. J. Furnivall's Introduction to the Play.*]

With this play of pathos and patriotism we open Shakspere's Second Period,—looking on *Richard II.* as the last play in which ryme plays a prominent part, we take the series of *Henry VI.* and *Richard III.* as the transition to the Second Period;—and on opening it we are struck with a greater fulness of characterization and power than we saw in the First-Period plays. But the whole work of Shakspere is continuous. *King John* is very closely linkt with *Richard III.* In both plays we have cruel uncles planning their nephews' murder, because the boys stand between them and the crown. In both we have distracted mothers overwhelmd with grief. In both we have prophecies of ruin and curses on the murderers, and in both the fulfilment of these. In both we have the kingdom divided against itself, and the horrors of civil

* *The Leopold Shakspere* (London, 1877), p. xl.

war. In both we have the same lesson of the danger of division taught to the discontented English parties of Shakspere's own day. *Richard III.* is an example of the misgovernment of a cruel tyrant; *King John* of the misgovernment of a selfish coward. But in *John* we have the mother's pathetic lament for her child far developt above that of Queen Elizabeth's for her murderd innocents, and far more touching than the laments of Queen Margaret and the Duchess of York, while the pathos of the stifled children's death is heightend in that of Arthur. The temptation scene of John and Hubert repeats that of Richard and Tyrrel. The Bastard's statement of his motives, "Gain, be my lord," etc., is like that of Richard the Third's about his villany. (The Bastard's speech on commodity may be compard with Lucrece's reproaches to opportunity.) Besides the boy's pleading for his life, besides his piteous death and the mother's cry for him, which comes home to every parent who has lost a child, we have in the play the spirit of Elizabethan England's defiance to the foreigner* and the Pope. *King John* is founded on the old play of *The Troublesome Raigne of King John*, 1591.† Shakspere alters the old play in eight

---

* "The great lesson taught in the last lines of the play should be more brought out. King, nobles, claimant, all lean on foreign help, and all find it a broken reed which pierces their hands."—C. Hargrove. Besides the passage usually cited from Andrew Boorde for these last lines, he has another nearer to Shakspere's words: "I think if all the world were set against England, it might neuer be conquered, they beyng treue within them selfe."—1542 (pr. 1547), *Introduction*, p. 164 of my ed. 1870.

† It is the old play re-written. The two *must* be read together and compard, to see what genius makes out of ordinary work. The extreme Protestant tone of the old play is much modified by Shakspere. And as Prof. Delius notices (*New Shakspere Society's Transactions*, 1875-6, Part II.), Shakspere only tells certain incidents that the old play acts, as Falconbridge ransacking the churches, arresting Peter of Pomfret on the stage; John's meal and poisoning, the death of the monk who poisons him, and Falconbridge's stabbing the abbot. Falconbridge's soliloquies are new too. On the many variations from history in *King John*, see

chief political points,—as shown by Mr. Richard Simpson in the *New Shakspere Society's Transactions*, 1874,*—in order to bring the play closer home to his hearers, and the circumstances of his time,—the disputed succession of Elizabeth,

T. P. Courtenay's *Commentaries on the Historical Plays of Shakspere*, two vols. Colburn, 1840, a book indispensable to the student of these plays. The old *Troublesome Raigne* of 1594 is reprinted in Hazlitt's *Shakspere's Library*, Part II. vol. i. p. 212 [also in Fleay's ed. of *King John*].

  * These points are stated by Mr. Simpson thus:

"1. In Shakspere, John is told by his own mother that he must rely on his 'strong possession,' not on his right; and the suggestion of the old play that Arthur, being 'but young and yet unmeet to reign,' was therefore to be passed over, is thrown out.

2. Elinor tells Constance that she can 'produce a will that bars the title' of Arthur.

3. History is altered to heighten and refine the characters of Arthur and Constance.

4. John's loss of his French possessions is accentuated by the exaggeration of the dowry given to Blanch.

5. The scenes where John first persuades Hubert to murder Arthur, and then reproaches him for it, are inventions of Shakspere.

6. The compression of John's four wars into two, though absolutely necessary for dramatic arrangement, is so managed as to have an Elizabethan bearing. Of these two wars the poet makes the first to concern Arthur's title, without any religious or ecclesiastical motive. The second he makes to be in revenge for Arthur's death, with an ecclesiastical motive added in John's excommunication. This is wholly unhistorical. No English lord interfered in behalf of Arthur, whose death raised no commotion in England, and was long past and forgotten before the controversy with the pope about Langton began. The confederacy between the barons and Lewis was ten years after Arthur's death, with which it had nothing to do. . . .

7. Pandulph insinuates to Lewis that it is his interest to abstain from interference till John's murder of his nephew should make interference profitable to himself.

8. Melun's confession of Lewis's intended treachery to the barons is the occasion of their return to allegiance.

Every one of these points, in which the poet deviates from the Chronicles, is so turned as to contain indirect references and allusions to contemporary politics, or to events which had a decisive influence on them."
—Ed.

and the interference of Spain and the Pope. The old play-
writer made the murder of Arthur, as Mr. Lloyd has notist,*
the turning-point between the high-spirited success of John
at first and his dejection and disgrace at last ; and he, too,
fixt on the assertion of national independence against invading Frenchmen and encroaching ecclesiastics as the true
principle of dramatic action of John's time. So long as John
is the impersonator of England, of defiance to the foreigner,
and opposition to the Pope, so long is he a hero. But he is
bold outside only, only politically; inside, morally, he is a
coward, sneak, and skunk. See how his nature comes out
in the hints for the murder of Arthur, his turning on Hubert
when he thinks the murder will bring evil to himself, and his
imploring Falconbridge to deny it. His death ought, of
course, dramatically to have followd from some act of his
in the play, as revenge for the murder of Arthur, or his plundering the abbots or abbeys, or opposing the Pope. The
author of *The Troublesome Raigne*, with a true instinct, made
a monk murder John out of revenge for his anti-Papal patriotism. But Shakspere, unfortunately, set this story aside,
though there was some warrant for it in Holinshed, and thus
left a serious blot on his drama which it is impossible to remove. The character which to me stands foremost in *John*
is Constance, with that most touching expression of grief for
the son she had lost. Beside her cry, the tender pleading
of Arthur for his life is heard, and both are backt by the
rough voice of Falconbridge, who, Englishman-like, depreci-
ates his own motives at first, but is lifted by patriotism into
a gallant soldier, while his deep moral nature shows itself in
his heartfelt indignation at Arthur's supposd murder. The
rhetoric of the earlier historical plays is kept up in *King
John*, and also Shakspere's power of creating situations,
which he had possesst from the first.

* *Critical Essays*, G. Bell and Sons, London, 1875.

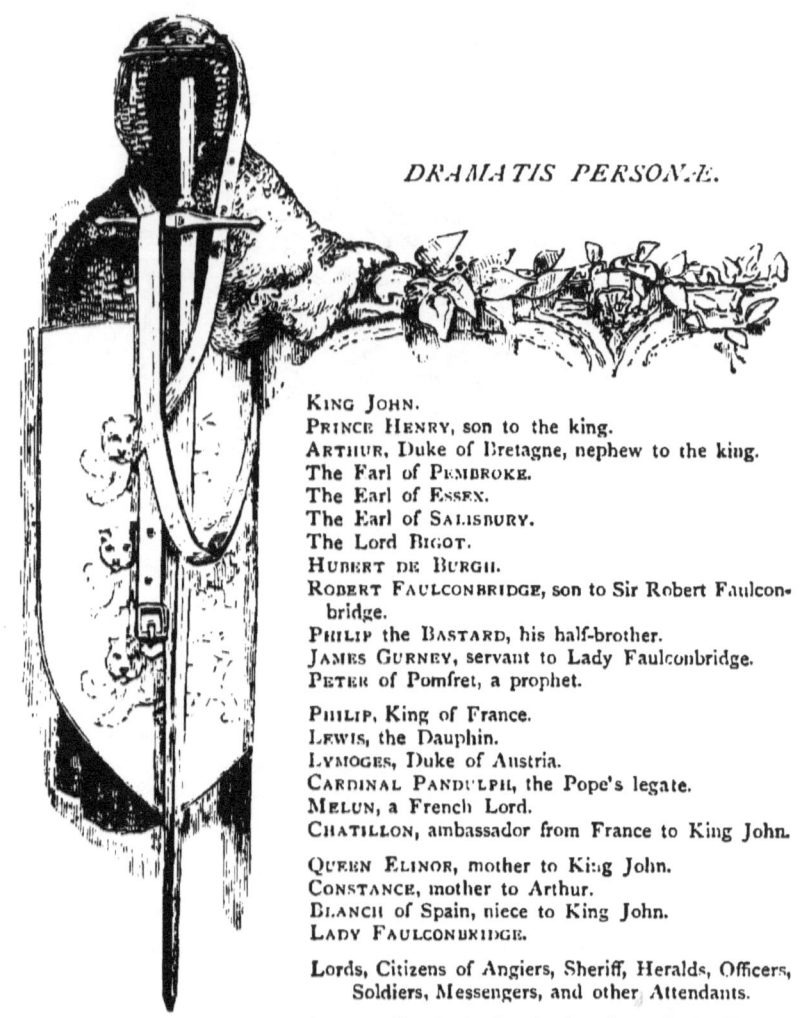

DRAMATIS PERSONÆ.

KING JOHN.
PRINCE HENRY, son to the king.
ARTHUR, Duke of Bretagne, nephew to the king.
The Earl of PEMBROKE.
The Earl of ESSEX.
The Earl of SALISBURY.
The Lord BIGOT.
HUBERT DE BURGH.
ROBERT FAULCONBRIDGE, son to Sir Robert Faulcon-
    bridge.
PHILIP the BASTARD, his half-brother.
JAMES GURNEY, servant to Lady Faulconbridge.
PETER of Pomfret, a prophet.

PHILIP, King of France.
LEWIS, the Dauphin.
LYMOGES, Duke of Austria.
CARDINAL PANDULPH, the Pope's legate.
MELUN, a French Lord.
CHATILLON, ambassador from France to King John.

QUEEN ELINOR, mother to King John.
CONSTANCE, mother to Arthur.
BLANCH of Spain, niece to King John.
LADY FAULCONBRIDGE.

Lords, Citizens of Angiers, Sheriff, Heralds, Officers,
    Soldiers, Messengers, and other Attendants.

SCENE: *Partly in England and partly in France.*

ROOM OF STATE IN THE PALACE.

ACT I.

SCENE I. *King John's Palace.*

Enter KING JOHN, QUEEN ELINOR, PEMBROKE, ESSEX, SALIS-
BURY, *and others; with* CHATILLON.

King John. Now, say, Chatillon, what would France with
  us?

Chatillon. Thus, after greeting, speaks the King of France

In my behaviour to the majesty,
The borrowed majesty, of England here.
   Elinor. A strange beginning!—borrowed majesty!
   King John. Silence, good mother; hear the embassy.
   Chatillon. Philip of France, in right and true behalf
Of thy deceased brother Geffrey's son,
Arthur Plantagenet, lays most lawful claim
To this fair island and the territories,   10
To Ireland, Poictiers, Anjou, Touraine, Maine,
Desiring thee to lay aside the sword
Which sways usurpingly these several titles,
And put the same into young Arthur's hand,
Thy nephew and right royal sovereign.
   King John. What follows if we disallow of this?
   Chatillon. The proud control of fierce and bloody war,
To enforce these rights so forcibly withheld.
   King John. Here have we war for war and blood for
      blood,
Controlment for controlment: so answer France.   20
   Chatillon. Then take my king's defiance from my mouth,
The farthest limit of my embassy.
   King John. Bear mine to him, and so depart in peace.
Be thou as lightning in the eyes of France;
For ere thou canst report I will be there,
The thunder of my cannon shall be heard.
So hence! Be thou the trumpet of our wrath
And sullen presage of your own decay.—
An honourable conduct let him have;
Pembroke, look to 't.—Farewell, Chatillon.   30
                [*Exeunt Chatillon and Pembroke.*
   Elinor. What now, my son! have I not ever said
How that ambitious Constance would not cease
Till she had kindled France and all the world,
Upon the right and party of her son?
This might have been prevented and made whole

With very easy arguments of love,
Which now the manage of two kingdoms must
With fearful bloody issue arbitrate.

  King John. Our strong possession and our right for us.

  Elinor. Your strong possession much more than your
     right,   40
Or else it must go wrong with you and me;
So much my conscience whispers in your ear,
Which none but heaven and you and I shall hear.

Enter a Sheriff.

  Essex. My liege, here is the strangest controversy
Come from the country to be judg'd by you
That e'er I heard; shall I produce the men?

  King John. Let them approach.—
Our abbeys and our priories shall pay
This expedition's charge.—

Enter Robert Faulconbr'dge, *and* Philip *his bastard
brother.*

               What men are you?

  Bastard. Your faithful subject I, a gentleman   50
Born in Northamptonshire, and eldest son,
As I suppose, to Robert Faulconbridge,—
A soldier, by the honour-giving hand
Of Cœur-de-lion knighted in the field.

  King John. What art thou?

  Robert. The son and heir to that same Faulconbridge.

  King John. Is that the elder, and art thou the heir?
You came not of one mother then, it seems.

  Bastard. Most certain of one mother, mighty king—
That is well known—and, as I think, one father;   60
But for the certain knowledge of that truth
I put you o'er to heaven and to my mother:
Of that I doubt, as all men's children may.

Elinor. Out on thee, rude man! thou dost shame thy mother
And wound her honour with this diffidence.
　Bastard. I, madam? no, I have no reason for it:
That is my brother's plea and none of mine;
The which if he can prove, a' pops me out
At least from fair five hundred pound a year.
Heaven guard my mother's honour—and my land!　　　70
　King John. A good blunt fellow.—Why, being younger born,
Doth he lay claim to thine inheritance?
　Bastard. I know not why, except to get the land.
But once he slander'd me with bastardy:
But whether I be as true begot or no,
That still I lay upon my mother's head;
But that I am as well begot, my liege,—
Fair fall the bones that took the pains for me!—
Compare our faces and be judge yourself.
If old Sir Robert did beget us both　　　　　80
And were our father, and this son like him,—
O old Sir Robert, father, on my knee
I give heaven thanks I was not like to thee!
　King John. Why, what a madcap hath heaven lent us here!
　Elinor. He hath a trick of Cœur-de-lion's face;
The accent of his tongue affecteth him.
Do you not read some tokens of my son
In the large composition of this man?
　King John. Mine eye hath well examined his parts,
And finds them perfect Richard.—Sirrah, speak,　　90
What doth move you to claim your brother's land?
　Bastard. Because he hath a half-face, like my father,
With that half-face would he have all my land;
A half-fac'd groat five hundred pound a year!
　Robert. My gracious liege, when that my father liv'd,
Your brother did employ my father much,—

Bastard. Well, sir, by this you cannot get my land;
Your tale must be how he employ'd my mother.
  Robert. And once dispatch'd him in an embassy
To Germany, there with the emperor   100
To treat of high affairs touching that time.
The advantage of his absence took the king
And in the mean time sojourn'd at my father's;
Where how he did prevail I shame to speak,
But truth is truth : large lengths of seas and shores
Between my father and my mother lay,
As I have heard my father speak himself,
When this same lusty gentleman was got.
Upon his death-bed he by will bequeath'd
His lands to me, and took it on his death   110
That this my mother's son was none of his;
And if he were, he came into the world
Full fourteen weeks before the course of time.
Then, good my liege, let me have what is mine,
My father's land, as was my father's will.
  King John. Sirrah, your brother is legitimate :
Your father's wife did after wedlock bear him,
And if she did play false, the fault was hers;
Which fault lies on the hazards of all husbands
That marry wives   Tell me, how if my brother,   120
Who, as you say, took pains to get this son,
Had of your father claim'd this son for his?
In sooth, good friend, your father might have kept
This calf bred from his cow from all the world;
In sooth he might : then, if he were my brother's,
My brother might not claim him, nor your father,
Being none of his, refuse him.   This concludes :
My mother's son did get your father's heir;
Your father's heir must have your father's land.
  Robert. Shall then my father's will be of no force 130
To dispossess that child which is not his?

Bastard. Of no more force to dispossess me, sir,
Than was his will to get me, as I think.

Elinor. Whether hadst thou rather be a Faulconbridge,
And like thy brother, to enjoy thy land,
Or the reputed son of Cœur-de-lion,
Lord of thy presence and no land beside?

Bastard. Madam, an if my brother had my shape,
And I had his, Sir Robert's his, like him;
And if my legs were two such riding-rods,   140
My arms such eel-skins stuff'd, my face so thin
That in mine ear I durst not stick a rose
Lest men should say 'Look, where three-farthings goes!'
And, to his shape, were heir to all this land,
Would I might never stir from off this place,
I would give it every foot to have this face;
I would not be Sir Nob in any case.

Elinor. I like thee well. Wilt thou forsake thy fortune,
Bequeath thy land to him, and follow me?
I am a soldier, and now bound to France.   150

Bastard. Brother, take you my land, I'll take my chance.
Your face hath got five hundred pound a year,
Yet sell your face for five pence and 't is dear.—
Madam, I'll follow you unto the death.

Elinor. Nay, I would have you go before me thither.

Bastard. Our country manners give our betters way.

King John. What is thy name?

Bastard. Philip, my liege, so is my name begun;
Philip, good old Sir Robert's wife's eldest son.

King John. From henceforth bear his name whose form
    thou bear'st;   160
Kneel thou down Philip, but arise more great,
Arise Sir Richard and Plantagenet.

Bastard. Brother, by the mother's side, give me your
    hand;
My father gave me honour, yours gave land.—

Now blessed be the hour, by night or day,
When I was got, Sir Robert was away!
    Elinor. The very spirit of Plantagenet!
I am thy grandam, Richard; call me so.
    Bastard. Madam, by chance but not by truth; what
        though?
Something about, a little from the right,   170
    In at the window, or else o'er the hatch;
Who dares not stir by day must walk by night,
    And have is have, however men do catch:
Near or far off, well won is still well shot,
And I am I, howe'er I was begot.
    King John. Go, Faulconbridge: now hast thou thy de-
        sire;
A landless knight makes thee a landed squire.—
Come, madam, and come, Richard, we must speed
For France, for France, for it is more than need.
    Bastard. Brother, adieu; good fortune come to thee!   180
For thou wast got i' the way of honesty.
                                    [*Exeunt all but Bastard.*
A foot of honour better than I was,
But many a many foot of land the worse.
Well, now can I make any Joan a lady.
' Good den, Sir Richard!'—' God-a-mercy, fellow!'—
And if his name be George, I'll call him Peter;
For new-made honour doth forget men's names:
'T is too respective and too sociable
For your conversion. Now your traveller,—
He and his toothpick at my worship's mess,   190
And when my knightly stomach is suffic'd,
Why then I suck my teeth and catechise
My picked man of countries: ' My dear sir,'—
Thus, leaning on mine elbow, I begin,—
' I shall beseech you'—that is question now;
And then comes answer like an Absey book:

'O sir,' says answer, 'at your best command;
At your employment; at your service, sir :'—
'No, sir,' says question, 'I, sweet sir, at yours :'—
And so, ere answer knows what question would,　　200
Saving in dialogue of compliment,
And talking of the Alps and Apennines,
The Pyrenean and the river Po,
It draws toward supper in conclusion so.
But this is worshipful society
And fits the mounting spirit like myself,
For he is but a bastard to the time
That doth not smack of observation :
And so am I, whether I smack or no;
And not alone in habit and device,　　210
Exterior form, outward accoutrement,
But from the inward motion to deliver
Sweet, sweet, sweet poison for the age's tooth;
Which, though I will not practise to deceive,
Yet, to avoid deceit, I mean to learn,
For it shall strew the footsteps of my rising.—
But who comes in such haste in riding-robes?
What woman-post is this? hath she no husband
That will take pains to blow a horn before her?

　　Enter LADY FAULCONBRIDGE *and* JAMES GURNEY.

O me! it is my mother.—How now, good lady!　　220
What brings you here to court so hastily?
　　Lady Faulconbridge. Where is that slave, thy brother?
　　　　where is he,
That holds in chase mine honour up and down?
　　Bastard. My brother Robert? old Sir Robert's son?
Colbrand the giant, that same mighty man?
Is it Sir Robert's son that you seek so?
　　Lady Faulconbridge. Sir Robert's son! Ay, thou unrever-
　　　　end boy,

Sir Robert's son; why scorn'st thou at Sir Robert?
He is Sir Robert's son, and so art thou.   225
   Bastard. James Gurney, wilt thou give us leave awhile?
   Gurney. Good leave, good Philip.
   Bastard.   Philip! sparrow!   James,
There 's toys abroad; anon I 'll tell thee more.—
                             [Exit Gurney.

Madam, I was not old Sir Robert's son;
Sir Robert might have eat his part in me
Upon Good-Friday and ne'er broke his fast.
Sir Robert could do well; marry, to confess,
Could he get me?   Sir Robert could not do it;
We know his handiwork: therefore, good mother,
To whom am I beholding for these limbs?
Sir Robert never holp to make this leg.   240
   Lady Faulconbridge. Hast thou conspired with thy brother
     too,
That for thine own gain shouldst defend mine honour?
What means this scorn, thou most untoward knave?
   Bastard. Knight, knight, good mother, Basilisco-like.
What!   I am dubb'd!   I have it on my shoulder.
But, mother, I am not Sir Robert's son:
I have disclaim'd Sir Robert and my land;
Legitimation, name, and all is gone.
Then, good my mother, let me know my father.—
Some proper man, I hope; who was it, mother?   250
   Lady Faulconbridge. Hast thou denied thyself a Faulcon-
     bridge?
   Bastard. As faithfully as I deny the devil.
   Lady Faulconbridge. King Richard Cœur-de-lion was thy
     father;
By long and vehement suit I was seduc'd.—
Heaven lay not my transgression to my charge!
Thou art the issue of my dear offence,
Which was so strongly urg'd past my defence.
                 D

Bastard. Now, by this light, were I to get again,
Madam, I would not wish a better father.
Some sins do bear their privilege on earth,   260
And so doth yours; your fault was not your folly:
Needs must you lay your heart at his dispose,
Subjected tribute to commanding love,
Against whose fury and unmatched force
The aweless lion could not wage the fight,
Nor keep his princely heart from Richard's hand.
He that perforce robs lions of their hearts
May easily win a woman's.   Ay, my mother,
With all my heart I thank thee for my father!
Who lives and dares but say thou didst not well   270
When I was got, I 'll send his soul to hell.
Come, lady, I will show thee to my kin;
   And they shall say, when Richard me begot,
If thou hadst said him nay, it had been sin:
   Who says it was, he lies; I say 't was not.   [*Exeunt.*

ANGIERS.

ACT II.

SCENE I. *France. Before Angiers.*

Enter AUSTRIA *and forces, drums, etc., on one side: on the other* KING PHILIP *of France and his power;* LEWIS, ARTHUR, CONSTANCE, *and attendants.*

King Philip. Before Angiers well met, brave Austria.—
Arthur, that great forerunner of thy blood,
Richard, that robb'd the lion of his heart
And fought the holy wars in Palestine,
By this brave duke came early to his grave;
And for amends to his posterity,
At our importance hither is he come,

To spread his colours, boy, in thy behalf,
And to rebuke the usurpation
Of thy unnatural uncle, English John :   12
Embrace him, love him, give him welcome hither.
    Arthur. God shall forgive you Cœur-de-lion's death
The rather that you give his offspring life,
Shadowing their right under your wings of war.
I give you welcome with a powerless hand,
But with a heart full of unstained love ;
Welcome before the gates of Angiers, duke.
    King Philip. A noble boy ! Who would not do thee right?
    Austria. Upon thy cheek lay I this zealous kiss,
As seal to this indenture of my love,   20
That to my home I will no more return,
Till Angiers and the right thou hast in France,
Together with that pale, that white-fac'd shore,
Whose foot spurns back the ocean's roaring tides
And coops from other lands her islanders,—
Even till that England, hedg'd in with the main,
That water-walled bulwark, still secure
And confident from foreign purposes,—
Even till that utmost corner of the west
Salute thee for her king ; till then, fair boy,   30
Will I not think of home, but follow arms.
    Constance. O, take his mother's thanks, a widow's thanks,
Till your strong hand shall help to give him strength
To make a more requital to your love !
    Austria. The peace of heaven is theirs that lift their swords
In such a just and charitable war.
    King Philip. Well then, to work. Our cannon shall be
      bent
Against the brows of this resisting town.—
Call for our chiefest men of discipline,
To cull the plots of best advantages.   40
We 'll lay before this town our royal bones,

Wade to the market-place in Frenchmen's blood,
But we will make it subject to this boy.
    Constance. Stay for an answer to your embassy,
Lest unadvis'd you stain your swords with blood.
My Lord Chatillon may from England bring
That right in peace which here we urge in war,
And then we shall repent each drop of blood
That hot rash haste so indirectly shed.

Enter CHATILLON.

    King Philip. A wonder, lady! lo, upon thy wish,   50
Our messenger Chatillon is arriv'd !—
What England says, say briefly, gentle lord ;
We coldly pause for thee ; Chatillon, speak.
    Chatillon. Then turn your forces from this paltry siege,
And stir them up against a mightier task.
England, impatient of your just demands,
Hath put himself in arms ; the adverse winds,
Whose leisure I have stay'd, have given him time
To land his legions all as soon as I.
His marches are expedient to this town,   60
His forces strong, his soldiers confident.
With him along is come the mother-queen,
An Ate, stirring him to blood and strife ;
With her her niece, the Lady Blanch of Spain ;
With them a bastard of the king's deceas'd ;
And all the unsettled humours of the land,
Rash, inconsiderate, fiery voluntaries,
With ladies' faces and fierce dragons' spleens,
Have sold their fortunes at their native homes,
Bearing their birthrights proudly on their backs,   70
To make a hazard of new fortunes here.
In brief, a braver choice of dauntless spirits
Than now the English bottoms have waft o'er
Did never float upon the swelling tide,

To do offence and scath in Christendom.　　　[*Drum beats.*
The interruption of their churlish drums
Cuts off more circumstance : they are at hand,
To parley or to fight; therefore prepare.
　　King Philip. How much unlook'd for is this expedition !
　　Austria. By how much unexpected, by so much　　　80
We must awake endeavour for defence ;
For courage mounteth with occasion.
Let them be welcome then; we are prepar'd.

Enter KING JOHN, ELINOR, BLANCH, *the* Bastard, Lords, *and forces.*

　　King John. Peace be to France, if France in peace permit
Our just and lineal entrance to our own;
If not, bleed France, and peace ascend to heaven,
Whiles we, God's wrathful agent, do correct
Their proud contempt that beats His peace to heaven.
　　King Philip. Peace be to England, if that war return
From France to England, there to live in peace.　　　90
England we love ; and for that England's sake
With burden of our armour here we sweat.
This toil of ours should be a work of thine ;
But thou from loving England art so far,
That thou hast under-wrought his lawful king,
Cut off the sequence of posterity,
Out-faced infant state and done a rape
'Upon the maiden virtue of the crown.
Look here upon thy brother Geffrey's face;
These eyes, these brows, were moulded out of his :　　　100
This little abstract doth contain that large
Which died in Geffrey, and the hand of time
Shall draw this brief into as huge a volume.
That Geffrey was thy elder brother born,
And this his son ; England was Geffrey's right
And this is Geffrey's : in the name of God

How comes it then that thou art call'd a king,
When living blood doth in these temples beat,
Which owe the crown that thou o'ermasterest?

King John. From whom hast thou this great commission,
    France, 110
To draw my answer from thy articles?

King Philip. From that supernal judge, that stirs good
    thoughts
In any breast of strong authority,
To look into the blots and stains of right.
That judge hath made me guardian to this boy;
Under whose warrant I impeach thy wrong,
And by whose help I mean to chastise it.

King John. Alack! thou dost usurp authority.

King Philip. Excuse, it is to beat usurping down.

Elinor. Who is it thou dost call usurper, France? 120

Constance. Let me make answer,—thy usurping son.

Elinor. Out, insolent! thy bastard shall be king,
That thou mayst be a queen, and check the world!

Constance. My bed was ever to thy son as true
As thine was to thy husband; and this boy
Liker in feature to his father Geffrey
Than thou and John in manners—being as like
As rain to water, or devil to his dam.
My boy a bastard! By my soul, I think
His father never was so true begot; 130
It cannot be, an if thou wert his mother.

Elinor. There's a good mother, boy, that blots thy
    father.

Constance. There's a good grandam, boy, that would blot
    thee.

Austria. Peace.

Bastard.   Hear the crier.

Austria.   What the devil art thou?

Bastard. One that will play the devil, sir, with you,

An a' may catch your hide and you alone.
You are the hare of whom the proverb goes,
Whose valour plucks dead lions by the beard.
I 'll smoke your skin-coat, an I catch you right:
Sirrah, look to 't; i' faith, I will, i' faith.   140

   Blanch. O, well did he become that lion's robe
That did disrobe the lion of that robe!

   Bastard. It lies as sightly on the back of him
As great Alcides' shows upon an ass;
But, ass, I 'll take that burthen from your back,
Or lay on that shall make your shoulders crack.

   Austria. What cracker is this same that deafs our ears
With this abundance of superfluous breath?
King Philip, determine what we shall do straight.

   King Philip. Women and fools, break off your conference.
King John, this is the very sum of all: 151
England and Ireland, Anjou, Touraine, Maine,
In right of Arthur do I claim of thee.
Wilt thou resign them and lay down thy arms?

   King John. My life as soon; I do defy thee, France.—
Arthur of Bretagne, yield thee to my hand;
And out of my dear love I 'll give thee more
Than e'er the coward hand of France can win:
Submit thee, boy.

   Elinor.   Come to thy grandam, child.

   Constance. Do, child, go to it grandam, child;   160
Give grandam kingdom, and it grandam will
Give it a plum, a cherry, and a fig;
There 's a good grandam.

   Arthur.   Good my mother, peace!
I would that I were low laid in my grave;
I am not worth this coil that 's made for me.

   Elinor. His mother shames him so, poor boy, he weeps.

   Constance. Now shame upon you, whether she does or no!
His grandam's wrongs, and not his mother's shames,

Draws those heaven-moving pearls from his poor eyes,
Which heaven shall take in nature of a fee;   170
Ay, with these crystal beads heaven shall be brib'd
To do him justice and revenge on you.
    Elinor. Thou monstrous slanderer of heaven and earth!
    Constance. Thou monstrous injurer of heaven and earth!
Call not me slanderer; thou and thine usurp
The dominations, royalties, and rights
Of this oppressed boy. This is thy eld'st son's son,
Infortunate in nothing but in thee:
Thy sins are visited in this poor child;
The canon of the law is laid on him,   180
Being but the second generation
Removed from thy sin-conceiving womb.
    King John. Bedlam, have done.
    Constance.   I have but this to say,—
That he is not only plagued for her sin,
But God hath made her sin and her the plague
On this removed issue, plagu'd for her
And with her plague; her sin his injury,
Her injury the beadle to her sin,
All punish'd in the person of this child,
And all for her; a plague upon her!   190
    Elinor. Thou unadvised scold, I can produce
A will that bars the title of thy son.
    Constance. Ay, who doubts that? a will! a wicked will;
A woman's will; a canker'd grandam's will!
    King Philip. Peace, lady! pause, or be more temperate.
It ill beseems this presence to cry aim
To these ill-tuned repetitions.—
Some trumpet summon hither to the walls
These men of Angiers: let us hear them speak
Whose title they admit, Arthur's or John's.   200

Trumpet sounds.   Enter certain Citizens *upon the walls.*

Citizen. Who is it that hath warn'd us to the walls?
King Philip. "T is France, for England.
King John.   England, for itself.
You men of Angiers, and my loving subjects,—
    King Philip. You loving men of Angiers, Arthur's sub-
        jects,
Our trumpet call'd you to this gentle parle—
    King John. For our advantage ; therefore hear us first.
These flags of France, that are advanced here
Before the eye and prospect of your town,
Have hither march'd to your endamagement.
The cannons have their bowels full of wrath,   210
And ready mounted are they to spit forth
Their iron indignation 'gainst your walls.
All preparation for a bloody siege
And merciless proceeding by these French
Confronts your city's eyes, your winking gates ;
And but for our approach those sleeping stones,
That as a waist doth girdle you about,
By the compulsion of their ordinance
By this time from their fixed beds of lime
Had been dishabited, and wide havoc made   22c
For bloody power to rush upon your peace.
But on the sight of us your lawful king,
Who painfully with much expedient march
Have brought a countercheck before your gates,
To save unscratch'd your city's threaten'd cheeks,
Behold, the French amaz'd vouchsafe a parle ;
And now, instead of bullets wrapp'd in fire,
To make a shaking fever in your walls,
They shoot but calm words folded up in smoke,
To make a faithless error in your ears :   230
Which trust accordingly, kind citizens,

And let us in, your king, whose labour'd spirits,
Forwearied in this action of swift speed,
Crave harbourage within your city walls.
  King Philip. When I have said, make answer to us both.
Lo, in this right hand, whose protection
Is most divinely vow'd upon the right
Of him it holds, stands young Plantagenet,
Son to the elder brother of this man,
And king o'er him and all that he enjoys.   240
For this down-trodden equity, we tread
In warlike march these greens before your town,
Being no further enemy to you
Than the constraint of hospitable zeal
In the relief of this oppressed child
Religiously provokes.   Be pleased then
To pay that duty which you truly owe
To him that owes it, namely this young prince;
And then our arms, like to a muzzled bear,
Save in aspect, hath all offence seal'd up.   250
Our cannons' malice vainly shall be spent
Against the invulnerable clouds of heaven;
And with a blessed and unvex'd retire,
With unhack'd swords and helmets all unbruis'd,
We will bear home that lusty blood again
Which here we came to spout against your town,
And leave your children, wives, and you in peace.
But if you fondly pass our proffer'd offer,
'T is not the roundure of your old-fac'd walls
Can hide you from our messengers of war,   260
Though all these English and their discipline
Were harbour'd in their rude circumference.
Then tell us, shall your city call us lord,
In that behalf which we have challeng'd it?
Or shall we give the signal to our rage,
And stalk in blood to our possession?

Citizen. In brief, we are the king of England's subjects;
For him, and in his right, we hold this town.

King John. Acknowledge then the king, and let me in.

Citizen. That can we not; but he that proves the king,
To him will we prove loyal: till that time   271
Have we ramm'd up our gates against the world.

King John. Doth not the crown of England prove the king?
And if not that, I bring you witnesses,
Twice fifteen thousand hearts of England's breed,—

Bastard. Bastards, and else.

King John. To verify our title with their lives.

King Philip. As many and as well-born bloods as those—

Bastard. Some bastards too.

King Philip. Stand in his face to contradict his claim.   280

Citizen. Till you compound whose right is worthiest,
We for the worthiest hold the right from both.

King John. Then God forgive the sin of all those souls
That to their everlasting residence,
Before the dew of evening fall, shall fleet,
In dreadful trial of our kingdom's king!

King Philip. Amen, amen!—Mount, chevaliers! to arms!

Bastard. Saint George, that swing'd the dragon, and e'er
        since
Sits on his horse back at mine hostess' door,
Teach us some fence!—[*To Austria*] Sirrah, were I at home,
At your den, sirrah, with your lioness,   291
I would set an ox-head to your lion's hide,
And make a monster of you.

Austria.   Peace! no more.

Bastard. O, tremble, for you hear the lion roar!

King John. Up higher to the plain; where we 'll set forth
In best appointment all our regiments.

Bastard. Speed then, to take advantage of the field.

King Philip. It shall be so;—and at the other hill
Command the rest to stand.— God and our right! [*Exeunt.*

Alarums and excursions; then enter a French Herald, *with trumpets, to the gates.*

French Herald. You men of Angiers, open wide your gates,
And let young Arthur, Duke of Bretagne, in,   301
Who by the hand of France this day hath made
Much work for tears in many an English mother,
Whose sons lie scatter'd on the bleeding ground.
Many a widow's husband grovelling lies,
Coldly embracing the discolour'd earth;
And victory, with little loss, doth play
Upon the dancing banners of the French,
Who are at hand, triumphantly display'd,
To enter conquerors and to proclaim   310
Arthur of Bretagne England's king and yours.

Enter English Herald, *with trumpets.*

English Herald. Rejoice, you men of Angiers, ring your
    bells;
King John, your king and England's, doth approach,
Commander of this hot malicious day.
Their armours, that march'd hence so silver-bright,
Hither return all gilt with Frenchmen's blood.
There stuck no plume in any English crest
That is removed by a staff of France;
Our colours do return in those same hands
That did display them when we first march'd forth;   320
And, like a jolly troop of huntsmen, come
Our lusty English, all with purpled hands,
Dyed in the dying slaughter of their foes.
Open your gates and give the victors way.

Citizen. Heralds, from off our towers we might behold,
From first to last, the onset and retire
Of both your armies; whose equality
By our best eyes cannot be censured.

Blood hath bought blood, and blows have answer'd blows ;
Strength match'd with strength, and power confronted power :
Both are alike ; and both alike we like.   331
One must prove greatest ; while they weigh so even,
We hold our town for neither, yet for both.

Re-enter the two KINGS, *with their powers, severally.*

King John. France, hast thou yet more blood to cast away ?
Say, shall the current of our right run on ?
Whose passage, vex'd with thy impediment,
Shall leave his native channel and o'erswell
With course disturb'd even thy confining shores,
Unless thou let his silver water keep
A peaceful progress to the ocean.   340
   King Philip. England, thou hast not sav'd one drop of
      blood,
In this hot trial, more than we of France ;
Rather, lost more.   And by this hand I swear,
That sways the earth this climate overlooks,
Before we will lay down our just-borne arms,
We 'll put thee down, 'gainst whom these arms we bear,
Or add a royal number to the dead,
Gracing the scroll that tells of this war's loss
With slaughter coupled to the name of kings.
   Bastard. Ha, majesty ! how high thy glory towers,   350
When the rich blood of kings is set on fire !
O, now doth Death line his dead chaps with steel :
The swords of soldiers are his teeth, his fangs ;
And now he feasts, mousing the flesh of men,
In undetermin'd differences of kings.—
Why stand these royal fronts amazed thus ?
Cry havoc, kings ! back to the stained field,
You equal potents, fiery kindled spirits !
Then let confusion of one part confirm
The other's peace ; till then, blows, blood, and death !   360

King John. Whose party do the townsmen yet admit?
King Philip. Speak, citizens, for England; who's your
    king?
Citizen. The king of England, when we know the king.
King Philip. Know him in us, that here hold up his right.
King John. In us, that are our own great deputy,
And bear possession of our person here,
Lord of our presence, Angiers, and of you.
    Citizen. A greater power than we denies all this;
And till it be undoubted, we do lock
Our former scruple in our strong-barr'd gates;   370
King'd of our fears, until our fears, resolv'd,
Be by some certain king purg'd and depos'd.
    Bastard. By heaven, these scroyles of Angiers flout you,
    kings,
And stand securely on their battlements,
As in a theatre, whence they gape and point
At your industrious scenes and acts of death.
Your royal presences be rul'd by me:
Do like the mutines of Jerusalem;
Be friends awhile, and both conjointly bend
Your sharpest deeds of malice on this town.   380
By east and west let France and England mount
Their battering cannon charged to the mouths,
Till their soul-fearing clamours have brawl'd down
The flinty ribs of this contemptuous city.
I'd play incessantly upon these jades,
Even till unfenced desolation
Leave them as naked as the vulgar air.
That done, dissever your united strengths,
And part your mingled colours once again,
Turn face to face and bloody point to point;   390
Then, in a moment, Fortune shall cull forth
Out of one side her happy minion,
To whom in favour she shall give the day,

And kiss him with a glorious victory.
How like you this wild counsel, mighty states?
Smacks it not something of the policy?

King John. Now, by the sky that hangs above our heads,
I like it well.—France, shall we knit our powers
And lay this Angiers even with the ground,
Then after fight who shall be king of it?   400

Bastard. An if thou hast the mettle of a king,
Being wrong'd as we are by this peevish town,
Turn thou the mouth of thy artillery,
As we will ours, against these saucy walls;
And when that we have dash'd them to the ground,
Why then defy each other, and pell-mell
Make work upon ourselves, for heaven or hell.

King Philip. Let it be so.—Say, where will you assault?

King John. We from the west will send destruction
Into this city's bosom.   410

Austria. I from the north.

King Philip.   Our thunder from the south
Shall rain their drift of bullets on this town.

Bastard. O prudent discipline! From north to south,
Austria and France shoot in each other's mouth:
I'll stir them to it.—Come, away, away!

Citizen. Hear us, great kings; vouchsafe awhile to stay,
And I shall show you peace and fair-fac'd league,
Win you this city without stroke or wound,
Rescue those breathing lives to die in beds,
That here come sacrifices for the field.   420
Persever not, but hear me, mighty kings.

King John. Speak on with favour; we are bent to hear.

Citizen. That daughter there of Spain, the Lady Blanch,
Is niece to England; look upon the years
Of Lewis the Dauphin and that lovely maid.
If lusty love should go in quest of beauty,
Where should he find it fairer than in Blanch?

If zealous love should go in search of virtue,
Where should he find it purer than in Blanch?
If love ambitious sought a match of birth,   430
Whose veins bound richer blood than Lady Blanch?
Such as she is, in beauty, virtue, birth,
Is the young Dauphin every way complete:
If not complete of, say he is not she;
And she again wants nothing, to name want,
If want it be not that she is not he.
He is the half part of a blessed man,
Left to be finished by such a she;
And she a fair divided excellence,
Whose fulness of perfection lies in him.   440
O, two such silver currents, when they join,
Do glorify the banks that bound them in;
And two such shores to two such streams made one,
Two such controlling bounds shall you be, kings,
To these two princes, if you marry them.
This union shall do more than battery can
To our fast-closed gates; for at this match,
With swifter spleen than powder can enforce,
The mouth of passage shall we fling wide ope,
And give you entrance: but without this match,   450
The sea enraged is not half so deaf,
Lions more confident, mountains and rocks
More free from motion, no, not Death himself
In mortal fury half so peremptory,
As we to keep this city.
    Bastard.   Here's a stay
That shakes the rotten carcass of old Death
Out of his rags! Here's a large mouth, indeed,
That spits forth death and mountains, rocks and seas,
Talks as familiarly of roaring lions
As maids of thirteen do of puppy-dogs!   460
What cannoneer begot this lusty blood?

E

He speaks plain cannon fire, and smoke and bounce;
He gives the bastinado with his tongue:
Our ears are cudgell'd; not a word of his
But buffets better than a fist of France.
Zounds! I was never so bethump'd with words
Since I first call'd my brother's father dad.

 Elinor. Son, list to this conjunction, make this match;
Give with our niece a dowry large enough:
For by this knot thou shalt so surely tie   170
Thy now unsur'd assurance to the crown,
That yon green boy shall have no sun to ripe
The bloom that promiseth a mighty fruit.
I see a yielding in the looks of France;
Mark, how they whisper: urge them while their souls
Are capable of this ambition,
Lest zeal, now melted, by the windy breath
Of soft petitions, pity, and remorse,
Cool and congeal again to what it was.

 Citizen. Why answer not the double majesties   480
This friendly treaty of our threaten'd town?

 King Philip. Speak England first, that hath been forward
   first
To speak unto this city; what say you?

 King John. If that the Dauphin there, thy princely son,
Can in this book of beauty read 'I love,'
Her dowry shall weigh equal with a queen;
For Anjou and fair Touraine, Maine, Poictiers,
And all that we upon this side the sea,
Except this city now by us besieg'd,
Find liable to our crown and dignity,   490
Shall gild her bridal bed and make her rich
In titles, honours, and promotions,
As she in beauty, education, blood,
Holds hand with any princess of the world.

 King Philip. What say'st thou, boy? look in the lady's face.

Lewis. I do, my lord; and in her eye I find
A wonder, or a wondrous miracle,
The shadow of myself form'd in her eye;
Which, being but the shadow of your son,
Becomes a sun and makes your son a shadow. 500
I do protest I never lov'd myself
Till now infixed I beheld myself
Drawn in the flattering table of her eye.
　　　　　　　　　　[*Whispers with Blanch.*
Bastard. Drawn in the flattering table of her eye!
Hang'd in the frowning wrinkle of her brow!
And quarter'd in her heart! he doth espy
Himself love's traitor; this is pity now,
That, hang'd and drawn and quarter'd, there should be
In such a love so vile a lout as he.
Blanch. My uncle's will in this respect is mine: 510
If he see aught in you that makes him like,
That any thing he sees, which moves his liking,
I can with ease translate it to my will;
Or if you will, to speak more properly,
I will enforce it easily to my love.
Further I will not flatter you, my lord,
That all I see in you is worthy love,
Than this,—that nothing do I see in you,
Though churlish thoughts themselves should be your judge,
That I can find should merit any hate. 520
　King John. What say these young ones?—What say you,
　　my niece?
Blanch. That she is bound in honour still to do
What you in wisdom still vouchsafe to say.
　King John. Speak then, prince Dauphin; can you love
　　this lady?
Lewis. Nay, ask me if I can refrain from love;
For I do love her most unfeignedly.
　King John. Then do I give Volquessen, Touraine, Maine,

Poictiers, and Anjou, these five provinces,
With her to thee; and this addition more,
Full thirty thousand marks of English coin.—   530
Philip of France, if thou be pleas'd withal,
Command thy son and daughter to join hands.

    King Philip. It likes us well.—Young princes, close your
        hands.

    Austria. And your lips too; for I am well assur'd
That I did so when I was first assur'd.

    King Philip. Now, citizens of Angiers, ope your gates,
Let in that amity which you have made;
For at St. Mary's chapel presently
The rites of marriage shall be solemniz'd.—
Is not the Lady Constance in this troop?   540
I know she is not, for this match made up
Her presence would have interrupted much.
Where is she and her son? tell me, who knows.

    Lewis. She is sad and passionate at your highness'
        tent.

    King Philip. And, by my faith, this league that we have
        made
Will give her sadness very little cure.—
Brother of England, how may we content
This widow lady? In her right we came;
Which we, God knows, have turn'd another way,
To our own vantage.

    King John.   We will heal up all;   550
For we 'll create young Arthur Duke of Bretagne
And Earl of Richmond; and this rich fair town
We make him lord of.—Call the lady Constance;
Some speedy messenger bid her repair
To our solemnity.—I trust we shall,
If not fill up the measure of her will,
Yet in some measure satisfy her so
That we shall stop her exclamation.

Go we, as well as haste will suffer us,
To this unlook'd for, unprepared pomp.   560
                    [*Exeunt all but the Bastard.*
  Bastard. Mad world! mad kings! mad composition!
John, to stop Arthur's title in the whole,
Hath willingly departed with a part;
And France, whose armour conscience buckled on,
Whom zeal and charity brought to the field
As God's own soldier, rounded in the ear
With that same purpose-changer, that sly devil,
That broker, that still breaks the pate of faith,
That daily break-vow, he that wins of all,
Of kings, of beggars, old men, young men, maids,   570
Who, having no external thing to lose
But the word maid, cheats the poor maid of that,
That smooth-fac'd gentleman, tickling Commodity,—
Commodity, the bias of the world,
The world, who of itself is peized well,
Made to run even upon even ground,
Till this advantage, this vile-drawing bias,
This sway of motion, this Commodity,
Makes it take head from all indifferency,
From all direction, purpose, course, intent;—   580
And this same bias, this Commodity,
This bawd, this broker, this all-changing word,
Clapp'd on the outward eye of fickle France,
Hath drawn him from his own determin'd aid,
From a resolv'd and honourable war,
To a most base and vile-concluded peace.
And why rail I on this Commodity?
But for because he hath not woo'd me yet:
Not that I have the power to clutch my hand,
When his fair angels would salute my palm;   590
But for my hand, as unattempted yet,
Like a poor beggar, raileth on the rich.

Well, whiles I am a beggar, I will rail
And say there is no sin but to be rich;
And being rich, my virtue then shall be
To say there is no vice but beggary.
Since kings break faith upon commodity,
Gain, be my lord, for I will worship thee!   [*Exit.*

QUEEN ELINOR.

THE BATTLE NEAR ANGIERS.

ACT III.

Scene I. *The French King's Pavilion.*

Enter CONSTANCE, ARTHUR, *and* SALISBURY.

Constance. Gone to be married! gone to swear a peace!
False blood to false blood join'd! gone to be friends!
Shall Lewis have Blanch, and Blanch those provinces?
It is not so; thou hast misspoke, misheard;
Be well advis'd, tell o'er thy tale again:
It cannot be; thou dost but say 't is so.
I trust I may not trust thee; for thy word
Is but the vain breath of a common man.
Believe me, I do not believe thee, man;
I have a king's oath to the contrary.   10
Thou shalt be punish'd for thus frighting me,

For I am sick and capable of fears,
Oppress'd with wrongs and therefore full of fears,
A widow, husbandless, subject to fears,
A woman, naturally born to fears;
And though thou now confess thou didst but jest,
With my vex'd spirits I cannot take a truce,
But they will quake and tremble all this day.
What dost thou mean by shaking of thy head?
Why dost thou look so sadly on my son?   20
What means that hand upon that breast of thine?
Why holds thine eye that lamentable rheum,
Like a proud river peering o'er his bounds?
Be these sad signs confirmers of thy words?
Then speak again; not all thy former tale,
But this one word, whether thy tale be true.
     Salisbury. As true as I believe you think them false
That give you cause to prove my saying true.
     Constance. O, if thou teach me to believe this sorrow,
Teach thou this sorrow how to make me die,   30
And let belief and life encounter so
As doth the fury of two desperate men
Which in the very meeting fall and die!
Lewis marry Blanch! O boy, then where art thou?
France friend with England, what becomes of me?—
Fellow, be gone: I cannot brook thy sight;
This news hath made thee a most ugly man.
     Salisbury. What other harm have I, good lady, done,
But spoke the harm that is by others done?
     Constance. Which harm within itself so heinous is   40
As it makes harmful all that speak of it.
     Arthur. I do beseech you, madam, be content.
     Constance. If thou, that bid'st me be content, wert grim,
Ugly, and slanderous to thy mother's womb,
Full of unpleasing blots and sightless stains,
Lame, foolish, crooked, swart, prodigious,

Patch'd with foul moles and eye-offending marks,
I would not care, I then would be content;
For then I should not love thee, no, nor thou
Become thy great birth nor deserve a crown. 50
But thou art fair, and at thy birth, dear boy,
Nature and Fortune join'd to make thee great;
Of Nature's gifts thou mayst with lilies boast
And with the half-blown rose. But Fortune, O,
She is corrupted, chang'd, and won from thee;
She adulterates hourly with thine uncle John,
And with her golden hand hath pluck'd on France
To tread down fair respect of sovereignty,
And made his majesty the bawd to theirs.
France is a bawd to Fortune and King John, 60
That strumpet Fortune, that usurping John!—
Tell me, thou fellow, is not France forsworn?
Envenom him with words, or get thee gone
And leave those woes alone which I alone
Am bound to underbear.
    Salisbury.   Pardon me, madam,
I may not go without you to the kings.
    Constance. Thou mayst, thou shalt; I will not go with thee.
I will instruct my sorrows to be proud;
For grief is proud and makes his owner stoop.
To me and to the state of my great grief 70
Let kings assemble; for my grief's so great
That no supporter but the huge firm earth
Can hold it up. Here I and sorrows sit;
Here is my throne, bid kings come bow to it.
                    [Seats herself on the ground.

Enter KING JOHN, KING PHILIP, LEWIS, BLANCH, ELINOR,
    the BASTARD, AUSTRIA, *and* Attendants.

    King Philip. 'T is true, fair daughter; and this blessed
    day

Ever in France shall be kept festival.
To solemnize this day the glorious sun
Stays in his course and plays the alchemist,
Turning with splendour of his precious eye
The meagre cloddy earth to glittering gold.   80
The yearly course that brings this day about
Shall never see it but a holiday.

    Constance. A wicked day, and not a holy day!   [*Rising.*
What hath this day deserv'd? what hath it done,
That it in golden letters should be set
Among the high tides in the calendar?
Nay, rather turn this day out of the week,
This day of shame, oppression, perjury;
Or, if it must stand still, let wives with child
Pray that their burthens may not fall this day,   90
Lest that their hopes prodigiously be cross'd.
But on this day let seamen fear no wrack;
No bargains break that are not this day made:
This day, all things begun come to ill end,
Yea, faith itself to hollow falsehood change!

    King Philip. By heaven, lady, you shall have no cause
To curse the fair proceedings of this day.
Have I not pawn'd to you my majesty?

    Constance. You have beguil'd me with a counterfeit
Resembling majesty, which, being touch'd and tried,   100
Proves valueless: you are forsworn, forsworn;
You came in arms to spill mine enemies' blood,
But now in arms you strengthen it with yours.
The grappling vigour and rough frown of war
Is cold in amity and painted peace,
And our oppression hath made up this league.—
Arm, arm, you heavens, against these perjur'd kings!
A widow cries; be husband to me, heavens!
Let not the hours of this ungodly day
Wear out the day in peace; but, ere sunset,   110

Set armed discord 'twixt these perjur'd kings!
Hear me, O, hear me!
    Austria.   Lady Constance, peace!
    Constance. War! war! no peace! peace is to me a war.—
O Lymoges! O Austria! thou dost shame
That bloody spoil; thou slave, thou wretch, thou coward!
Thou little valiant, great in villany!
Thou ever strong upon the stronger side!
Thou Fortune's champion that dost never fight
But when her humorous ladyship is by
To teach thee safety! thou art perjur'd too,   120
And sooth'st up greatness.   What a fool art thou,
A ramping fool, to brag and stamp and swear
Upon my party! Thou cold-blooded slave,
Hast thou not spoke like thunder on my side,
Been sworn my soldier, bidding me depend
Upon thy stars, thy fortune, and thy strength,
And dost thou now fall over to my foes?
Thou wear a lion's hide! doff it for shame,
And hang a calf's-skin on those recreant limbs.   129
    Austria. O, that a man should speak those words to me!
    Bastard. And hang a calf's-skin on those recreant limbs.
    Austria. Thou dar'st not say so, villain, for thy life.
    Bastard. And hang a calf's-skin on those recreant limbs.
    King John. We like not this; thou dost forget thyself.

          Enter PANDULPH.

    King Philip. Here comes the holy legate of the pope.
    Pandulph. Hail, you anointed deputies of heaven!
To thee, King John, my holy errand is.
I Pandulph, of fair Milan cardinal,
And from Pope Innocent the legate here,
Do in his name religiously demand   140
Why thou against the church, our holy mother,
So wilfully dost spurn, and force perforce

Keep Stephen Langton, chosen archbishop
Of Canterbury, from that holy see?
This, in our foresaid holy father's name,
Pope Innocent, I do demand of thee.

    King John. What earthly name to interrogatories
Can task the free breath of a sacred king?
Thou canst not, cardinal, devise a name
So slight, unworthy, and ridiculous,   150
To charge me to an answer, as the pope.
Tell him this tale; and from the mouth of England
Add thus much more,—that no Italian priest
Shall tithe or toll in our dominions:
But as we, under heaven, are supreme head,
So under Him that great supremacy,
Where we do reign, we will alone uphold,
Without the assistance of a mortal hand.
So tell the pope, all reverence set apart
To him and his usurp'd authority.   160

    King Philip. Brother of England, you blaspheme in this.

    King John. Though you and all the kings of Christen-
      dom
Are led so grossly by this meddling priest,
Dreading the curse that money may buy out,
And by the merit of vile gold, dross, dust,
Purchase corrupted pardon of a man,
Who in that sale sells pardon from himself,
Though you and all the rest, so grossly led,
This juggling witchcraft with revenue cherish,
Yet I alone, alone do me oppose   170
Against the pope, and count his friends my foes.

    Pandulph. Then, by the lawful power that I have,
Thou shalt stand curs'd and excommunicate:
And blessed shall he be that doth revolt
From his allegiance to an heretic;
And meritorious shall that hand be call'd,

Canonized and worshipp'd as a saint,
That takes away by any secret course
Thy hateful life.
 Constance. O, lawful let it be
That I have room with Rome to curse awhile! 180
Good father cardinal, cry thou amen
To my keen curses; for without my wrong
There is no tongue hath power to curse him right.
 Pandulph. There 's law and warrant, lady, for my curse.
 Constance. And for mine too; when law can do no right,
Let it be lawful that law bar no wrong.
Law cannot give my child his kingdom here,
For he that holds his kingdom holds the law;
Therefore, since law itself is perfect wrong,
How can the law forbid my tongue to curse? 190
 Pandulph. Philip of France, on peril of a curse,
Let go the hand of that arch-heretic,
And raise the power of France upon his head,
Unless he do submit himself to Rome.
 Elinor. Look'st thou pale, France? do not let go thy
  hand.
 Constance. Look to that, devil; lest that France repent,
And by disjoining hands hell lose a soul.
 Austria. King Philip, listen to the cardinal.
 Bastard. And hang a calf's-skin on his recreant limbs.
 Austria. Well, ruffian, I must pocket up these wrongs, 200
Because—
 Bastard. Your breeches best may carry them.
 King John. Philip, what say'st thou to the cardinal?
 Constance. What should he say, but as the cardinal?
 Lewis. Bethink you, father; for the difference
Is purchase of a heavy curse from Rome,
Or the light loss of England for a friend:
Forego the easier.
 Blanch. That 's the curse of Rome.

 Constance. O Lewis, stand fast! the devil tempts thee
  here
In likeness of a new untrimmed bride.   209

 Blanch. The Lady Constance speaks not from her faith,
But from her need.

 Constance.   O, if thou grant my need,
Which only lives but by the death of faith,
That need must needs infer this principle,
That faith would live again by death of need.
O then, tread down my need, and faith mounts up;
Keep my need up, and faith is trodden down!

 King John. The king is mov'd, and answers not to this.

 Constance. O, be remov'd from him, and answer well!

 Austria. Do so, King Philip; hang no more in doubt. 219

 Bastard. Hang nothing but a calf's-skin, most sweet lout.

 King Philip. I am perplex'd, and know not what to say.

 Pandulph. What canst thou say but will perplex thee
  more,
If thou stand excommunicate and curs'd?

 King Philip. Good reverend father, make my person yours,
And tell me how you would bestow yourself.
This royal hand and mine are newly knit,
And the conjunction of our inward souls
Married in league, coupled and link'd together
With all religious strength of sacred vows.
The latest breath that gave the sound of words 230
Was deep-sworn faith, peace, amity, true love
Between our kingdoms and our royal selves;
And even before this truce, but new before,
No longer than we well could wash our hands
To clap this royal bargain up of peace,
Heaven knows, they were besmear'd and overstain'd
With slaughter's pencil, where revenge did paint
The fearful difference of incensed kings:
And shall these hands, so lately purg'd of blood,

So newly join'd in love, so strong in both,   240
Unyoke this seizure and this kind regreet?
Play fast and loose with faith? so jest with heaven,
Make such unconstant children of ourselves,
As now again to snatch our palm from palm,
Unswear faith sworn, and on the marriage-bed
Of smiling peace to march a bloody host,
And make a riot on the gentle brow
Of true sincerity? O, holy sir,
My reverend father, let it not be so!
Out of your grace, devise, ordain, impose   250
Some gentle order; and then we shall be blest
To do your pleasure and continue friends.
    Pandulph. All form is formless, order orderless,
Save what is opposite to England's love.
Therefore to arms! be champion of our church,
Or let the church, our mother, breathe her curse,
A mother's curse, on her revolting son.
France, thou mayst hold a serpent by the tongue,
A chafed lion by the mortal paw,
A fasting tiger safer by the tooth,   260
Than keep in peace that hand which thou dost hold.
    King Philip. I may disjoin my hand, but not my faith.
    Pandulph. So mak'st thou faith an enemy to faith,
And like a civil war set'st oath to oath,
Thy tongue against thy tongue. O, let thy vow
First made to heaven, first be to heaven perform'd,
That is, to be the champion of our church!
What since thou swor'st is sworn against thyself,
And may not be performed by thyself;
For that which thou hast sworn to do amiss   270
Is not amiss when it is truly done,
And being not done, where doing tends to ill,
The truth is then most done not doing it.
The better act of purposes mistook

Is to mistake again; though indirect,
Yet indirection thereby grows direct,
And falsehood falsehood cures, as fire cools fire
Within the scorched veins of one new-burn'd.
It is religion that doth make vows kept;
But thou hast sworn against religion,   280
By which thou swear'st against the thing thou swear'st,
And mak'st an oath the surety for thy truth
Against an oath: the truth thou art unsure
To swear swears only not to be forsworn;
Else what a mockery should it be to swear!
But thou dost swear only to be forsworn;
And most forsworn, to keep what thou dost swear.
Therefore thy later vows against thy first
Is in thyself rebellion to thyself;
And better conquest never canst thou make   290
Than arm thy constant and thy nobler parts
Against these giddy loose suggestions:
Upon which better part our prayers come in,
If thou vouchsafe them.   But if not, then know
The peril of our curses light on thee
So heavy as thou shalt not shake them off,
But in despair die under their black weight.
    Austria. Rebellion! flat rebellion!
    Bastard.   Will 't not be?
Will not a calf's-skin stop that mouth of thine?
    Lewis. Father, to arms!
    Blanch.   Upon thy wedding-day?   300
Against the blood that thou hast married?
What, shall our feast be kept with slaughter'd men?
Shall braying trumpets and loud churlish drums,
Clamours of hell, be measures to our pomp?
O husband, hear me!—ay, alack, how new
Is husband in my mouth!—even for that name,
Which till this time my tongue did ne'er pronounce,

Upon my knee I beg, go not to arms
Against mine uncle.
   Constance.   O, upon my knee,
Made hard with kneeling, I do pray to thee,   310
Thou virtuous Dauphin, alter not the doom
Forethought by heaven!
   Blanch. Now shall I see thy love; what motive may
Be stronger with thee than the name of wife?
   Constance. That which upholdeth him that thee upholds,
His honour.—O, thine honour, Lewis, thine honour!
   Lewis. I muse your majesty doth seem so cold,
When such profound respects do pull you on.
   Pandulph. I will denounce a curse upon his head.
   King Philip. Thou shalt not need.—England, I will fall
     from thee.   320
   Constance. O fair return of banish'd majesty!
   Elinor. O foul revolt of French inconstancy!
   King John. France, thou shalt rue this hour within this
     hour.
   Bastard. Old Time the clock - setter, that bald sexton
     Time,
Is it as he will? well then, France shall rue.
   Blanch. The sun's o'ercast with blood; fair day, adieu!
Which is the side that I must go withal?
I am with both: each army hath a hand;
And in their rage, I having hold of both,
They whirl asunder and dismember me.   330
Husband, I cannot pray that thou mayst win;
Uncle, I needs must pray that thou mayst lose;
Father, I may not wish the fortune thine;
Grandam, I will not wish thy wishes thrive;
Whoever wins, on that side shall I lose;
Assured loss before the match be play'd.
   Lewis. Lady, with me, with me thy fortune lies.
   Blanch. There where my fortune lives, there my life dies.

F

King John. Cousin, go draw our puissance together.—

         [*Exit Bastard.*

France, I am burn'd up with inflaming wrath ;   340

A rage whose heat hath this condition,

That nothing can allay, nothing but blood,

The blood, and dearest-valued blood, of France.

 King Philip. Thy rage shall burn thee up, and thou shalt turn

To ashes, ere our blood shall quench that fire ;

Look to thyself, thou art in jeopardy.

 King John. No more than he that threats.—To arms let 's

  hie !   [*Exeunt.*

   Scene II. *The Same. Plains near Angiers.*

Alarums, excursions. Enter the Bastard, *with* Austria's
head.

 Bastard. Now, by my life, this day grows wondrous hot ;

Some airy devil hovers in the sky

And pours down mischief. Austria's head lie there,

While Philip breathes.

   Enter King John, Arthur, *and* Hubert.

 King John. Hubert, keep this boy.—Philip, make up ;

My mother is assailed in our tent,

And ta'en, I fear.

 Bastard.   My lord, I rescued her ;

Her highness is in safety, fear you not :

But on, my liege ; for very little pains   9

Will bring this labour to an happy end.   [*Exeunt.*

SCENE III. *The Same.*

Alarums, excursions, retreat. Enter KING JOHN, ELINOR,
ARTHUR, *the* BASTARD, HUBERT, *and* Lords.

King John. [*To Elinor*] So shall it be ; your grace shall
    stay behind
So strongly guarded.—[*To Arthur*] Cousin, look not sad :
Thy grandam loves thee ; and thy uncle will
As dear be to thee as thy father was.
    Arthur. O, this will make my mother die with grief!
    King John. [*To the Bastard*] Cousin, away for England !
    haste before ;
And, ere our coming, see thou shake the bags
Of hoarding abbots. Set at liberty
Imprison'd angels ; the fat ribs of peace
Must by the hungry now be fed upon.   10
Use our commission in his utmost force.
    Bastard. Bell, book, and candle shall not drive me back,
When gold and silver becks me to come on.
I leave your highness.—Grandam, I will pray,
If ever I remember to be holy,
For your fair safety ; so, I kiss your hand.
    Elinor. Farewell, gentle cousin.
    King John.   Coz, farewell. [*Exit Bastard.*
    Elinor. Come hither, little kinsman ; hark, a word.
    King John. Come hither, Hubert. O my gentle Hu-
    bert,
We owe thee much ! within this wall of flesh   20
There is a soul counts thee her creditor
And with advantage means to pay thy love ;
And, my good friend, thy voluntary oath
Lives in this bosom, dearly cherished.
Give me thy hand. I had a thing to say,—
But I will fit it with some better time.

By heaven, Hubert, I am almost asham'd
To say what good respect I have of thee.

   Hubert. I am much bounden to your majesty.

   King John. Good friend, thou hast no cause to say so yet.
But thou shalt have; and creep time ne'er so slow,   31
Yet it shall come for me to do thee good.
I had a thing to say,—but let it go.
The sun is in the heaven, and the proud day,
Attended with the pleasures of the world,
Is all too wanton and too full of gawds
To give me audience.   If the midnight bell
Did, with his iron tongue and brazen mouth,
Sound on into the drowsy race of night;
If this same were a churchyard where we stand,   40
And thou possessed with a thousand wrongs,
Or if that surly spirit, melancholy,
Had bak'd thy blood and made it heavy-thick,
Which else runs tickling up and down the veins,
Making that idiot, laughter, keep men's eyes
And strain their cheeks to idle merriment,
A passion hateful to my purposes,
Or if that thou couldst see me without eyes,
Hear me without thine ears, and make reply
Without a tongue, using conceit alone,   50
Without eyes, ears, and harmful sound of words;
Then, in despite of brooded watchful day,
I would into thy bosom pour my thoughts.
But, ah, I will not!—yet I love thee well;
And, by my troth, I think thou lov'st me well.

   Hubert. So well, that what you bid me undertake,
Though that my death were adjunct to my act,
By heaven, I would do it!

   King John.   Do not I know thou wouldst?
Good Hubert, Hubert,—Hubert, throw thine eye
On yon young boy: I'll tell thee what, my friend,   60

He is a very serpent in my way;
And wheresoe'er this foot of mine doth tread,
He lies before me.   Dost thou understand me?
Thou art his keeper.
  Hubert.   And I 'll keep him so,
That he shall not offend your majesty.
  King John.   Death.
  Hubert. My lord?
  King John.   A grave.
  Hubert.   He shall not live.
  King John.   Enough.
I could be merry now.   Hubert, I love thee;
Well, I 'll not say what I intend for thee:
Remember.—Madam, fare you well;
I 'll send those powers o'er to your majesty.   70
  Elinor. My blessing go with thee!
  King John.   For England, cousin, go;
Hubert shall be your man, attend on you
With all true duty.—On toward Calais, ho!   [*Exeunt.*

  SCENE IV. *The Same.   The French King's Tent.*

Enter KING PHILIP, LEWIS, PANDULPH, *and* Attendants.

  King Philip. So, by a roaring tempest on the flood,
A whole armado of convicted sail
Is scatter'd and disjoin'd from fellowship.
  Pandulph. Courage and comfort! all shall yet go well.
  King Philip. What can go well, when we have run so ill?
Are we not beaten?   Is not Angiers lost?
Arthur ta'en prisoner? divers dear friends slain?
And bloody England into England gone,
O'erbearing interruption, spite of France?
  Lewis. What he hath won, that hath he fortified;   10
So hot a speed with such advice dispos'd,
Such temperate order in so fierce a cause,

Doth want example : who hath read or heard
Of any kindred action like to this?

   King Philip. Well could I bear that England had this
      praise,
So we could find some pattern of our shame.—

           Enter CONSTANCE.

Look, who comes here! a grave unto a soul;
Holding the eternal spirit, against her will,
In the vile prison of afflicted breath.—
I prithee, lady, go away with me.　　　　　　　　　　20

   Constance. Lo, now! now see the issue of your peace.

   King Philip. Patience, good lady! comfort, gentle Con-
      stance!

   Constance. No, I defy all counsel, all redress,
But that which ends all counsel, true redress,
Death, death.—O amiable lovely death!
Thou odoriferous stench! sound rottenness!
Arise forth from the couch of lasting night,
Thou hate and terror to prosperity,
And I will kiss thy detestable bones,
And put my eyeballs in thy vaulty brows,　　　　　　30
And ring these fingers with thy household worms,
And stop this gap of breath with fulsome dust,
And be a carrion monster like thyself!
Come, grin on me, and I will think thou smil'st,
And buss thee as thy wife!　Misery's love,
O come to me!

   King Philip.　　O fair affliction, peace!

   Constance. No, no, I will not, having breath to cry.—
O, that my tongue were in the thunder's mouth!
Then with a passion would I shake the world,
And rouse from sleep that fell anatomy　　　　　　40
Which cannot hear a lady's feeble voice,
Which scorns a modern invocation.

Pandulph. Lady, you utter madness, and not sorrow.
Constance. Thou art not holy to belie me so.
I am not mad : this hair I tear is mine ;
My name is Constance ; I was Geffrey's wife ;
Young Arthur is my son, and he is lost !
I am not mad ; I would to heaven I were !
For then, 't is like I should forget myself ;
O, if I could, what grief should I forget !—   50
Preach some philosophy to make me mad,
And thou shalt be canoniz'd, cardinal ;
For being not mad but sensible of grief,
My reasonable part produces reason
How I may be deliver'd of these woes,
And teaches me to kill or hang myself.
If I were mad, I should forget my son,
Or madly think a babe of clouts were he.
I am not mad ; too well, too well I feel
The different plague of each calamity.   60
    King Philip. Bind up those tresses.—O, what love I note
In the fair multitude of those her hairs !
Where but by chance a silver drop hath fallen,
Even to that drop ten thousand wiry friends
Do glue themselves in sociable grief,
Like true, inseparable, faithful loves,
Sticking together in calamity.
    Constance. To England, if you will.
    King Philip.   Bind up your hairs.
    Constance. Yes, that I will ; and wherefore will I do it ?
I tore them from their bonds, and cried aloud,   70
' O that these hands could so redeem my son,
As they have given these hairs their liberty !'
But now I envy at their liberty,
And will again commit them to their bonds,
Because my poor child is a prisoner.—
And, father cardinal, I have heard you say

That we shall see and know our friends in heaven :
If that be true, I shall see my boy again;
For since the birth of Cain, the first male child,
To him that did but yesterday suspire,   84
There was not such a gracious creature born.
But now will canker-sorrow eat my bud,
And chase the native beauty from his cheek,
And he will look as hollow as a ghost,
As dim and meagre as an ague's fit,
And so he 'll die; and, rising so again,
When I shall meet him in the court of heaven
I shall not know him : therefore never, never
Must I behold my pretty Arthur more.

    Pandulph. You hold too heinous a respect of grief.   90
    Constance. He talks to me that never had a son.
    King Philip. You are as fond of grief as of your child.
    Constance. Grief fills the room up of my absent child,
Lies in his bed, walks up and down with me,
Puts on his pretty looks, repeats his words,
Remembers me of all his gracious parts,
Stuffs out his vacant garments with his form;
Then, have I reason to be fond of grief?
Fare you well; had you such a loss as I,
I could give better comfort than you do.—   100
I will not keep this form upon my head,
When there is such disorder in my wit.
O Lord! my boy, my Arthur, my fair son!
My life, my joy, my food, my all the world!
My widow-comfort, and my sorrow's cure!   [*Exit.*
    King Philip. I fear some outrage, and I 'll follow her.
                                          [*Exit.*
    Lewis. There 's nothing in this world can make me
      joy :
Life is as tedious as a twice-told tale
Vexing the dull ear of a drowsy man;

And bitter shame hath spoil'd the sweet world's taste,   110
That it yields nought but shame and bitterness.
   Pandulph. Before the curing of a strong disease,
Even in the instant of repair and health,
The fit is strongest; evils that take leave,
On their departure most of all show evil.
What have you lost by losing of this day?
   Lewis. All days of glory, joy, and happiness.
   Pandulph. If you had won it, certainly you had.
No, no; when Fortune means to men most good,
She looks upon them with a threatening eye.   120
'T is strange to think how much King John hath lost
In this which he accounts so clearly won;
Are not you griev'd that Arthur is his prisoner?
   Lewis. As heartily as he is glad he hath him.
   Pandulph. Your mind is all as youthful as your blood.
Now hear me speak with a prophetic spirit;
For even the breath of what I mean to speak
Shall blow each dust, each straw, each little rub,
Out of the path which shall directly lead
Thy foot to England's throne; and therefore mark.   130
John hath seiz'd Arthur; and it cannot be
That, whiles warm life plays in that infant's veins,
The misplac'd John should entertain an hour,
One minute, nay, one quiet breath of rest.
A sceptre snatch'd with an unruly hand
Must be as boisterously maintain'd as gain'd;
And he that stands upon a slippery place
Makes nice of no vile hold to stay him up.
That John may stand, then Arthur needs must fall;
So be it, for it cannot be but so.   140
   Lewis. But what shall I gain by young Arthur's fall?
   Pandulph. You, in the right of Lady Blanch your wife,
May then make all the claim that Arthur did.
   Lewis. And lose it, life and all, as Arthur did.

Pandulph. How green you are and fresh in this old
   world!
John lays you plots; the times conspire with you;
For he that steeps his safety in true blood
Shall find but bloody safety and untrue.
This act so evilly born shall cool the hearts
Of all his people and freeze up their zeal,   150
That none so small advantage shall step forth
To check his reign, but they will cherish it;
No natural exhalation in the sky,
No scope of nature, no distemper'd day,
No common wind, no customed event,
But they will pluck away his natural cause
And call them meteors, prodigies, and signs,
Abortives, presages, and tongues of heaven,
Plainly denouncing vengeance upon John.
   Lewis. May be he will not touch young Arthur's life,   160
But hold himself safe in his prisonment.
   Pandulph. O, sir, when he shall hear of your approach,
If that young Arthur be not gone already,
Even at that news he dies; and then the hearts
Of all his people shall revolt from him,
And kiss the lips of unacquainted change,
And pick strong matter of revolt and wrath
Out of the bloody fingers' ends of John.
Methinks I see this hurly all on foot;
And, O, what better matter breeds for you   170
Than I have nam'd! The bastard Faulconbridge
Is now in England, ransacking the church,
Offending charity; if but a dozen French
Were there in arms, they would be as a call
To train ten thousand English to their side,
Or as a little snow, tumbled about,
Anon becomes a mountain. O noble Dauphin,
Go with me to the king; 't is wonderful

What may be wrought out of their discontent,
Now that their souls are topfull of offence.   180
For England go; I will whet on the king.
   Lewis. Strong reasons make strong actions; let us go:
If you say ay, the king will not say no.   [*Exeunt.*

THE MARRIAGE OF LEWIS AND BLANCH.

All murthers past do stand excus'd in this (iv. 3. 51).

ACT IV.

SCENE I. *A Room in a Castle.*

Enter HUBERT *and two* Attendants.

Hubert. Heat me these irons hot; and look thou stand
Within the arras: when I strike my foot
Upon the bosom of the ground, rush forth,
And bind the boy which you shall find with me
Fast to the chair.   Be heedful; hence, and watch.

1 Attendant. I hope your warrant will bear out the deed.
Hubert. Uncleanly scruples! fear not you; look to 't.—
          [*Exeunt Attendants.*
Young lad, come forth; I have to say with you.

     Enter ARTHUR.

Arthur. Good morrow, Hubert.
Hubert.   Good morrow, little prince.
Arthur. As little prince, having so great a title   10
To be more prince, as may be. You are sad.
Hubert. Indeed, I have been merrier.
Arthur.   Mercy on me!
Methinks nobody should be sad but I;
Yet, I remember, when I was in France,
Young gentlemen would be as sad as night,
Only for wantonness. By my christendom,
So I were out of prison and kept sheep,
I should be as merry as the day is long;
And so I would be here, but that I doubt
My uncle practises more harm to me: 20
He is afraid of me and I of him.
Is it my fault that I was Geffrey's son?
No, indeed, is 't not; and I would to heaven
I were your son, so you would love me, Hubert.
Hubert. [*Aside*] If I talk to him, with his innocent prate
He will awake my mercy which lies dead;
Therefore I will be sudden and dispatch.
Arthur. Are you sick, Hubert? you look pale to-day.
In sooth, I would you were a little sick,
That I might sit all night and watch with you;   30
I warrant I love you more than you do me.
Hubert. [*Aside*] His words do take possession of my bos-
  om.—
Read here, young Arthur.—   [*Showing a paper.*
      [*Aside*] How now, foolish rheum!

Turning dispiteous torture out of door!
I must be brief, lest resolution drop
Out at mine eyes in tender womanish tears.—
Can you not read it? is it not fair writ?
    Arthur. Too fairly, Hubert, for so foul effect.
Must you with hot irons burn out both mine eyes?
    Hubert. Young boy, I must.
    Arthur.   And will you?
    Hubert.   And I will.
    Arthur. Have you the heart? When your head did but
        ache,   41
I knit my handkercher about your brows,—
The best I had, a princess wrought it me,—
And I did never ask it you again;
And with my hand at midnight held your head,
And like the watchful minutes to the hour,
Still and anon cheer'd up the heavy time,
Saying, 'What lack you?' and 'Where lies your grief?'
Or 'What good love may I perform for you?'
Many a poor man's son would have lien still,   50
And ne'er have spoke a loving word to you;
But you at your sick service had a prince.
Nay, you may think my love was crafty love
And call it cunning. Do, an if you will.
If heaven be pleas'd that you must use me ill,
Why then you must. Will you put out mine eyes?
These eyes that never did nor never shall
So much as frown on you.
    Hubert.   I have sworn to do it,
And with hot irons must I burn them out.
    Arthur. Ah, none but in this iron age would do it!   60
The iron of itself, though heat red-hot,
Approaching near these eyes, would drink my tears
And quench his fiery indignation
Even in the matter of mine innocence;

Nay, after that, consume away in rust,
But for containing fire to harm mine eye.
Are you more stubborn-hard than hammer'd iron?
An if an angel should have come to me
And told me Hubert should put out mine eyes,
I would not have believ'd him,—no tongue but Hubert's. 70
    Hubert. Come forth.   [*Stamps.*

    Re-enter Attendants, *with a cord, irons, etc.*
Do as I bid you do.
    Arthur. O, save me, Hubert, save me! my eyes are out
Even with the fierce looks of these bloody men.
    Hubert. Give me the iron, I say, and bind him here.
    Arthur. Alas, what need you be so boisterous-rough?
I will not struggle, I will stand stone-still.
For heaven sake, Hubert, let me not be bound!
Nay, hear me, Hubert, drive these men away,
And I will sit as quiet as a lamb;   80
I will not stir, nor wince, nor speak a word,
Nor look upon the iron angerly.
Thrust but these men away, and I 'll forgive you,
Whatever torment you do put me to.
    Hubert. Go, stand within; let me alone with him.
    1 *Attendant.* I am best pleas'd to be from such a deed.
                            [*Exeunt Attendants.*
    Arthur. Alas, I then have chid away my friend!
He hath a stern look, but a gentle heart;
Let him come back, that his compassion may
Give life to yours.
    Hubert.   Come, boy, prepare yourself.   90
    Arthur. Is there no remedy?
    Hubert.   None, but to lose your eyes.
    Arthur. O heaven, that there were but a mote in yours,
A grain, a dust, a gnat, a wandering hair,
Any annoyance in that precious sense!

Then feeling what small things are boisterous there,
Your vile intent must needs seem horrible.

   Hubert. Is this your promise? go to, hold your tongue.

   Arthur. Hubert; the utterance of a brace of tongues
Must needs want pleading for a pair of eyes:
Let me not hold my tongue, let me not, Hubert;   100
Or, Hubert, if you will, cut out my tongue,
So I may keep mine eyes. O, spare mine eyes,
Though to no use but still to look on you!
Lo, by my troth, the instrument is cold
And would not harm me.

   Hubert.   I can heat it, boy.

   Arthur. No, in good sooth; the fire is dead with grief,
Being create for comfort, to be us'd
In undeserv'd extremes. See else yourself:
There is no malice in this burning coal;
The breath of heaven has blown his spirit out,   110
And strew'd repentant ashes on his head.

   Hubert. But with my breath I can revive it, boy.

   Arthur. An if you do, you will but make it blush
And glow with shame of your proceedings, Hubert:
Nay, it perchance will sparkle in your eyes;
And like a dog that is compell'd to fight,
Snatch at his master that doth tarre him on.
All things that you should use to do me wrong
Deny their office; only you do lack
That mercy which fierce fire and iron extends,   120
Creatures of note for mercy-lacking uses.

   Hubert. Well, see to live; I will not touch thine eye
For all the treasure that thine uncle owes:
Yet am I sworn, and I did purpose, boy,
With this same very iron to burn them out.

   Arthur. O, now you look like Hubert! all this while
You were disguised.

   Hubert.   Peace! no more. Adieu.

Your uncle must not know but you are dead:
I 'll fill these dogged spies with false reports;
And, pretty child, sleep doubtless and secure,   130
That Hubert, for the wealth of all the world,
Will not offend thee.

   Arthur.   O heaven! I thank you, Hubert.

   Hubert. Silence! no more. Go closely in with me;
Much danger do I undergo for thee.   [*Exeunt.*

      SCENE II. *King John's Palace.*

Enter KING JOHN, PEMBROKE, SALISBURY, *and other* Lords.

   King John. Here once again we sit, once again crown'd,
And look'd upon, I hope, with cheerful eyes.

   Pembroke. This once again, but that your highness pleas'd,
Was once superfluous: you were crown'd before,
And that high royalty was ne'er pluck'd off,
The faiths of men ne'er stained with revolt;
Fresh expectation troubled not the land
With any long'd-for change or better state.

   Salisbury. Therefore, to be possess'd with double pomp,
To guard a title that was rich before,   10
To gild refined gold, to paint the lily,
To throw a perfume on the violet,
To smooth the ice, or add another hue
Unto the rainbow, or with taper-light
To seek the beauteous eye of heaven to garnish,
Is wasteful and ridiculous excess.

   Pembroke. But that your royal pleasure must be done,
This act is as an ancient tale new told,
And in the last repeating troublesome,
Being urged at a time unseasonable.   20

   Salisbury. In this the antique and well noted face
Of plain old form is much disfigured;
And, like a shifted wind unto a sail,

                G

It makes the course of thoughts to fetch about,
Startles and frights consideration,
Makes sound opinion sick and truth suspected,
For putting on so new a fashion'd robe.

  Pembroke. When workmen strive to do better than well,
They do confound their skill in covetousness ;
And oftentimes excusing of a fault   30
Doth make the fault the worse by the excuse,—
As patches set upon a little breach
Discredit more in hiding of the fault
Than did the fault before it was so patch'd.

  Salisbury. To this effect, before you were new crown'd,
We breath'd our counsel ; but it pleas'd your highness
To overbear it, and we are all well pleas'd,
Since all and every part of what we would
Doth make a stand at what your highness will.

  King John. Some reasons of this double coronation   40
I have possess'd you with and think them strong ;
And more, more strong, when lesser is my fear,
I shall indue you with : meantime but ask
What you would have reform'd that is not well,
And well shall you perceive how willingly
I will both hear and grant you your requests.

  Pembroke. Then I,—as one that am the tongue of these,
To sound the purposes of all their hearts,
Both for myself and them, but, chief of all,
Your safety, for the which myself and them   50
Bend their best studies,—heartily request
The enfranchisement of Arthur ; whose restraint
Doth move the murmuring lips of discontent
To break into this dangerous argument,—
If what in rest you have in right you hold,
Why then your fears, which, as they say, attend
The steps of wrong, should move you to mew up
Your tender kinsman, and to choke his days

With barbarous ignorance, and deny his youth
The rich advantage of good exercise?   60
That the time's enemies may not have this
To grace occasions, let it be our suit
That you have bid us ask his liberty;
Which for our goods we do no further ask
Than whereupon our weal, on you depending,
Counts it your weal he have his liberty.

Enter HUBERT.

King John. Let it be so; I do commit his youth
To your direction.—Hubert, what news with you?
                                                     [*Taking him apart.*
Pembroke. This is the man should do the bloody deed;
He show'd his warrant to a friend of mine.   70
The image of a wicked heinous fault
Lives in his eye: that close aspect of his
Does show the mood of a much troubled breast;
And I do fearfully believe 't is done,
What we so fear'd he had a charge to do.
Salisbury. The colour of the king doth come and go
Between his purpose and his conscience,
Like heralds 'twixt two dreadful battles set;
His passion is so ripe, it needs must break.
Pembroke. And when it breaks, I fear will issue thence   80
The foul corruption of a sweet child's death.
King John. We cannot hold mortality's strong hand.—
Good lords, although my will to give is living,
The suit which you demand is gone and dead;
He tells us Arthur is deceas'd to-night.
Salisbury. Indeed we fear'd his sickness was past cure.
Pembroke. Indeed we heard how near his death he was
Before the child himself felt he was sick.
'This must be answer'd either here or hence.
King John. Why do you bend such solemn brows on me?

Think you I bear the shears of destiny?   91
Have I commandment on the pulse of life?
 Salisbury. It is apparent foul play; and 't is shame
That greatness should so grossly offer it.
So thrive it in your game! and so, farewell.
 Pembroke. Stay yet, Lord Salisbury; I 'll go with thee,
And find the inheritance of this poor child,
His little kingdom of a forced grave.
That blood which owed the breadth of all this isle,
Three foot of it doth hold; bad world the while!   100
This must not be thus borne; this will break out
To all our sorrows, and ere long I doubt.   [*Exeunt Lords.*
 King John. They burn in indignation.   I repent;
There is no sure foundation set on blood,
No certain life achiev'd by others' death.—

    Enter a Messenger.

A fearful eye thou hast; where is that blood
That I have seen inhabit in those cheeks?
So foul a sky clears not without a storm;
Pour down thy weather.—How goes all in France?
 Messenger. From France to England. Never such a power
For any foreign preparation   111
Was levied in the body of a land.
The copy of your speed is learn'd by them;
For when you should be told they do prepare,
The tidings comes that they are all arriv'd.
 King John. O, where hath our intelligence been drunk?
Where hath it slept? Where is my mother's care,
That such an army could be drawn in France,
And she not hear of it?
 Messenger.   My liege, her ear
Is stopp'd with dust; the first of April died   120
Your noble mother: and, as I hear, my lord,
The Lady Constance in a frenzy died

Three days before. But this from rumour's tongue
I idly heard; if true or false I know not.
   King John. Withhold thy speed, dreadful Occasion!
O, make a league with me, till I have pleas'd
My discontented peers!—What! mother dead!
How wildly then walks my estate in France!—
Under whose conduct came those powers of France
That thou for truth giv'st out are landed here?   130
   Messenger. Under the Dauphin.
   King John.   Thou hast made me giddy
With these ill tidings.—

     Enter the BASTARD *and* PETER *of Pomfret.*

               Now, what says the world
To your proceedings? do not seek to stuff
My head with more ill news, for it is full.
   Bastard. But if you be afeard to hear the worst,
Then let the worst unheard fall on your head.
   King John. Bear with me, cousin; for I was amaz'd
Under the tide: but now I breathe again
Aloft the flood, and can give audience
To any tongue, speak it of what it will.   140
   Bastard. How I have sped among the clergymen,
The sums I have collected shall express.
But as I travell'd hither through the land,
I find the people strangely fantasied;
Possess'd with rumours, full of idle dreams,
Not knowing what they fear, but full of fear:
And here's a prophet, that I brought with me
From forth the streets of Pomfret, whom I found
With many hundreds treading on his heels;
To whom he sung, in rude harsh-sounding rhymes,   150
That, ere the next Ascension-day at noon,
Your highness should deliver up your crown.
   King John. Thou idle dreamer, wherefore didst thou so?

Peter. Foreknowing that the truth will fall out so.
King John. Hubert, away with him; imprison him;
And on that day at noon, whereon he says
I shall yield up my crown, let him be hang'd.
Deliver him to safety; and return,
For I must use thee.—   [*Exit Hubert with Peter.*
                    O my gentle cousin,
Hear'st thou the news abroad, who are arriv'd?   160
Bastard. The French, my lord; men's mouths are full of
        it:
Besides, I met Lord Bigot and Lord Salisbury,
With eyes as red as new-enkindled fire,
And others more, going to seek the grave
Of Arthur, whom they say is kill'd to-night
On your suggestion.
King John.   Gentle kinsman, go,
And thrust thyself into their companies.
I have a way to win their loves again;
Bring them before me.
Bastard.   I will seek them out.
King John. Nay, but make haste; the better foot be-
        fore.—   170
O, let me have no subject enemies,
When adverse foreigners affright my towns
With dreadful pomp of stout invasion!—
Be Mercury, set feathers to thy heels,
And fly like thought from them to me again.
Bastard. The spirit of the time shall teach me speed.
                                                [*Exit.*
King John. Spoke like a sprightful noble gentleman.—
Go after him; for he perhaps shall need
Some messenger betwixt me and the peers,
And be thou he.
Messenger.   With all my heart, my liege.   [*Exit.*
King John. My mother dead!   181

Re-enter HUBERT.

Hubert. My lord, they say five moons were seen to-night;
Four fixed, and the fifth did whirl about
The other four in wondrous motion.
    King John. Five moons!
    Hubert.   Old men and beldams in the streets
Do prophesy upon it dangerously.
Young Arthur's death is common in their mouths :
And when they talk of him, they shake their heads
And whisper one another in the ear ;
And he that speaks doth gripe the hearer's wrist,   190
Whilst he that hears makes fearful action,
With wrinkled brows, with nods, with rolling eyes.
I saw a smith stand with his hammer, thus,
The whilst his iron did on the anvil cool,
With open mouth swallowing a tailor's news ;
Who, with his shears and measure in his hand,
Standing on slippers, which his nimble haste
Had falsely thrust upon contrary feet,
Told of a many thousand warlike French
That were embattailed and rank'd in Kent.   200
Another lean unwash'd artificer
Cuts off his tale and talks of Arthur's death.
    King John. Why seek'st thou to possess me with these
        fears ?
Why urgest thou so oft young Arthur's death ?
Thy hand hath murther'd him ; I had a mighty cause
To wish him dead, but thou hadst none to kill him.
    Hubert. No had, my lord ! why, did you not provoke me ?
    King John. It is the curse of kings to be attended
By slaves that take their humours for a warrant
To break within the bloody house of life,   210
And on the winking of authority
To understand a law, to know the meaning

Of dangerous majesty, when perchance it frowns
More upon humour than advis'd respect.
  Hubert. Here is your hand and seal for what I did.
  King John. O, when the last account 'twixt heaven and
   earth
Is to be made, then shall this hand and seal
Witness against us to damnation !
How oft the sight of means to do ill deeds
Make deeds ill done! Hadst not thou been by,   220
A fellow by the hand of nature mark'd,
Quoted, and sign'd to do a deed of shame,
This murther had not come into my mind ;
But taking note of thy abhorr'd aspect,
Finding thee fit for bloody villany,
Apt, liable to be employ'd in danger,
I faintly broke with thee of Arthur's death ;
And thou, to be endeared to a king,
Made it no conscience to destroy a prince.
  Hubert. My lord,—   230
  King John. Hadst thou but shook thy head or made a
   pause
When I spake darkly what I purposed,
Or turn'd an eye of doubt upon my face,
As bid me tell my tale in express words,
Deep shame had struck me dumb, made me break off,
And those thy fears might have wrought fears in me ;
But thou didst understand me by my signs,
And didst in signs again parley with sin,
Yea, without stop, didst let thy heart consent,
And consequently thy rude hand to act   240
The deed, which both our tongues held vile to name.
Out of my sight, and never see me more !
My nobles leave me ; and my state is brav'd,
Even at my gates, with ranks of foreign powers:
Nay, in the body of this fleshly land,

This kingdom, this confine of blood and breath,
Hostility and civil tumult reigns
Between my conscience and my cousin's death.

   Hubert. Arm you against your other enemies,
I 'll make a peace between your soul and you. 250
Young Arthur is alive; this hand of mine
Is yet a maiden and an innocent hand,
Not painted with the crimson spots of blood.
Within this bosom never enter'd yet
The dreadful motion of a murtherous thought;
And you have slander'd nature in my form,
Which, howsoever rude exteriorly,
Is yet the cover of a fairer mind
Than to be butcher of an innocent child.

   King John. Doth Arthur live? O, haste thee to the peers,
Throw this report on their incensed rage, 261
And make them tame to their obedience!
Forgive the comment that my passion made
Upon thy feature; for my rage was blind,
And foul imaginary eyes of blood
Presented thee more hideous than thou art.
O, answer not, but to my closet bring
The angry lords with all expedient haste.
I conjure thee but slowly; run more fast.   [*Exeunt.*

SCENE III. *Before the Castle.*

Enter ARTHUR, *on the walls.*

   Arthur. The wall is high, and yet will I leap down.—
Good ground, be pitiful and hurt me not!—
There 's few or none do know me; if they did,
This ship-boy's semblance hath disguis'd me quite.
I am afraid; and yet I 'll venture it.
If I get down, and do not break my limbs,
I 'll find a thousand shifts to get away;

As good to die and go, as die and stay.   [*Leaps down.*
O me! my uncle's spirit is in these stones.—   9
Heaven take my soul, and England keep my bones!   [*Dies.*

Enter PEMBROKE, SALISBURY, *and* BIGOT.

Salisbury. Lords, I will meet him at Saint Edmundsbury;
It is our safety, and we must embrace
This gentle offer of the perilous time.
     Pembroke. Who brought that letter from the cardinal?
     Salisbury. The Count Melun, a noble lord of France;
Whose private with me of the Dauphin's love
Is much more general than these lines import.
     Bigot. To-morrow morning let us meet him then.
     Salisbury. Or rather then set forward; for 't will be
Two long days' journey, lords, or ere we meet.   20

Enter the BASTARD.

Bastard. Once more to-day well met, distemper'd lords!
The king by me requests your presence straight.
     Salisbury. The king hath dispossess'd himself of us:
We will not line his thin bestained cloak
With our pure honours, nor attend the foot
That leaves the print of blood where'er it walks.
Return and tell him so; we know the worst.
     Bastard. Whate'er you think, good words, I think, were best.
     Salisbury. Our griefs, and not our manners, reason now.
     Bastard. But there is little reason in your grief;   30
Therefore 't were reason you had manners now.
     Pembroke. Sir, sir, impatience hath his privilege.
     Bastard. 'T is true, to hurt his master, no man else.
     Salisbury. This is the prison.   What is he lies here?
                                        [*Seeing Arthur.*
     Pembroke. O death, made proud with pure and princely
          beauty!
The earth had not a hole to hide this deed.

Salisbury. Murther, as hating what himself hath done,
Doth lay it open to urge on revenge.
  Bigot. Or, when he doom'd this beauty to a grave,
Found it too precious-princely for a grave.   40
  Salisbury. Sir Richard, what think you? have you be-
    held,
Or have you read or heard? or could you think?
Or do you almost think, although you see,
That you do see? could thought, without this object,
Form such another? This is the very top,
The height, the crest, or crest unto the crest,
Of murther's arms; this is the bloodiest shame,
The wildest savagery, the vilest stroke,
That ever wall-eyed wrath or staring rage
Presented to the tears of soft remorse.   50
  Pembroke. All murthers past do stand excus'd in this;
And this, so sole and so unmatchable,
Shall give a holiness, a purity,
To the yet unbegotten sin of times,
And prove a deadly bloodshed but a jest,
Exampled by this heinous spectacle.
  Bastard. It is a damned and a bloody work;
The graceless action of a heavy hand,
If that it be the work of any hand.
  Salisbury. If that it be the work of any hand!   60
We had a kind of light what would ensue.
It is the shameful work of Hubert's hand,
The practice and the purpose of the king;
From whose obedience I forbid my soul,
Kneeling before this ruin of sweet life,
And breathing to his breathless excellence
The incense of a vow, a holy vow,
Never to taste the pleasures of the world,
Never to be infected with delight,
Nor conversant with ease and idleness,   70

Till I have set a glory to this head,
By giving it the worship of revenge.
Pembroke. } Our souls religiously confirm thy words.
Bigot. }

Enter HUBERT.

Hubert. Lords, I am hot with haste in seeking you.
Arthur doth live; the king hath sent for you.
Salisbury. O, he is bold and blushes not at death.—
Avaunt, thou hateful villain, get thee gone!
Hubert. I am no villain.
Salisbury.   Must I rob the law?
                                    [*Drawing his sword.*
Bastard. Your sword is bright, sir; put it up again.
Salisbury. Not till I sheathe it in a murtherer's skin.   80
Hubert. Stand back, Lord Salisbury, stand back, I say;
By heaven, I think my sword 's as sharp as yours.
I would not have you, lord, forget yourself,
Nor tempt the danger of my true defence;
Lest I, by marking of your rage, forget
Your worth, your greatness, and nobility.
Bigot. Out, dunghill! dar'st thou brave a nobleman?
Hubert. Not for my life; but yet I dare defend
My innocent life against an emperor.   89
Salisbury. Thou art a murtherer.
Hubert.   Do not prove me so.
Yet I am none: whose tongue soe'er speaks false,
Not truly speaks; who speaks not truly, lies.
Pembroke. Cut him to pieces.
Bastard.   Keep the peace, I say.
Salisbury. Stand by, or I shall gall you, Faulconbridge.
Bastard. Thou wert better gall the devil, Salisbury;
If thou but frown on me, or stir thy foot,
Or teach thy hasty spleen to do me shame,
I 'll strike thee dead. Put up thy sword betime;

Or I 'll so maul you and your toasting-iron,
That you shall think the devil is come from hell.   100
 Bigot. What wilt thou do, renowned Faulconbridge?
Second a villain and a murtherer? .
 Hubert. Lord Bigot, I am none.
 Bigot.   Who kill'd this prince?
 Hubert. 'T is not an hour since I left him well;
I honour'd him, I lov'd him, and will weep
My date of life out for his sweet life's loss.
 Salisbury. Trust not those cunning waters of his eyes,
For villany is not without such rheum ;
And he, long traded in it, makes it seem
Like rivers of remorse and innocency.   110
Away with me, all you whose souls abhor
The uncleanly savours of a slaughter-house ;
For I am stifled with this smell of sin.
 Bigot. Away toward Bury, to the Dauphin there !
 Pembroke. There tell the king he may inquire us out.
          [*Exeunt Lords.*
 Bastard. Here 's a good world!—Knew you of this fair
    work ?
Beyond the infinite and boundless reach
Of mercy, if thou didst this deed of death,
Art thou damn'd, Hubert.
 Hubert.   Do but hear me, sir.
 Bastard. Ha! I 'll tell thee what ;   120
Thou 'rt damn'd as black—nay, nothing is so black ;
Thou art more deep damn'd than Prince Lucifer :
There is not yet so ugly a fiend of hell
As thou shalt be, if thou didst kill this child.
 Hubert. Upon my soul—
 Bastard.   If thou didst but consent
To this most cruel act, do but despair ;
And if thou want'st a cord, the smallest thread
That ever spider twisted from her womb

Will serve to strangle thee ; a rush will be a beam
To hang thee on; or wouldst thou drown thyself,   130
Put but a little water in a spoon,
And it shall be as all the ocean,
Enough to stifle such a villain up.
I do suspect thee very grievously.

    Hubert. If I in act, consent, or sin of thought,
Be guilty of the stealing that sweet breath
Which was embounded in this beauteous clay,
Let hell want pains enough to torture me !
I left him well.

    Bastard.   Go, bear him in thine arms.
I am amaz'd, methinks, and lose my way   140
Among the thorns and dangers of this world.
How easy dost thou take all England up!
From forth this morsel of dead royalty,
The life, the right, and truth of all this realm
Is fled to heaven ; and England now is left
To tug and scamble and to part by the teeth
The unowed interest of proud-swelling state.
Now for the bare-pick'd bone of majesty
Doth dogged war bristle his angry crest,
And snarleth in the gentle eyes of peace :   150
Now powers from home and discontents at home
Meet in one line; and vast confusion waits,
As doth a raven on a sick-fall'n beast,
The imminent decay of wrested pomp.
Now happy he whose cloak and cincture can
Hold out this tempest.—Bear away that child
And follow me with speed; I 'll to the king.
A thousand businesses are brief in hand,
And heaven itself doth frown upon the land.   [*Exeunt.*

Upon the altar at St. Edmundsbury (v. 4. 18).

ACT V.

Scene I. *King John's Palace.*

Enter King John, Pandulph, *and* Attendants.

King John. Thus have I yielded up into your hand
The circle of my glory.   [*Giving the crown.*

Pandulph.   Take again
From this my hand, as holding of the pope
Your sovereign greatness and authority.
    King John. Now keep your holy word; go meet the
        French,
And from his holiness use all your power
To stop their marches fore we are inflam'd.
Our discontented counties do revolt;   .
Our people quarrel with obedience,
Swearing allegiance and the love of soul   10
To stranger blood, to foreign royalty.
This inundation of mistemper'd humour
Rests by you only to be qualified :
Then pause not; for the present time 's so sick,
That present medicine must be minister'd,
Or overthrow incurable ensues.
    Pandulph. It was my breath that blew this tempest up,
Upon your stubborn usage of the pope;
But since you are a gentle convertite,
My tongue shall hush again this storm of war,   20
And make fair weather in your blustering land.
On this Ascension-day, remember well,
Upon your oath of service to the pope,
Go I to make the French lay down their arms.   [*Exit.*
    King John. Is this Ascension-day?   Did not the prophet
Say that before Ascension-day at noon
My crown I should give off?   Even so I have :
I did suppose it should be on constraint;
But, heaven be thank'd, it is but voluntary.

                    Enter the BASTARD.

    Bastard. All Kent hath yielded; nothing there holds out
But Dover castle : London hath receiv'd,   31
Like a kind host, the Dauphin and his powers.
Your nobles will not hear you, but are gone

To offer service to your enemy,
And wild amazement hurries up and down
The little number of your doubtful friends.
   King John. Would not my lords return to me again,
After they heard young Arthur was alive?
   Bastard. They found him dead and cast into the streets,
An empty casket, where the jewel of life   40
By some damn'd hand was robb'd and ta'en away.
   King John. That villain Hubert told me he did live.
   Bastard. So, on my soul, he did, for aught he knew.
But wherefore do you droop? why look you sad?
Be great in act, as you have been in thought;
Let not the world see fear and sad distrust
Govern the motion of a kingly eye.
Be stirring as the time ; be fire with fire ;
Threaten the threatener, and outface the brow
Of bragging horror : so shall inferior eyes,   50
That borrow their behaviours from the great,
Grow great by your example and put on
The dauntless spirit of resolution.
Away, and glister like the god of war,
When he intendeth to become the field ;
Show boldness and aspiring confidence.
What, shall they seek the lion in his den,
And fright him there? and make him tremble there?
O, let it not be said ; forage, and run
To meet displeasure farther from the doors,   60
And grapple with him ere he comes so nigh.
   King John. The legate of the pope hath been with me,
And I have made a happy peace with him ;
And he hath promis'd to dismiss the powers
Led by the Dauphin.
   Bastard.   O inglorious league !
Shall we, upon the footing of our land,
Send fair-play orders and make compromise,

Insinuation, parley, and base truce
To arms invasive? shall a beardless boy,
A cocker'd silken wanton, brave our fields,   7◦
And flesh his spirit in a warlike soil,
Mocking the air with colours idly spread,
And find no check?   Let us, my liege, to arms :
Perchance the cardinal cannot make your peace;
Or :f he do, let it at least be said
They saw we had a purpose of defence.
    King John. Have thou the ordering of this present time.
    Bastard. Away, then, with good courage ! yet, I know,
Our party may well meet a prouder foe.   [*Exeunt.*

    SCENE II.   *The Dauphin's Camp at St. Edmundsbury.*

Enter, in arms, LEWIS, SALISBURY, MELUN, PEMBROKE, BIGOT,
        and Soldiers.

    Lewis. My Lord Melun, let this be copied out,
And keep it safe for our remembrance.
Return the precedent to these lords again ;
That, having our fair order written down,
Both they and we, perusing o'er these notes,
May know wherefore we took the sacrament,
And keep our faiths firm and inviolable.
    Salisbury. Upon our sides it never shall be broken.
And, noble Dauphin, albeit we swear
A voluntary zeal and an unurg'd faith   10
To your proceedings, yet, believe me, prince,
I am not glad that such a sore of time
Should seek a plaster by contemn'd revolt,
And heal the inveterate canker of one wound
By making many.   O, it grieves my soul,
That I must draw this metal from my side
To be a widow-maker ! O, and there
Where honourable rescue and defence

Cries out upon the name of Salisbury!
But such is the infection of the time,   20
That, for the health and physic of our right,
We cannot deal but with the very hand
Of stern injustice and confused wrong.—
And is 't not pity, O my grieved friends,
That we, the sons and children of this isle,
Were born to see so sad an hour as this;
Wherein we step after a stranger march
Upon her gentle bosom, and fill up
Her enemies' ranks,—I must withdraw and weep
Upon the spot of this enforced cause,—   30
To grace the gentry of a land remote,
And follow unacquainted colours here?
What, here?   O nation, that thou couldst remove!
That Neptune's arms, who clippeth thee about,
Would bear thee from the knowledge of thyself,
And grapple thee unto a pagan shore;
Where these two Christian armies might combine
The blood of malice in a vein of league,
And not to spend it so unneighbourly!
   Lewis. A noble temper dost thou show in this;   40
And great affections wrestling in thy bosom
Doth make an earthquake of nobility.
O, what a noble combat hast thou fought
Between compulsion and a brave respect!
Let me wipe off this honourable dew,
That silverly doth progress on thy cheeks.
My heart hath melted at a lady's tears,
Being an ordinary inundation;
But this effusion of such manly drops,
This shower, blown up by tempest of the soul,   50
Startles mine eyes, and makes me more amaz'd
Than had I seen the vaulty top of heaven
Figur'd quite o'er with burning meteors.

Lift up thy brow, renowned Salisbury,
And with a great heart heave away this storm;
Commend these waters to those baby eyes
That never saw the giant world enrag'd,
Nor met with fortune other than at feasts,
Full of warm blood, of mirth, of gossiping.
Come, come; for thou shalt thrust thy hand as deep　60
Into the purse of rich prosperity
As Lewis himself:—so, nobles, shall you all,
That knit your sinews to the strength of mine.—
And even there, methinks, an angel spake;

　　　　　　Enter PANDULPH.

Look, where the holy legate comes apace,
To give us warrant from the hand of heaven,
And on our actions set the name of right
With holy breath.
　　Pandulph.　　　　Hail, noble prince of France!
The next is this: King John hath reconcil'd
Himself to Rome; his spirit is come in,　　　　70
That so stood out against the holy church,
The great metropolis and see of Rome.
Therefore thy threatening colours now wind up,
And tame the savage spirit of wild war,
That, like a lion foster'd up at hand,
It may lie gently at the foot of peace,
And be no further harmful than in show.
　　Lewis. Your grace shall pardon me, I will not back;
I am too high-born to be propertied,
To be a secondary at control,　　　　　　80
Or useful serving-man and instrument,
To any sovereign state throughout the world.
Your breath first kindled the dead coal of wars
Between this chastis'd kingdom and myself,
And brought in matter that should feed this fire;

And now 't is far too huge to be blown out
With that same weak wind which enkindled it.
You taught me how to know the face of right,
Acquainted me with interest to this land,
Yea, thrust this enterprise into my heart;   90
And come ye now to tell me John hath made
His peace with Rome? What is that peace to me?
I, by the honour of my marriage-bed,
After young Arthur, claim this land for mine;
And, now it is half-conquer'd, must I back
Because that John hath made his peace with Rome?
Am I Rome's slave? What penny hath Rome borne,
What men provided, what munition sent,
To underprop this action? Is 't not I
That undergo this charge? who else but I,   100
And such as to my claim are liable,
Sweat in this business and maintain this war?
Have I not heard these islanders shout out
'Vive le roi!' as I have bank'd their towns?
Have I not here the best cards for the game,
To win this easy match play'd for a crown?
And shall I now give o'er the yielded set?
No, no, on my soul, it never shall be said.
   Pandulph. You look but on the outside of this work.
   Lewis. Outside or inside, I will not return   110
Till my attempt so much be glorified
As to my ample hope was promised
Before I drew this gallant head of war,
And cull'd these fiery spirits from the world,
To outlook conquest and to win renown
Even in the jaws of danger and of death.—
                               [Trumpet sounds.
What lusty trumpet thus doth summon us?

Enter the BASTARD, *attended.*

Bastard. According to the fair play of the world,
Let me have audience ; I am sent to speak.—
My holy lord of Milan, from the king   120
I come, to learn how you have dealt for him ;
And, as you answer, I do know the scope
And warrant limited unto my tongue.
    Pandulph. The Dauphin is too wilful-opposite,
And will not temporize with my entreaties ;
He flatly says he 'll not lay down his arms.
    Bastard. By all the blood that ever fury breath'd,
The youth says well.   Now hear our English king ;
For thus his royalty doth speak in me.
He is prepar'd, and reason too he should :   130
This apish and unmannerly approach,
This harness'd masque and unadvised revel,
This unhair'd sauciness and boyish troops,
The king doth smile at ; and is well prepar'd
To whip this dwarfish war, these pigmy arms,
From out the circle of his territories.
That hand which had the strength, even at your door,
To cudgel you and make you take the hatch,
To dive like buckets in concealed wells,
To crouch in litter of your stable planks,   140
To lie like pawns lock'd up in chests and trunks,
To hug with swine, to seek sweet safety out
In vaults and prisons, and to thrill and shake
Even at the crying of your nation's crow,
Thinking his voice an armed Englishman,—
Shall that victorious hand be feebled here,
That in your chambers gave you chastisement ?
No ! know the gallant monarch is in arms,
And like an eagle o'er his aery towers,
To souse annoyance that comes near his nest.—   150

And you degenerate, you ingrate revolts,
You bloody Neroes, ripping up the womb
Of your dear mother England, blush for shame;
For your own ladies and pale-visag'd maids
Like Amazons come tripping after drums,
Their thimbles into armed gauntlets change,
Their needles to lances, and their gentle hearts
To fierce and bloody inclination.

    Lewis. There end thy brave, and turn thy face in peace;
We grant thou canst outscold us. Fare thee well;   160
We hold our time too precious to be spent
With such a brabbler.

    Pandulph.   Give me leave to speak.

    Bastard. No, I will speak.

    Lewis.   We will attend to neither.
Strike up the drums; and let the tongue of war
Plead for our interest and our being here.

    Bastard. Indeed, your drums, being beaten, will cry out;
And so shall you, being beaten. Do but start
An echo with the clamour of thy drum,
And even at hand a drum is ready brac'd
That shall reverberate all as loud as thine;   170
Sound but another, and another shall
As loud as thine rattle the welkin's ear
And mock the deep-mouth'd thunder: for at hand,
Not trusting to this halting legate here,
Whom he hath us'd rather for sport than need,
Is warlike John; and in his forehead sits
A bare-ribb'd death, whose office is this day
To feast upon whole thousands of the French.

    Lewis. Strike up our drums, to find this danger out.

    Bastard. And thou shalt find it, Dauphin, do not doubt.

                            [*Exeunt.*

SCENE III. *The Field of Battle.*

Alarums. Enter KING JOHN *and* HUBERT.

King John. How goes the day with us? O, tell me, Hubert.

Hubert. Badly, I fear. How fares your majesty?

King John. This fever, that hath troubled me so long,
Lies heavy on me ; O, my heart is sick !

Enter a Messenger.

Messenger. My lord, your valiant kinsman, Faulconbridge,
Desires your majesty to leave the field
And send him word by me which way you go.

King John. Tell him, toward Swinstead, to the abbey there.

Messenger. Be of good comfort; for the great supply
That was expected by the Dauphin here,   10
Are wrack'd three nights ago on Goodwin Sands.
This news was brought to Richard but even now;
The French fight coldly, and retire themselves.

King John. Ay me! this tyrant fever burns me up,
And will not let me welcome this good news.—
Set on toward Swinstead : to my litter straight ;
Weakness possesseth me, and I am faint.   [*Exeunt.*

SCENE IV. *Another Part of the Field.*

Enter SALISBURY, PEMBROKE, *and* BIGOT.

Salisbury. I did not think the king so stor'd with friends.

Pembroke. Up once again ; put spirit in the French :
If they miscarry, we miscarry too.

Salisbury. That misbegotten devil, Faulconbridge,
In spite of spite, alone upholds the day.

Pembroke. They say King John sore sick hath left the field.

Enter MELUN, *wounded.*

Melun. Lead me to the revolts of England here.

Salisbury. When we were happy we had other names..

Pembroke. It is the Count Melun.

Salisbury.   Wounded to death.

Melun. Fly, noble English, you are bought and sold ;   10
Unthread the rude eye of rebellion,
And welcome home again discarded faith.
Seek out King John and fall before his feet ;
For if the French be lords of this loud day,
He means to recompense the pains you take
By cutting off your heads.   Thus hath he sworn
And I with him, and many moe with me,
Upon the altar at Saint Edmundsbury ;
Even on that altar where we swore to you
Dear amity and everlasting love.   20

   Salisbury. May this be possible? may this be true?

   Melun. Have I not hideous death within my view,
Retaining but a quantity of life,
Which bleeds away, even as a form of wax
Resolveth from his figure 'gainst the fire ?
What in the world should make me now deceive,
Since I must lose the use of all deceit?
Why should I then be false, since it is true
That I must die here and live hence by truth ?
I say again, if Lewis do win the day,   30
He is forsworn, if e'er those eyes of yours
Behold another day break in the east ;
But even this night, whose black contagious breath
Already smokes about the burning crest
Of the old, feeble, and day-wearied sun,
Even this ill night, your breathing shall expire,
Paying the fine of rated treachery
Even with a treacherous fine of all your lives,

If Lewis by your assistance win the day.
Commend me to one Hubert with your king ;   40
The love of him, and this respect besides,
For that my grandsire was an Englishman,
Awakes my conscience to confess all this.
In lieu whereof, I pray you, bear me hence
From forth the noise and rumour of the field,
Where I may think the remnant of my thoughts
In peace, and part this body and my soul
With contemplation and devout desires.
     Salisbury. We do believe thee ; and beshrew my soul
But I do love the favour and the form   50
Of this most fair occasion, by the which
We will untread the steps of damned flight,
And like a bated and retired flood,
Leaving our rankness and irregular course,
Stoop low within those bounds we have o'erlook'd,
And calmly run on in obedience
Even to our ocean, to our great King John.
My arm shall give thee help to bear thee hence,
For I do see the cruel pangs of death
Right in thine eye.—Away, my friends ! New flight,   60
And happy newness, that intends old right.
                         [*Exeunt, leading off Melun.*

          SCENE V.   *The French Camp.*
          Enter LEWIS *and his train.*

     Lewis. The sun of heaven methought was loath to set,
But stay'd and made the western welkin blush,
When English measure backward their own ground
In faint retire.   O, bravely came we off,
When with a volley of our needless shot,
After such bloody toil we bid good night,
And wound our tottering colours clearly up,
Last in the field, and almost lords of it !

Enter a Messenger.

Messenger. Where is my prince, the Dauphin?
Lewis. Here; what news?
Messenger. The Count Melun is slain; the English lords
By his persuasion are again fall'n off,   11
And your supply, which you have wish'd so long,
Are cast away and sunk on Goodwin Sands.
    Lewis. Ah, foul shrewd news! beshrew thy very heart!
I did not think to be so sad to-night
As this hath made me.—Who was he that said
King John did fly an hour or two before
The stumbling night did part our weary powers?
    Messenger. Whoever spoke it, it is true, my lord.   19
    Lewis. Well; keep good quarter and good care to-night.
The day shall not be up so soon as I,
To try the fair adventure of to-morrow.   [*Exeunt.*

SCENE VI. *An Open Place in the Neighborhood of Swinstead Abbey.*

Enter the BASTARD *and* HUBERT, *severally.*

    Hubert. Who 's there? speak, ho! speak quickly, or I
      shoot.
    Bastard. A friend.—What art thou?
    Hubert. Of the part of England.
    Bastard. Whither dost thou go?
    Hubert. What 's that to thee? why may not I demand
Of thine affairs, as well as thou of mine?
    Bastard. Hubert, I think?
    Hubert. Thou hast a perfect thought;
I will upon all hazards well believe
Thou art my friend, that know'st my tongue so well.
Who art thou?
    Bastard. Who thou wilt; and if thou please,

Thou mayst befriend me so much as to think   10
I come one way of the Plantagenets.

Hubert. Unkind remembrance! thou and eyeless night
Have done me shame.—Brave soldier, pardon me,
That any accent breaking from thy tongue
Should scape the true acquaintance of mine ear.

Bastard. Come, come; sans compliment, what news
    abroad?

Hubert. Why, here walk I in the black brow of night,
To find you out.

Bastard.   Brief, then; and what 's the news?

Hubert. O, my sweet sir, news fitting to the night,
Black, fearful, comfortless, and horrible.   20

Bastard. Show me the very wound of this ill news;
I am no woman, I 'll not swoon at it.

Hubert. The king, I fear, is poison'd by a monk;
I left him almost speechless, and broke out
To acquaint you with this evil, that you might
The better arm you to the sudden time,
Than if you had at leisure known of this.

Bastard. How did he take it? who did taste to him?

Hubert. A monk, I tell you; a resolved villain,
Whose bowels suddenly burst out: the king   30
Yet speaks, and peradventure may recover.

Bastard. Who didst thou leave to tend his majesty?

Hubert. Why, know you not? the lords are all come back,
And brought Prince Henry in their company;
At whose request the king hath pardon'd them,
And they are all about his majesty.

Bastard. Withhold thine indignation, mighty heaven,
And tempt us not to bear above our power!—
I 'll tell thee, Hubert, half my power this night,
Passing these flats, are taken by the tide,   40
These Lincoln Washes have devoured them;
Myself, well mounted, hardly have escap'd.

Away before : conduct me to the king ;
I doubt he will be dead or ere I come.   [*Exeunt.*

SCENE VII.   *The Orchard of Swinstead Abbey.*

Enter PRINCE HENRY, SALISBURY, *and* BIGOT.

Prince Henry. It is too late ; the life of all his blood
Is touch'd corruptibly, and his pure brain,
Which some suppose the soul's frail dwelling-house,
Doth by the idle comments that it makes
Foretell the ending of mortality.

Enter PEMBROKE.

Pembroke. His highness yet doth speak, and holds be-
    lief
That, being brought into the open air,
It would allay the burning quality
Of that fell poison which assaileth him.   9
Prince Henry. Let him be brought into the orchard here.—
Doth he still rage ?   [*Exit Bigot.*
Pembroke.   He is more patient
Than when you left him ; even now he sung.
Prince Henry. O vanity of sickness ! fierce extremes
In their continuance will not feel themselves.
Death, having prey'd upon the outward parts,
Leaves them insensible, and his siege is now
Against the mind, the which he pricks and wounds
With many legions of strange fantasies,
Which, in their throng and press to that last hold,
Confound themselves.   'T is strange that death should
    sing.   20
I am the cygnet to this pale faint swan,
Who chants a doleful hymn to his own death,
And from the organ-pipe of frailty sings
His soul and body to their lasting rest.

Salisbury. Be of good comfort, prince ; for you are born
To set a form upon that indigest
Which he hath left so shapeless and so rude.

Enter Attendants, *and* BIGOT, *carrying* KING JOHN *in a
chair.*

King John. Ay, marry, now my soul hath elbow-room ;
It would not out at windows nor at doors.
There is so hot a summer in my bosom,   30
That all my bowels crumble up to dust :
I am a scribbled form, drawn with a pen
Upon a parchment, and against this fire
Do I shrink up.
    Prince Henry. How fares your majesty ?
    King John. Poison'd,—ill fare—dead, forsook, cast off ;
And none of you will bid the winter come
To thrust his icy fingers in my maw,
Nor let my kingdom's rivers take their course
Through my burn'd bosom, nor entreat the north
To make his bleak winds kiss my parched lips   40
And comfort me with cold. I do not ask you much :
I beg cold comfort ; and you are so strait
And so ingrateful, you deny me that.
    Prince Henry. O that there were some virtue in my tears,
That might relieve you !
    King John.   The salt in them is hot.
Within me is a hell ; and there the poison
Is as a fiend confin'd to tyrannize
On unreprievable condemned blood.

Enter the BASTARD.

    Bastard. O, I am scalded with my violent motion
And spleen of speed to see your majesty !   50
    King John. O cousin, thou art come to set mine eye.
The tackle of my heart is crack'd and burn'd,

And all the shrouds wherewith my life should sail
Are turned to one thread, one little hair;
My heart hath one poor string to stay it by,
Which holds but till thy news be uttered,
And then all this thou seest is but a clod
And module of confounded royalty.

 Bastard. The Dauphin is preparing hitherward,
Where heaven He knows how we shall answer him; 60
For in a night the best part of my power,
As I upon advantage did remove,
Were in the Washes all unwarily
Devoured by the unexpected flood. [*The king dies.*

 Salisbury. You breathe these dead news in as dead an
  ear.—
My liege! my lord!—But now a king, now thus.

 Prince Henry. Even so must I run on, and even so stop.
What surety of the world, what hope, what stay,
When this was now a king, and now is clay?

 Bastard. Art thou gone so? I do but stay behind 70
To do the office for thee of revenge,
And then my soul shall wait on thee to heaven,
As it on earth hath been thy servant still.—
Now, now, you stars that move in your right spheres,
Where be your powers? show now your mended faiths,
And instantly return with me again,
To push destruction and perpetual shame
Out of the weak door of our fainting land.
Straight let us seek, or straight we shall be sought;
The Dauphin rages at our very heels. 80

 Salisbury. It seems you know not, then, so much as we.
The Cardinal Pandulph is within at rest,
Who half an hour since came from the Dauphin,
And brings from him such offers of our peace
As we with honour and respect may take,
With purpose presently to leave this war.

Bastard. He will the rather do it when he sees
Ourselves well sinewed to our defence.

Salisbury. Nay, it is in a manner done already :
For many carriages he hath dispatch'd   90
To the sea-side, and put his cause and quarrel
To the disposing of the cardinal ;
With whom yourself, myself, and other lords,
If you think meet, this afternoon will post
To consummate this business happily.

Bastard. Let it be so.—And you, my noble prince,
With other princes that may best be spar'd,
Shall wait upon your father's funeral.

Prince Henry. At Worcester must his body be interr'd ;
For so he will'd it.

Bastard.   Thither shall it then.   100
And happily may your sweet self put on
The lineal state and glory of the land !
To whom, with all submission, on my knee
I do bequeath my faithful services
And true subjection everlastingly.

Salisbury. And the like tender of our love we make,
To rest without a spot for evermore.

Prince Henry. I have a kind soul that would give you
            thanks,
And knows not how to do it but with tears.

Bastard. O, let us pay the time but needful woe,   110
Since it hath been beforehand with our griefs.—
This England never did, nor never shall,
Lie at the proud foot of a conqueror,
But when it first did help to wound itself.
Now these her princes are come home again,
Come the three corners of the world in arms,
And we shall shock them.   Nought shall make us rue,
If England to itself do rest but true.   [*Exeunt.*

NOTES.

I

ABBREVIATIONS USED IN THE NOTES.

Abbott (or Gr.), Abbott's *Shakespearian Grammar* (third edition).
A. S., Anglo-Saxon.
A. V., Authorized Version of the Bible (1611).
B. and F., Beaumont and Fletcher.
B. J., Ben Jonson.
Camb. ed., "Cambridge edition" of *Shakespeare*, edited by Clark and Wright.
Cf. (*confer*), compare.
Clarke, "Cassell's Illustrated Shakespeare," edited by Charles and Mary Cowden Clarke (London, n. d.).
Coll., Collier (second edition).
Coll. MS., Manuscript Corrections of Second Folio, edited by Collier.
D., Dyce (second edition).
Fl., F. G. Fleay's ed. of *King John* (London and Glasgow, 1878).
H., Hudson (first edition).
Halliwell, J. O. Halliwell (folio ed. of Shakespeare).
Id. (*idem*), the same.
K., Knight (second edition).
Nares, *Glossary*, edited by Halliwell and Wright (London, 1859).
Prol., Prologue.
S , Shakespeare.
Schmidt, A. Schmidt's *Shakespeare-Lexicon* (Berlin, 1874).
Sr., Singer.
St., Staunton.
Theo., Theobald
V., Verplanck.
W., White.
Walker, Wm. Sidney Walker's *Critical Examination of the Text of Shakespeare* (London, 1860).
Warb., Warburton.
Wb., Webster's Dictionary (revised quarto edition of 1879).
Worc., Worcester's Dictionary (quarto edition).

The abbreviations of the names of Shakespeare's Plays will be readily understood; as *T. N.* for *Twelfth Night*, *Cor.* for *Coriolanus*, *3 Hen. VI.* for *The Third Part of King Henry the Sixth*, etc. *P. P.* refers to *The Passionate Pilgrim*; *V. and A.* to *Venus and Adonis*; *L. C.* to *Lover's Complaint*; and *Sonn.* to the *Sonnets*.

When the abbreviation of the name of a play is followed by a reference to *page*, Rolfe's edition of the play is meant.

The numbers of the lines (except for *King John*) are those of the "Globe" ed. or of Crowell's reprint of that ed.

NOTES.

TOMB OF KING JOHN IN WORCESTER CATHEDRAL.

ACT I.

DRAMATIS PERSONÆ.—We give these as in the Camb. and Globe eds. The Var. of 1821 and most of the modern eds. add sundry historical details; as the fact that Prince Henry was "afterwards King Henry III.," etc. The Earl of Pembroke was William Mareshall; the Earl of Essex was Geffrey Fitz-Peter, who held the office of Chief Justiciary of England; the Earl of Salisbury was William Longsword; and Lord Bigot was Robert Bigot, Earl of Norfolk. "Faulconbridge" is the spelling of the folio, followed by the majority of the modern editors. Fleay retains also the old forms "Gourney" and "Chatillion."

SCENE I.—Most of the eds. give the scene as "*Northampton. A Room of State in the King's Palace.*" There is no doubt that the court was then held at Northampton ; but with regard to the locality of some of the other scenes we cannot speak so positively. The 1st scene of act iv., for instance, is laid by Capell in "Northampton," by Halliwell in "Dover," and by W. in "Canterbury." As the Camb. editors remark, "nothing is gained by an attempt to harmonize the plot with historical facts gathered from Holinshed and elsewhere, when it is plain that S. was either ignorant of them or indifferent to minute accuracy."

3. *In my behaviour.* "In the *character* which I here assume" (Johnson) ; "in the words and action that I am going to use" (Malone) ; "not only in my words, but in my bearing and manner—my assumption of superiority to the 'borrowed majesty' of John" (Fl.).

4. *Borrowed.* The folio form, retained by the Camb. ed. and W. Most eds. give it "borrow'd."

11. *Touraine.* The 1st folio has "Torayne," the later folios "Lorayne" or "Loraine." The old play has "Torain" in the corresponding passage.

16. *Disallow.* Used by S. nowhere else ; but we have *allow of* in *W. T.* iv. 1. 29 and *T. N.* iv. 2. 63.

17. *Control.* Constraint, compulsion. Cf. *Rich. III.* iii. 5. 84 : "without control " (that is, restraint). See also *Hen. V.* ii. 4. 96 :

> "*French King.* Or else what follows?
> "*Exeter.* Bloody constraint ; for if you hide the crown
> Even in your hearts, there will he rake for it."

19. *War for war*, etc. Steevens compares *Jeronimo*, 1588–89 :

> "*And.* Thou shalt pay tribute, Portugal, with blood.
> "*Bal.* Tribute for tribute then ; and foes for foes."

24. *As lightning.* Johnson finds fault with the simile, because "the lightning is destructive, and the thunder innocent ;" but it is the quickness with which the thunder *follows* the lightning to which the poet alludes. Besides, as Farmer notes, the thunder was not then thought to be harmless. Cf. *Temp.* ii. 1. 204, ii. 2. 112, *M. for M.* ii. 2. 110 fol., *J. C.* i. 3. 49, *Cymb.* iv. 2. 271, etc.

Of course the mention of *cannon* here is an anachronism, as it is in *Macbeth* and *Hamlet.* Gunpowder was not invented until at least a century later, and artillery is commonly said to have been first used at the battle of Cressy. As K. remarks, S. "uses terms which were familiar to his audience, to present a particular image to their senses. Had he, instead of cannon, spoken of the mangonell and the petraria—the stone-flinging machines of the time of John—he would have addressed himself to the very few who might have appreciated his exactness ; but his words would have fallen dead upon the ears of the many."

27. *Trumpet.* Trumpeter, herald. See *Ham.* p. 176 or *W. T.* p. 168.

28. *Sullen.* Sad, dismal. Cf. *R. and J.* iv. 5. 88 : "sullen dirges." See also *Rich. II.* p. 222.

29. *Conduct.* Escort ; as in *Hen. V.* i. 2. 297 : "safe conduct," etc. This use of the word is still retained in military parlance.

30. *Chatillon.* A quadrisyllable, like the "Chatillion" of the folio.

34. *Party.* Part, side ; as in ii. 1. 361 and iii. 1. 123 below. See also *Rich. II.* p. 195.

37. *Manage.* Administration. Cf. *Temp.* i. 2. 70 : "the manage of my state ;" *M. of V.* iii. 4. 25 : "The husbandry and manage of my house," etc.

39. *Our strong possession,* etc. See p. 32 above.

49. *Charge.* Cost, expense. See *Rich. II.* p. 175. The 1st folio has "expeditious," which Fl. retains, making it = "urgent, sudden."

50. *Your faithful subject,* etc. Steevens remarks that the character of the Bastard, adopted from the old play, is "compounded of two distinct personages :" "Falcasius de Brente" of Matthew Paris's *Chronicle,* and the natural son of Richard I. "named Philip," mentioned by Holinshed. Malone suggests that the author of the old play was led to affix the name of *Faulconbridge* to this son of King Richard by a passage in the continuation of Harding's *Chronicle,* 1543, where he is called "one Faulconbridge, therle of Kent, his bastarde, a stoute-hearted man." It is said that his mother was a lady of Poictou, and that King Richard bestowed upon her son a lordship in that province. The old play gives only this slight hint of the character which S. has made so much of :

> " Next them a bastard of the king's deceas'd,
> A hardie wild-head, rough, and venturous."

54. *Cœur-de-lion.* Spelt uniformly "Cordelion" in the folios.

62. *Put you o'er.* Refer you ; the only instance of the phrase in S.

64. *Rude man.* Fl. gives "rude-man" (like *goodman,* etc.) and compares "rudesby" in *T. of S.* iii. 2. 10 and *T. N.* iv. 1. 55.

65. *Diffidence.* Distrust, suspicion ; the only sense of the word in S. Cf. 1 *Hen. VI.* iii. 3. 10 :

> " We have been guided by thee hitherto,
> And of thy cunning had no diffidence :"

and *Lear,* i. 2. 161 : "needless diffidences."

68. *A'.* A corruption of *he,* common in the language of the vulgar, but sometimes put into the mouth of the well-bred (Schmidt). The early eds. print it without the apostrophe ; the modern ones give *a'* or *'a.*

69. *Pound.* S. uses both *pound* and *pounds* for the plural. See *Rich. II.* p. 182.

75. *Whether.* The folios (except the 4th) have "where," as in ii. 1. 167 below and not a few other passages. W. prints "whe'r," which is another contraction found in the old eds. In 134 below the folios have "whether," though the word is metrically equivalent to a monosyllable, as here. See Gr. 466.

78. *Fair fall,* etc. Good luck befall the frame that bore the pains of maternity for me ! Cf. *V. and A.* 472 : "Fair fall the wit that can so well defend her !" See also *L. L. L.* ii. 1. 124, 125.

82. *O old Sir Robert, father.* Perhaps Fl. is right in omitting the comma after *Robert.*

84. *Lent.* Heath conjectured "sent;" but cf. *R. of L.* 17, *A. IV.* ii. 2. 8, *Per.* prol. 24, etc.

85. *Trick.* "Peculiarity" (Schmidt); as in *W. T.* ii. 3. 100: "The trick of 's frown;" *Lear,* iv. 6. 108: "The trick of that voice I do well remember," etc. Some connect this use of the word with its heraldic application = copy. Mr. Wilbraham, in his MS. notes (cited in the Camb. ed.), gives from an old account-book: "July 21st, 1691, received of Mr. Cole for a trick of Consure's arms, 2s. 6d."

86. *Affecteth.* Resembles; a sense not found elsewhere in S., but somewhat like its use = imitate, as in *T. of A.* iv. 3. 199: "Thou dost affect my manners," etc.

88. *The large composition,* etc. "This expression finely brings to the eye those magnificent proportions of manly strength that characterized Richard I., and which helped to make him the heroic ideal of English hearts" (Clarke).

93. *With that half-face.* The early eds. have "With half that face;" corrected by Theo. Some editors put a period at the end of 92.

94. *A half-fac'd groat.* A silver groat (or fourpence) with the king's profile on it; first coined in the reign of Henry VII. The groat was not coined at all until the time of Edward III. But S. did not mind these little anachronisms. For the contemptuous use of *half-faced,* cf. *2 Hen. IV.* iii. 2. 283: "this same half-faced fellow, Shadow." Here there is a play upon the word.

100. *The emperor.* Henry VI.

110. *Took it,* etc. Took his oath, protested. Cf. *1 Hen. IV.* v. 4. 154: "I 'll take it upon my death, I gave him this wound; *Id.* ii. 4. 9: "They take it already upon their salvation, that though I be but Prince of Wales, yet I am the king of courtesy," etc. Fl. quotes *Lover's Progress,* v. 3:

> "Upon my death I take it, uncompell'd,
> That they are guilty."

119. *Which fault.* Cf. iii. 1. 40 below: "Which harm," etc. Gr. 269. *Lies on the hazards of* = is risked by; a gambling phrase (Fl.). Cf. *M. for M.* iv. 2. 166: "I 'll lay myself in hazard," etc.

127. *This concludes.* "This is a *decisive argument.* As your father, if he liked him, could not be forced to resign him, so, not liking him, he is not at liberty to reject him" (Johnson). Perhaps it is simply = this is the conclusion.

137. *Lord of thy presence.* "Master of that fine manly person inherited from Cœur-de-lion;" with perhaps the added idea, as Clarke suggests, of "master of thine own individuality or identity." Cf. ii. 1. 367 and 377 below. Halliwell quotes Sir Henry Wotton's description of *The Happy Man:*

> "Lord of himself, though not of lands,
> And having nothing, yet hath all."

138. *An if.* The folios have "And if," as often. Gr. 101, 105.

139. *And I,* etc. The folio reads: "And I had his, sir *Roberts* his like him," etc. The modern editors arrange it in as many different ways

as a Chinese puzzle. The majority give it, "And I had his, Sir Robert his, like him." Fleay has "And I had his Sir Robert's ; his, like him ;" that is, "his (my brother's) shape of Sir Robert ; *his* (my brother's) ; like *him* (my brother)—Philip pointing at his brother at the words *his* and *him*." The reading in the text is that of the Camb. ed. *Sir Robert's his* may perhaps be=his, derived from Sir Robert, or Sir Robert's shape as seen in him ; spoken contemptuously, the repeated *his* being treated as a noun. Johnson explains "Sir Robert his" as=Sir Robert's, the *his* being used instead of the possessive *'s*, as in "Mars his sword" (*Sonn.* 55. 7), "Lewis his satisfaction" (*Hen. V.* i. 2. 88), etc. ; but we doubt whether that form of the possessive was ever used with the thing possessed "understood," not expressed. Schmidt considers that in *Sir Robert's his* we have "the *'s* of the genitive and *his* combined."

140. *Riding-rods.* Switches.

142. *Rose.* It was the fashion in Elizabeth's time to wear rosettes of ribbon, and sometimes real roses, stuck behind the ear. Steevens cites Marston, B. J., Davenant, and Burton in illustration of the custom.

To understand the allusion in *three-farthings*, it is necessary to know that Elizabeth coined pieces of that value which had her head and the emblematic *rose* of England upon them. These coins, as Malone states, were of silver and so *thin* that they were liable to be cracked. Hence B. J., in his *Every Man in His Humour*, says : "He values me at a cracked three-farthings."

144. *To.* In addition to, besides. Gr. 185.

146. *Face.* Fl. reads "hand," as being "necessary for the rhyme, and also for the antithesis to *foot*, which, after Shakespeare's usual custom, is used in a double sense, one meaning being merely glanced at."

147. *Nob.* Contemptuous for *Robert*. The folio prints it "sir nobbe." Clarke thinks there is a kind of pun on *nob*, the cant word for head.

154. *Unto the death.* Though death be the consequence ; the Fr. *à la mort.* Cf. *Much Ado*, i. 3. 72, *L. L. L.* v. 2. 146, etc.

161. *Arise.* Steevens's emendation of the "rise" of the folios.

162. *Plantagenet.* Originally not a family name, but a nickname, by which a grandson of Geffrey, the first earl of Anjou, was distinguished, from his wearing a broom-stalk (*planta genista*) in his bonnet ; afterwards popularly assigned as a surname to the royal family of England from Henry II. to Richard II. (Malone).

169. *Truth.* Honesty (Johnson). Cf. 181 below. *What though* = what of it? what matters it? Cf. *M. W.* i. 1. 286, *A. Y. L.* iii. 3. 31, *Hen. V.* ii. 1. 9, etc.

170. *Something about,* etc. "*I am*, says the sprightly knight, *your grandson*, a little *irregularly*, but every man cannot get what he wishes the legal way. He that *dares not go* about his designs *by day* must *make his motions* in the *night ; he* to whom the door is shut must climb *the window* or leap the *hatch*. This, however, shall not depress me ; for the world never inquires how any man got what he is known to possess, but allows that *to have* is *to have*, however it was *caught*, and that he *who wins shot well*, whatever was his skill, whether the arrow fell *near* the mark or *far* off it" (Johnson). *In at the window* and *over the hatch* were

proverbial phrases for illegitimacy, as Steevens shows by sundry quotations. A *hatch* is a half-door (the lower half of the door arranged to shut, leaving the upper half open like a window) such as is still commonly seen in English cottages. Cf. v. 2. 138 below: "take the hatch;" and *Lear*, iii. 6. 76: "Dogs leap the hatch."

177. *A landless knight.* Not the king ("John *Sans-terre*" or "Lackland," as he was called), but Philip.

180. *Good fortune come to thee*, etc. The *thee* is emphatic. He intimates that he himself does not need the good wish, as, according to the proverb, "bastards are born lucky."

182. *A foot.* A step, *un pas* (Johnson).

184. *Joan.* A peasant girl. Cf. *L. L. L.* iii. 1. 207: "Some men must love my lady and some Joan;" *Id.* v. 2. 930: "While greasy Joan doth keel the pot," etc.

185. *Good den.* Good evening. See *R. and J.* p. 148. "Faulconbridge is now entertaining himself with ideas of greatness, suggested by his recent knighthood. *Good den, Sir Richard* he supposes to be the salutation of a vassal; *God-a-mercy, fellow*, his own supercilious reply to it" (Steevens). *God-a-mercy* = God have mercy. Cf. *T. of S.* iv. 3. 154, *Ham.* iv. 5. 199, etc.

188. *Respective.* Regardful, or considerate. Cf. *M. of V.* v. 1. 156: "You should have been respective, and have kept it;" *R. and J.* iii. 1. 128: "Away to heaven, respective lenity," etc.

189. *Conversion.* Change of condition; needlessly changed by Pope to "conversing."

Your traveller. "It is said in *A. W.* [ii. 5. 30] that 'a *traveller* is a good thing after dinner.' In that age of newly excited curiosity, one of the entertainments at great tables seems to have been the discourse of a traveller" (Johnson).

190. *Toothpick.* The use of a toothpick was considered a foreign affectation in the time of S. See *W. T.* p. 206. For *mess*, see *W. T.* p. 157, note on *Lower messes.*

191. *Suffic'd.* Satisfied; as in *A. Y. L.* ii. 7. 131:

> "till he be first suffic'd,
> Oppress'd with two weak evils, age and hunger,
> I will not touch a bit."

192. *I suck my teeth.* Not using a toothpick, like the traveller.

193. *Picked.* Refined. Cf. *L. L. L.* v. 1. 14: "He is too picked, too spruce, too affected, too odd, as it were, too peregrinate, as I may call it." See also *Ham.* p. 262. *My picked man of countries* = "my travelled fop" (Holt White).

196. *Absey book.* ABC book, or primer, which often included a catechism, like the old *New England Primer.* Halliwell quotes Cotgrave, *Fr. Dict.*: "*Abecé*, an abcee, the crosse-row, an alphabet."

201. *Compliment.* Tollet cites Sir W. Cornwallis's *Essays*, 1601, in which the extravagance of compliment in that day is thus ridiculed: "We spend even at his [a friend's or stranger's] entrance a whole volume of words. What a deal of synamon and ginger is sacrificed to dissimulation! 'O, how blessed do I take mine eyes for presenting me

with this sight! O Signior, the star that governs my life in content-
ment, give me leave to interre myself in your arms!—Not so, sir, it is too
unworthy an inclosure to contain such preciousness,' &c. &c. This, and
a cup of drink, makes the time as fit for a departure as can be."

203. *The Pyrenean.* The Pyrenees.

207. *For he is but a bastard*, etc. "He is accounted but a mean man,
in the present age, who does not show, by his dress, his deportment, and
his talk, that he has travelled, and made observations in foreign countries" (Malone). For *smack* in 208 the folio has "smoake;" corrected
by Theo.

212. *Motion.* Impulse ; as in iv. 2. 255 below : "The dreadful motion
of a murtherous thought," etc.

214. *Which.* Referring to *to deliver sweet poison.* Cf. Gr. 271.

219. *To blow a horn.* "He means that a woman who travelled about
like a *post* was likely to *horn* her husband" (Johnson). Cf. *Much Ado,*
p. 123, notes on *Rechcat* and *Baldrick.*

220. *Gurney.* S. may have got this name from Holinshed, who, in his
history of King John, mentions a Hugh Gourney (Malone).

225. *Colbrand.* A Danish giant, whom Guy of Warwick discomfited
in the presence of King Athelstan (Johnson). Cf. *Hen. VIII.* v. 4. 22 :
"I am not Samson, nor Sir Guy, nor Colbrand," etc.

227. *Unreverend.* Used by S. interchangeably with *unreverent*, and =
irreverent, disrespectful. Cf. *T. G. of V.* ii. 6. 14 : "Fie, fie, unreverend
tongue ! to call her bad," etc. *Irreverent* does not occur in S.

228. *Scorn'st thou at.* Scoffest thou at. Cf. *Rich. III.* iv. 4. 102 :
"one that scorn'd at me." See also *R. and J.* p. 160.

230. *Give us leave awhile.* Leave us alone ; a courteous expression
of the time. See *R. and J.* p. 150, note on *Give leave awhile.*

231. *Good leave, good Philip.* Coleridge, in one of his Table-Talks,
said : "For an instance of Shakespeare's power *in minimis.* I generally
quote James Gurney's character in *King John.* How individual and
comical he is with the four words allowed to his dramatic life !" Clarke
adds : "They certainly suffice to show us the free-and-easy style of the
confidential servitor ; one intrusted with the family secrets of this country household ; one accustomed to treat the eldest son, but not the heir,
with a coolly easy familiarity tolerated by the good-humoured young
man, and only lightly waved aside by the new-made knight."

Sparrow! The sparrow was called *Philip* from its note. Holt White
quotes Lyly, *Mother Bombie :*

> "cry
> Phip phip the sparrowes as they fly."

From the note of the bird, Catullus, in his *Elegy on Lesbia's Sparrow*, has
formed a verb : "Ad solam dominam usque *pipilabat.*" Cf. Gascoigne's
Praise of Philip Sparrow :

> "Of all the byrds that I doo know,
>   Philip my sparrow hath no peere.
> *   *   *   *   *   *   *
> Let other prayse what byrd they will,
> Sweete Philip shall be my byrd still."

Sir Richard sportively rebukes Gurney for calling him by his former name : " *Philip!* do you take me for a *sparrow?*"

232. *There 's toys abroad.* "Certain trifling changes have come to pass" (Sr.). For *toy*=trifle, see *Ham.* p. 247 or *M. N. D.* p. 179.

234. *Sir Robert might have eat,* etc. Steevens quotes Heywood, *Dia- logues upon Proverbs,* 1562 :

> "he may his parte on good Fridaie eate,
> And fast never the wurs, for ought he shall geate."

236. *To confess.* To be honest, to tell the truth.

239. *Beholding.* Beholden, indebted. See *M. of V.* p. 135, or Gr. 372.

240. *Holp.* Helped ; the form regularly used by S. except in *Rich. III.* v. 3. 167 and *Oth.* ii. 1. 138, where we find *helped.* It is also the more common form for the participle, being used ten times, while *helped* occurs only four times. *Holpen* is found in the A. V. in *Ps.* lxxxiii. 8, *Dan.* xi. 34, *Luke,* i. 54, etc.

243. *Untoward.* Unmannerly ; as in the only other instance of the word in S., *T. of S.* iv. 5. 79 : "Then hast thou taught Hortensio to be untoward."

244. *Basilisco-like.* An allusion, as Theo. explains, to *Soliman and Perseda,* a stupid play printed in 1599 :

> "*Basilisco.* O, I swear, I swear.
> "*Piston.* By the contents of this blade,—
> "*Basilisco.* By the contents of this blade,—
> "*Piston.* I, the aforesaid Basilisco,—
> "*Basilisco.* I, the aforesaid Basilisco,—knight,
> Good fellow. knight.
> "*Piston.* Knave, good fellow, knave, knave."

The Bastard, *Basilisco-like,* insists on being called *knight* instead of *knave.*

250. *Proper.* Comely, handsome. See *M. of V.* p. 132, note on *A proper man's picture.* Cf. *Heb.* xi. 23.

Who was it, mother? "No one like Shakespeare for setting straight before the imagination the very look, gesture, and tone with which a few simple words could be uttered. By the way in which he has written these two lines, introducing this little sentence at the close, we see the son's hugging arm thrown round her, the close drawing her to him, the manly wooing voice by which he accompanies the coaxing question" (Clarke).

256. *Dear.* Grievous. Cf. *Hen. V.* ii. 2. 181 : "your dear offences ;" *Rich. III.* i. 4. 215 :

> "How canst thou urge God's dreadful law to us,
> When thou hast broke it in so dear degree?"

Cf. *Temp.* p. 124 (note on *The dear'st o' th' loss*) or *Rich. II.* p. 151.

260. *Some sins,* etc. "There are *sins* that, whatever be determined of them above, are not much censured *on earth*" (Johnson).

262. *Dispose.* Cf. *T. G. of V.* ii. 7. 86 : "All that is mine I leave at thy dispose" (see also *Id.* iv. 1. 76). For *dispose*=disposition, temper, see *Oth.* p. 170.

265. *Aweless.* Fearless. Fl. makes it ="unruled, lawless," compar-

ing the use of *awe* in *Nobody and Somebody:* "Subjects unto the awe of Elidun."

266. *Nor keep*, etc. The allusion is to the old legend that Richard derived his name of *Cœur-de-lion* from having torn out the heart of a lion to which he had been exposed by the Duke of Austria in revenge for having killed his son. A metrical form of the story may be found in Percy's *Reliques.*

267. *Perforce.* By force. See *A. Y. L.* p. 141 or *M. N. D.* p. 138.

272. *My kin.* The king and the dowager queen. Cf. 168 above.

ACT II.

SCENE I.—In the folio this scene is headed "*Scæna Secunda;*" and the next (iii. 1), "*Actus Secundus.*" The latter ends with iii. 1. 74, making the act consist of only 74 lines ; and "*Actus Tertius, Scæna prima*" then begins, continuing to end of iii. 1. "*Scæna Secunda*" includes iii. 2 and iii. 3, and "*Scæna Tertia*" is iii. 4. The divisions of the last two acts are the same as in the modern eds. Fl. makes the first 299 lines of this scene a second scene of act i., taking the remainder as ii. 1 ; and he divides iii. 1 into ii. 2 (74 lines) and iii. 1. W. also makes this division of iii. 1, and gives good reasons for it ; but for convenience in cross references we follow the arrangement (first made by Theo.) in the "Globe" ed. and most of the modern eds.

1. *Before Angiers*, etc. The folio gives this speech, and the one in 18 below, to "*Lewis,*" but it clearly belongs to King Philip, as D., Clarke, and some others assign it. The expression "At *our* importance" in 7 is alone sufficient to show that it belongs to the king, who would also be more likely to refer to Arthur as "noble *boy*" than would Lewis, who was of about the same age. As Mr. Williams has remarked, those who adhere to the folio, which is often inaccurate in its prefixes (see, for instance, on 368 below), forget that S. has crowded into this drama the events of several years. "In the later acts Lewis plays a conspicuous part, and heads the invasion of England ; but at the period in question he was a mere youth, and was evidently so considered by the dramatist." Cf. 495 below, where the king addresses him as "boy," and 521, where he and Blanch are called "young ones." It is hardly probable that this "beardless boy," as the Bastard afterwards calls him (v. 1. 69) would be the first to welcome the Duke of Austria here, and that in the presence of his royal father. As a rule, S. "makes his monarchs and great personages open and conclude the dialogue whenever they appear." It may be added that in the old play the corresponding speech is given to King Philip.

Fl. believes that the first 200 lines of this scene (with iii. 2. 1-10) were "inserted hurriedly after the rest of the play had been written," and after the death of the poet's son, Hamnet, in 1596 ; and that the blunders in names "are to be attributed to the confusion caused by grief in Shakespeare's mind."

The introduction of *Austria* here is an anachronism, as Leopold, Duke of Austria, by whom Richard I. had been thrown into prison in 1193, died in 1195, while the action of this play begins in 1199 (Malone). Cf. the old play (i. 2. 4) :

> "Brave Austria, cause of Cordelion's death,
> Is also come to aid thee in thy wars."

7. *Importance.* Importunity. See *T. N.* p. 168 ; and cf. *Much Ado*, p. 129, note on *Important.*

12. *God shall forgive you*, etc. "S. has made Arthur of younger age at this period than historical truth warrants ; but he well knew that the truth of tragic story would be more perfectly fulfilled by having a child the subject of injury here. The way in which he has drawn the innocent boy throughout is intensely pathetic—a sweet and gentle nature hurled to and fro like a flower amid tempests ; bruised, wounded, and finally crushed by the stormy passions and ruthless ambitions of the merciless natures around him. That the dramatist has nowise violated natural and characteristic truth, by making the little prince speak with a grace and propriety beyond those generally belonging to children of his age, we have confirmatory evidence in a record made by Froissart in his *Chronicles*, where he describes the conduct of the Princess of France, then 'a yonge childe of eyght yere of age'" (Clarke).

16. *Unstained.* The Coll. MS. makes the bad alteration "unstrained." As Sr. remarks, "the antithesis of the hand without *power*, but love without *stain*, is both lucid and forcible."

20. *Indenture.* Contract. See *Ham.* p. 262, note on *A pair of indentures.*

23. *Pale* and *white-fac'd* refer of course to the chalk cliffs of the southern coast of England. Hence *Albion*, from the Latin *albus*, white.

26. *With.* By. Gr. 193. On the passage, cf. *Rich. II.* ii. 1. 46 fol.

34. *A more requital.* A greater return. Cf. *V. and A.* 78 : "a more delight ;" *R. of L.* 332 : "a more rejoicing ;" *C. of E.* ii. 2. 174 : "a more contempt," etc.

37. *Well then*, etc. The first speech given to King Philip in the folio ; but the form of expression rather implies that he has spoken before. See on 1 above.

39. *Chiefest.* A superlative often used by S. See *M. of V.* ii. 8. 43, *Macb.* iii. 5. 33, *Ham.* i. 2. 117, etc.

40. *Plots of best advantages.* Most advantageous positions.

45. *Unadvis'd.* Inconsiderate, rash. Cf. *R. and J.* ii. 2. 118 : "It is too rash, too unadvis'd, too sudden," etc. See also 191 and v. 2. 132 below.

49. *Indirectly.* Wrongfully ; as in *Hen. V.* ii. 4. 94 : "Your crown and kingdom, indirectly held," etc. So *indirection* = wrong, in iii. 1. 276 below, and in *J. C.* iv. 3. 75.

50. *A wonder.* "The wonder is only that Chatillon happened to arrive at the moment when Constance mentioned him ; which the French king, according to a superstition which prevails more or less in every mind agitated by great affairs, turns into a miraculous interposition, or omen of good" (Johnson).

53. *We coldly pause for thee.* That is, we restrain ourself, and calmly wait to hear thy message. Cf. *Much Ado,* p. 145, note on *Bear it coldly.*

58. *Stay'd.* Waited for. See *Ham.* p. 268.

59. *All as soon.* For this "intensive" use of *all,* see Gr. 28.

60. *Expedient.* Expeditious, rapid; used by S. in this sense only in plays before 1596 (Fl.). See *Rich. II.* p. 169; and cf. 223 and iv. 2. 268 below.

63. *Ate.* See *Much Ado,* p. 132. The folio misprints "Ace."

65. *King's.* The later folios have "king." The old play has "Next t' them, a bastard of the king's deceast."

66. *Unsettled humours.* Restless spirits.

67. *Voluntaries.* Volunteers. Cf. *T. and C.* ii. 1. 106: "Ajax was here the voluntary."

68. *Fierce dragons' spleens.* Cf. *Rich. III.* v. 3. 350: "Inspire us with the spleen of fiery dragons!" *Spleen* = impetuosity, ardour.

69. *Have sold their fortunes,* etc. Cf. *Hen. VIII.* i. 1. 83:

> "O, many
> Have broke their backs with laying manors on 'em
> For this great journey."

73. *Bottoms.* Ships. See *T. N.* p. 162. *Waft* = wafted; as in *M. of V.* v. 1. 11. Gr. 341. Cf. *heat* = heated, in iv. 1. 61 below. Halliwell quotes *The Affectionate Shepheard,* 1594:

> "And from Deaths quiver fell a fatall shaft,
> That under Cupid by the wind was waft."

75. *Scath.* Harm, mischief. See *R. and J.* p. 161. Spenser uses the noun often; as in *F. Q.* i. 12. 34: "To worke new woe and improvided scath," etc.

77. *More circumstance.* Further particulars. See *R. and J.* p. 178, note on *Stay the circumstance.*

85. *Lineal.* By lineal or hereditary right.

87. *Whiles.* See on iii. 4. 132 below; and for *if that* in 89, Gr. 287.

95. *Underwrought.* Undermined; used by S. nowhere else. Rowe changed *his* to "its," and the Coll. MS. has "her."

97. *Outfaced infant state.* "Brazenly outraged a child's right" (Clarke); that is, his right to the throne. For *outfaced,* cf. v. 1. 49 below.

101. *This little abstract,* etc. Cf. *W. T.* ii. 3. 97:

> "Behold, my lords,
> Although the print be little. the whole matter
> And copy of the father," etc.

103. *Brief.* Equivalent to *abstract* above. Cf. *M. W.* i. 1. 146, *M. N. D.* v. 1. 42, etc.

106. *This is Geffrey's.* This is Geffrey's heir. Mason's change of *this* to "his" (adopted by W.) does not seem to be necessary. Clarke makes *this is Geffrey's* = this boy's (that is, his right) is Geffrey's.

109. *Owe.* Own, are entitled to. Cf. 248 and iv. 2. 99 below. *O'ermasterest* = hast become master of, hast got by force.

111. *To draw my answer,* etc. "To make me answer according to thy articles" (Schmidt); "to draw up my replication out of the clauses of your own brief" (Fl.). It is legal phraseology.

113. *Breast.* The 1st folio has "beast ;" corrected in 2d folio.

119. *Excuse.* Schmidt is probably right in making this a noun. It seems to be elliptical = my excuse is. Fl. explains it " pardon me."

123. *Check.* "Treat as a bondman" (Schmidt). Cf. *3 Hen. VI.* iii. 2. 166 :

> "to command, to check, to o'erbear such
> As are of better person than myself."

Malone quotes Holinshed : "Surely Queen Eleanor, the kyngs mother, was sore against her nephew Arthur, rather moved thereto by envye conceyved against his mother, than upon any just occasion, given in the behalfe of the childe ; for that she saw, if he were king, how his mother Constance would looke to beare the most rule within the realme of Englande, till her sonne should come to a lawfull age to governe of himselfe. So hard a thing it is, to bring women to agree in one minde, their natures commonly being so contrary."

127. *Than thou,* etc. The folio reads "Then thou and *Iohn,* in manners being as like," etc. ; and Fl. prefers that pointing.

128. *Dam.* Here used contemptuously ; but not always so. See *IV. T.* p. 178.

131. *If thou wert his mother.* "Constance alludes to Elinor's infidelity to her husband, Louis VII., when they were in the Holy Land ; on account of which he was divorced from her. She afterwards (1151) married our King Henry II." (Malone).

134. *Hear the crier!* A sarcastic allusion to the crier's proclamation of silence in courts of justice, suggested by Austria's *Peace!*

136. *An a' may catch you,* etc. It is said that Austria wore a lion's hide which he had taken as a spoil from Richard when he killed him (Pope). As Johnson adds, S. assumed that this story would be familiar to his audience, and therefore does not refer to it in the play as the ground of the Bastard's hostility to Austria.

137. *The proverb.* "Mortuo leoni et lepores insultant" (Erasmus, *Adagia,* quoted by Malone). Steevens cites *The Spanish Tragedy :* "So hares may pull dead lions by the beard."

139. *I'll smoke your skin-coat.* Halliwell quotes Cotgrave : "*L'en auray,*—blowes being understood—I shall be well beaten ; my skin-coat will be soundly curried." In the North of England *smoke* is a provincialism = "to beat severely."

141. *O, well,* etc. Clarke is inclined to assign this speech to Constance rather than Blanch, "who seems intended by the dramatist to take no part in what is going forward until there is question of her marriage with the Dauphin, and she is addressed by him ;" but S. follows the old play, in which Blanch says :

> "Joy tide his soul, to whom that spoil belong'd :
> Ah, Richard, how thy glory here is wrong'd!"

144. *As great Alcides' shows,* etc. The folio reads "As great *Alcides* shooes vpon an Asse ;" and "shoes" was defended by Malone and Steevens, who cited sundry passages referring to the shoes of Hercules on feet too small for them. Fl. also retains "shoes," but changes *ass* to "ape." The emendation in the text is due to Theo., and is adopted by

most of the recent editors. Keightley conjectures "Alcides' should," and Vaughan "Alcides' does."

147. *Cracker.* A play upon the various meanings of the word, including that of boaster. Halliwell quotes *Nomenclator*, 1585 : " *Grand menteur ou vanteur*, a bragger ; a boster ; a vaunter ; a craker ; a vaine praiser of his owne virtue." Cf. the modern vulgarism, "cracking himself up."

149. *King Philip, determine*, etc. The folio reads :

> "King *Lewis*, determine what we shall doe strait.
> "*Lew.* Women & fooles," etc.

The emendation in the text was made by Theo. Capell's reading, adopted by many of the editors, is

> " *King Philip.* Lewis, determine what we shall do straight.
> "*Lewis.* Women and fools," etc.

The objection to this is implied in the note on 1 above. The King would not be likely to refer the matter to a mere "boy" for decision. For Austria's form of address, cf. iii. 1. 198: " King Philip, listen to the cardinal;" and again in 219: "Do so, King Philip; hang no more in doubt." As Clarke remarks, the reply of John, " I do defy thee, *France*," appears conclusively to settle the point that we ought to assign the present speech to King Philip.

152. *Anjou.* The folio has "*Angiers;*" corrected by Theo. Cf. 487 below.

160. *It.* For the possessive *it*, see *W. T.* p. 172, note on *It own.* Here it is apparently used in imitation of the language of children, or the " baby-talk " of mothers to their children.

163. *Good my mother, peace !* See on p. 34 above.

165. *Coil.* Ado, disturbance. See *Much Ado*, p. 146, or *M. N. D.* p. 168.

169. *Draws.* Changed by Capell to "Draw." See Gr. 333.

S. is fond of comparing tears to *pearls.* Cf. *V. and A.* 980, *R. of L.* 1213, 1553, *Sonn.* 34. 13, *T. G. of V.* iii. 1. 224, *Rich. III.* iv. 4. 322, and *Lear*, iv. 3. 24.

170. *Beads.* Cf. *J. C.* iii. 1. 284: "those beads of sorrow." Fl. sees a play on beads of a rosary.

177. *Eld'st.* For the contraction of superlatives, see Gr. 473.

178. *Infortunate.* Used by S. occasionally instead of *unfortunate ;* as *incertain, ingrateful, insociable*, etc. See Gr. 442.

180. *The canon of the law.* See *Exod.* xx. 5.

183. *Bedlam.* Lunatic ; from Bedlam (or *Bethlehem*) Hospital in London. Cf. *Lear*, iii. 7. 103 : "get the Bedlam To lead him," etc.

184. *That he is not only plagued*, etc. Another Chinese puzzle for the critics (see on i. 1. 139 above). The folio gives the passage thus :

> "*Con.* I haue but this to say,
> That he is not one'y plagued for her sin,
> But God hath made her sinne and her, the plague
> On this remoued issue, plagued for her,
> And with her plague her sinne : his iniury
> Her iniurie the Beadle to her sinne,
> All punish'd in the person of this childe,
> And all for her, a plague vpon her."

The pointing in the text (adopted by K. and the Camb. ed.) is that of Mr. Roby, who explains the passage thus : "God hath made her sin and herself to be a plague to this distant child, who is punished for her and with the punishment belonging to her ; God has made her sin to be an injury to Arthur, and her injurious deeds to be the executioner to punish her sin ; all which (namely, her first sin and her now injurious deeds) are punished in the person of this child."

Many of the editors adopt Roderick's conjecture of "plagued" for *plague* in 187. Sr. points the lines thus :

> "But God hath made her sin and her the plague
> On this removed issue ;—plagu d for her,
> And with her plagu'd ; her sin, his injury ;
> Her injury, the beadle to her sin :" etc.,

which he explains (abridging Henley) as follows : "Young Arthur is here represented as not only suffering *from* the guilt of his grandmother, but also by *her* in person, she being made the very instrument of his sufferings. So that he is *plagued on her account*, and plagued with her, that is, by her. *Her* sin brings upon him *his* injury, or the evil *he* suffers ; and *her* injury, or the evil *she* inflicts, is as the beadle to her sin, or executioner of the punishment annexed to it."

The only other reading and interpretation we will notice is that of Fl., who gives

> "But God hath made her sin and her the plague
> On this removed issue ; plagued for her,
> And with her plague, her sin : his injury
> Her injury, the beadle to her sin :" etc.

His explanation is : "Plagued on her account, and by means of her wrong-doing, which is a plague inflicted by her (cf. *her sin, the plague*, in line 185) ; the injury inflicted on him, the injury inflicted by her, being the beadle, the chastiser (in Arthur's sufferings) of her original wrong-doing."

W. points the passage essentially as in the text, but adopts Roderick's "plagued." H. follows Sr., reprinting his explanation as above. Clarke's reading is the same as Fleay's.

191. *Unadvised.* See on 45 above.

192. *Will.* There is a play upon the word.

194. *Canker'd.* Venomous, malignant ; as in I *Hen. IV.* i. 3. 137 : "ingrate and canker'd Bolingbroke," etc.

196. *Cry aim.* Encourage ; "an expression borrowed from archery = to encourage the archers by crying out *aim* when they were about to shoot, and then in a general sense to applaud, to encourage with cheers" (Schmidt). Cf. *M. W.* iii. 2. 45 : "to these violent proceedings all my neighbours shall cry aim." See also *Id.* ii. 3. 93. Halliwell, among other illustrations of the phrase, cites B. and F., *Love's Cure :* "Can I cry aim to this against myself ?"

197. *Ill-tuned repetitions.* "Discordant recriminations" (Clarke). *Repetitions* is metrically equivalent to five syllables, like *observation* in i. 1. 208 above.

198. *Trumpet.* Trumpeter. See on i. 1. 27 above.

205. *Gentle parle.* Friendly parley. For *parle*, see *Hen. V.* p. 164 ; and cf. 226 below.

209. *Endamagement.* Injury. S. uses the noun only here, but we find the verb *endamage* in *T. G. of V.* iii. 2. 43 and 1 *Hen. VI.* ii. 1. 77.

215. *Confronts your.* The 1st and 2d folios have "Comfort yours," the 3d and 4th "Comfort your;" corrected by Capell. The Coll. MS. gives "Come 'fore your." *Winking*=shut hastily, in apprehension of danger.

217. *Doth.* The form is to be explained by the proximity of *waist.* Cf. iii. 1. 295 below: "The peril of our curses light on thee." Gr. 412.

218. *Ordinance.* Ordnance. See *Hen. V.* p. 161.

220. *Dishabited.* Dislodged. Fl. gives "dishabit'." Cf. *waft* in 73 above.

223. *Expedient.* See on 60 above.

228. *A shaking fever.* Cf. *Macb.* ii. 3. 66:

> "some say, the earth
> Was feverous and did shake."

See also *Cor.* i. 4. 61.

229. *Words folded up in smoke.* Malone compares *R. of L.* 1027: "This helpless smoke of words doth me no right." See also *Id.* 1042 and *L. L. L.* iii. 1. 64.

230. *To make,* etc. That is, to deceive your ears, to delude you.

233. *Forwearied.* Wearied out, exhausted; used by S. only here. Cf. Spenser, *F. Q.* i. 1. 32: "Ye all forwearied be;" *Id.* i. 9. 13: "Forwearied with my sportes," etc.

236. *Protection.* A quadrisyllable. See on 197 above.

237. *Divinely.* "Religiously" (246 below), sacredly.

247. *Owe.* In the modern sense; but in the next line=owns, is entitled to, as in 109 above.

250. *Aspect.* The regular accent in S. Gr. 490.

252. *Invulnerable.* The 1st folio has "involuerable;" corrected in 2d folio.

253. *Unvex'd retire.* Unmolested return. For the noun, cf. 326 and v. 5. 4 below.

256. *Spout.* Cf. *T. and C.* iv. 5. 10: "let thy eyes spout blood," etc.

258. *Fondly pass.* Foolishly disregard or reject. *Proffer'd offer* has been suspected of corruption, and "love," "favour," "terms," etc., have been suggested in place of *offer;* but *proffer'd offer* may be a more emphatic *proffer* or *offer,* or a mere inadvertence of composition.

259. *Roundure.* Round or circle (Fr. *rondeur*). The folios have "rounder," which indicates the pronunciation. We have *rondure* in *Sonn.* 21. 8.

264. *In that behalf which.* That is, *in* which; a common ellipsis in relative clauses. See Gr. 394.

266. *Possession.* A quadrisyllable. Cf. *repetitions* in 197 and *protection* in 236 above, and *ocean* in 340 below. Gr. 479.

268. *For him,* etc. Cf. the old play: "to him will we remain firm subjects, and for him, and in his right, we hold our town."

278. *Bloods.* "Men of mettle" (Schmidt). Cf. *J. C.* i. 2. 151: "the breed of noble bloods." See also 461 below.

281. *Compound.* Agree, decide.

K

288. *Swing'd.* Whipped, conquered. Cf. *T. G. of V.* ii. 1. 88, iii. 1. 392, *M. for M.* v. 1. 130, etc. The folio has "swindg'd."

289. *Horse back.* As one word ("horsebacke") in the folio. See *Macb.* p. 204 (note on *Horses*) or Gr. 471.

292. *I would set an ox-head,* etc. Steevens quotes the old play:

> "But let the frolick Frenchman take no scorn,
> If Philip front him with an English horn."

On *monster*, cf. *Oth.* iv. 1. 63: "A horned man 's a monster," etc.

306. *Discolour'd.* The folio has "discoloured."

309. *Display'd.* Suggested by the *banners* (see 320 below), though re-ferring in a way to *the French.*

314. *Malicious.* Malignant, destructive.

316. *Gilt.* Stained. See *Macb.* p. 192, note on *I 'll gild,* etc.

321. *Like a jolly troop of huntsmen,* etc. Hunters used to stain their hands with the blood of the deer as a badge of their success. Cf. *J. C.* iii. 1. 204:

> "Here wast thou bay'd, brave hart,
> Here didst thou fall; and here thy hunters stand,
> Sign'd in thy spoil, and crimson'd in thy lethe."

323. *Dying.* There is an obvious play upon the word. The pun was a common one. Halliwell quotes Heywood, *Epigrams,* 1562: "Dyers be ever dying, but never dead;" and Davies, *Scourge of Folly,* 1611.

> "Turbine the dyer stalkes before his dore,
> Like Cæsar, that by dying oft did thrive;
> And though the beggar be as proud as pore,
> Yet (like the mortifide) he dyes to live."

325. *Might.* Could. Gr. 312. The folios give the speeches of this *Citizen* to "*Hub.*" (Hubert), a mistake probably due to the fact that both parts were taken by the same actor.

326. *Retire.* Retreat. See on 253 above.

328. *Censured.* Judged, determined. See *Much Ado,* p. 139; and for the noun = judgment, *Macb.* p. 251 or *Ham.* p. 190.

The *cannot* is not strictly consistent with the context. The meaning clearly is that the *equality* of the two armies is evident, or *both are alike;* the best judges cannot see any *variation* from the *equality.*

335. *Run.* The 1st folio has "rome," changed in the 2d to "runne." W. prefers "roam," as agreeing better with the *peaceful progress.* He believes that S. had in mind the same stream that suggested the beauti-ful description in *T. G. of V.* ii. 7. 25–32. Here, however, *roam* does not seem to fit the comparison so well as *run.* "The king would rather de-scribe his right as *running on* in a *direct* than in an *irregular* course, such as would be implied in the word *roam*" (Steevens). Cf. also the very similar passage in v. 4. 53–57, where we have

> "*calmly run on* in obedience
> Even to our ocean, to our great King John."

336. *Vex'd.* Disturbed Cf. *Lear,* iv. 4. 2: "the vex'd sea." See also *Temp.* i. 2. 229 and *R. and J.* i. 1. 198.

339. *Water.* The Coll. MS. has "waters," which W. adopts, on the ground that S. does not use the singular of water as a body, but only as a fluid.

340. *Ocean.* A trisyllable; as in *T. G. of V.* ii. 7. 32. Cf. Milton, *Hymn on Nativ.* 66: "Whispering new joys to the mild ocean."

344. *Climate.* Here apparently=sky, heavens. For its use =country, region, see *Rich. II.* p. 203.

354. *Mousing.* Tearing, as a cat does a mouse. Cf. *M. N. D.* v. 1. 274: "Well moused, lion!" Malone cites Dekker, *Wonderful Year*, 1603: "Whilst Troy was swilling sack and sugar, and mousing fat venison, the mad Greekes made bonfires of their houses." Pope changed the word to "mouthing."

355. *Differences.* Quarrels, dissensions.

356. *Fronts.* Brows, faces. See *Ham.* p. 236, note on *The front of Jove.*

357. *Cry havoc!* The signal that no quarter was to be given. Cf. *Cor.* iii. 1. 275:

> "Do not cry havoc, where you should but hunt
> With modest warrant."

See also *J. C.* iii. 1. 273, *Ham.* v. 2. 375, etc.

358. *Potents.* Potentates, powers; the only instance of the noun in S. The Coll. MS. has "potent."

367. *Lord of our presence.* "Master of our own identity or individuality" (Clarke). See on i. 1. 137 above.

368. *A greater power than we.* Theo. (following Warb.) changed *we* to "ye." "The reference may be to the Lord of hosts, who has not yet decided the superiority of either army; and till it be undoubted the people of Angiers will not open their gates" (Tollet). If this be not the meaning, the *power* must be *our fears.* All the folios assign this speech to the French king.

371. *King'd of.* Ruled by (Gr. 170). The folio has "Kings of our feare;" corrected by Tyrwhitt. *Resolv'd*=set at rest. Cf. its use = dissolved, in v. 4. 25 below.

373. *Scroyles.* Scabby fellows (Fr. *escrouelles*); a term of great contempt. Taylor the Water-Poet speaks of a "hungry sawcy scroyle." Cf. B. J., *Every Man in his Humour*, i. 1. "hang 'em, scroyles!" and *Poetaster*, iv. 3: "I cry thee mercy, my good scroyle, wast thou?"

376. *Industrious.* Capell conjectured "illustrious;" but, as Steevens remarks, the expression is=" your laborious *industry* of war."

378. *Mutines.* Mutineers, rebels. Cf. *Ham.* v. 2. 6: "the mutines in the bilboes." *Mutiner* occurs in *Cor.* i. 1. 254. Malone cites a *History of the Jews,* written in Hebrew by Joseph Ben Gorion, and translated into English by Peter Morwyn, 1575, which tells how three factions in Jerusalem, which had been engaged in "most cruel battailes" with one another, made peace, "intending to turne their cruelty upon the Romaines, confirming and ratifying the same atonement and purpose by swearing one to another," etc. S. had probably read this book, as the allusion is not in the old play.

383. *Soul-fearing.* Soul-affrighting. For *fear*=cause to fear, cf. *M. of V.* ii. 1. 9:

> "I tell thee, lady, this aspect of mine
> Hath fear'd the valiant,"

and see note in our ed. p. 137. Cf. *fearful* in iv. 2. 106 below.

385. *Jades.* The word meant originally a worthless or vicious horse. See *Hen. V.* p. 170 and *Much Ado,* p. 121. For the masculine use of *jade* as applied to persons, cf. *T. of S.* ii. 1. 202.

387. *Vulgar.* General, common to all.

392. *Minion.* Darling, favourite (Fr. *mignon*). Cf. *Temp.* iv. 1. 98: "Mars's hot minion;" and see our ed. p. 136.

396. *The policy.* "That which you call policy" (Schmidt); or "the politic art, the art of Machiavel" (Fl.).

398. *Knit.* Join, unite; as in iii. 1. 226 below.

400. *Fight who shall.* Fight *to decide* who shall. As Abbott (Gr. 382) remarks, "the Elizabethan writers objected to scarcely any ellipsis, provided the deficiency could be easily supplied from the context." *After=* afterwards; as in *Temp.* ii. 2. 10, etc. Gr. 26.

401. *Mettle.* The early eds. make no distinction between *mettle* and *metal,* using either for the literal or the metaphorical meaning. Thus, in *Rich. II.* i. 2. 23, the quartos have "mettall" or "mettal," the folios "mettle."

402. *Peevish.* Foolish; perhaps the only sense in S. See *Hen. V.* p. 171.

404. *Saucy.* Impudent, insolent; used by S. in a stronger sense than the modern one. Cf. *J. C.* i. 3. 12: "the world, too saucy with the gods," etc. See also *Macb.* p. 214.

406. *Pell-mell.* Cf. *Rich. III.* v. 3. 312: "let 's to 't pell-mell," etc.

411. *Thunder.* W. adopts Capell's conjecture of "thunders;" but the word may be used collectively=cannon.

418. *You.* For yon.

421. *Persever.* The regular spelling and accent in S. Cf. *A. W.* iv. 2. 36, 37, where it rhymes with *ever.* Gr. 492.

424. *Niece.* The folios have "neere" or "near." The emendation is from the Coll. MS. K. and Clarke retain and defend "near" as = nearly related.

425. *Dauphin.* It is "Dolphin" in the folios, as elsewhere; and W. retains that spelling, which indicates the pronunciation of the time. Cf. 1 *Hen. VI.* i. 4. 107, where there is a play on the word and the name of the fish.

426. *Lusty.* "Full of animal life and spirits" (Schmidt); as in 255 above and 461 below.

428. *Zealous.* Explained by Johnson and Schmidt as=pious, religious; which is favoured by the antithesis.

431. *Bound.* Confine, enclose; as in 442 below.

434. *Complete of.* "That is, full of those qualities" (Schmidt); complete *thereof,* or *therein.* Theo. gave "complete of,—say;" and Hanmer, "complete, oh! say."

438. *A she.* The folios have "as she;" but the analogy of other passages in S. favours Thirlby's emendation, which has been generally adopted. See *A. Y. L.* p. 170, or Gr. 224.

For the idea that woman was completed or perfected by marriage, see *T. N.* p. 121 (note on *Are fill'd,* etc.) and p. 140 (note on *Perfection*).

446. *Battery.* Battering, assault.

447. *Match.* Johnson is "loath to think" that there is a play on the word.

448. *Spleen.* See on 68 above ; and cf. iv. 3. 97 and v. 7. 50 below.

455. *Stay.* A word that has been a stumbling-block to the commentators. See a page and a half of discussion in the Var. of 1821. Probably Schmidt is right in explaining it as "the imperative of the verb used substantively." The Citizen has begun (416) by saying "vouchsafe awhile to *stay.*" Some make *stay*=support, prop ; and Clarke thinks there may be an indirect reference to that sense of the word. "That a *restraint* and a *support* should be personified sufficiently to be supposed capable of shaking 'the rotten carcass of old Death' is not beyond the license of poetry in figurative language." "Flaw," "say," "story," "storm," etc. have been suggested, but no change is necessary.

462. *He speaks plain cannon fire*, etc. Cf. *Hen. V.* v. 2. 156 : "I speak to thee plain soldier." See also *Much Ado*, ii. 1. 255, 343, *Ham.* iii. 2. 414, etc. *Bounce*="bang" (Schmidt).

465. *Buffets.* Boxes ; as in *Hen. V.* v. 2. 146 : "if I might buffet for my love," etc.

466. *Zounds.* Like *'swounds* (see *Ham.* p. 214), contracted from "God's wounds!"

468. *Conjunction.* Connection, union ; as in iii. 1. 227 below. Capell marks 468–479 as "*Aside to John.*"

471. *Unsur'd.* "Unsure" (iii. 1. 283 below), unassured.

476. *Capable.* Susceptible. Cf. iii. 1. 12 below.

477. *Lest zeal*, etc. Steevens thought that *zeal* is compared to "*metal* in a state of fusion," not to dissolving ice, as Johnson had explained it. Malone paraphrases the passage thus : "Lest the now *zealous* and to you well-affected *heart* of Philip, which but lately was cold and hard as ice, and has *newly* been *melted and softened*, should by the breath of supplications of Constance, and pity for Arthur, again *become congealed* and frozen." Cf. iii. 4. 149 below :

> "This act so evilly born shall cool the hearts
> Of all his people and freeze up their zeal."

W. makes *pity and remorse* the subject of *cool and congeal.*

481. *Treaty.* Here=proposal tending to a *treaty* or agreement ; as in *Cor.* ii. 2. 59 and *A. and C.* iii. 11. 62.

485. *This book of beauty.* For the metaphor, cf. *R. and J.* i. 3. 87 : "This precious book of love, this unbound lover ;" and see *Id.* iii. 2. 83, *Oth.* iv. 2. 71, etc. Malone compares *Macb.* i. 5. 63.

487. *Anjou.* The folios have "Angiers," as in 152 above ; corrected by Theo.

492. *Promotions.* A quadrisyllable. See on 266 above.

494. *Holds hand with.* Goes hand in hand with, equals.

498. *Shadow.* Reflection ; as in *V. and A.* 162 :

> "Narcissus so himself himself forsook,
> And died to kiss his shadow in the brook."

See also *Id.* 1099, *Rich. II.* iv. 1. 293 (where there is a play upon *shadow*, as here), and *J. C.* i. 2. 58.

502. *Infixed.* Imprinted. Cf. *A. W.* v. 3. 47 : "Where the impression of mine eye infixing," etc.

503. *Table.* Tablet, or that on which a picture is drawn or painted. Cf. *Sonn.* 24. 2 :

> "Mine eye hath play'd the painter and hath stell'd
> Thy beauty's form in table of my heart ;"

and *A. W.* i. 1. 106 :
> "to sit and draw
> His arched brows, his hawking eye, his curls,
> In our heart's table."

In the speech that follows, there is an allusion to the punishment of "drawing, hanging, and quartering." For similar quibbles, see *Much Ado*, p. 143, note on *Hang it first, and draw it afterwards.*

513. *Translate it to my will.* Cf. *M. W.* i. 3. 54 : "He hath studied her will, and translated her will, out of honesty into English." See also *A. Y. L.* ii. 1. 19.

527. *Volquessen.* The old name of a part of Normandy (the Latin *Pagus Velocassinus*) more recently known as *Le Vexin.* Cf. the old play :

> "*John.* First, Philip knows her dowry out of Spaine,
> To be so great as to content a king:
> But more to mend and amplify the same,
> I give in money thirty thousand marks.
> For land I leave it to thine own demand.
>   "*Phil.* Then I demand Volquesson, Torain, Main,
> Poiters, and Aniou, these five provinces,
> Which thou, as King of England, hold'st in France."

530. *Marks.* The *mark* was worth 13 shillings 4 pence.

532. *Join hands.* That is, for the formal betrothal. See *T. N.* p. 160 (note on *Plight me,* etc.) and p. 166 (note on *Contracted*).

533. *Likes.* Pleases. See *Ham.* pp. 202, 274. The folio points the line thus : "It likes vs well young Princes : close your hands ;" corrected by Rowe.

534. *And your lips too.* This was also a part of the ceremony of betrothal. See *T. N.* v. 1. 159 :

> "A contract of eternal bond of love,
> Confirm'd by mutual joinder of your hands,
> Attested by the holy close of lips,
> Strengthen'd by interchangement of your rings," etc.

535. *Assur'd.* Affianced. Walker conjectures "affied," but the repetition with a play on the word is quite in the poet's manner. Cf. 247, 248, and 498–500 above.

538. *Saint Mary's chapel.* This is said to be the so-called Church of Ronceray, dedicated to St. Mary the Virgin in 1028 and re-dedicated in 1119 by Pope Calixtus II. It is now used as a chapel for the students of the School of Arts.

544. *Passionate.* Full of *passion* or sorrow. Cf. *T. G. of V.* i. 2. 124 : "Poor, forlorn Proteus, passionate Proteus." *Passion* often = sorrow ; as in *L. L. L.* v. 2. 118 : "passion's solemn tears," etc.

550. *Vantage.* Advantage ; as in *Sonn.* 88. 12, *Rich. II.* i. 3. 218, etc.

558. *Exclamation.* Outcry, vociferous opposition. Cf. *2 Hen. IV.* ii. 1. 88 : "What man of good temper would endure this tempest of exclamation ?" See also *R. of L.* 705, *Rich. III.* iv. 4. 153, etc.

563. *Departed with.* Parted with. Cf. *L. L. L.* ii. 1. 147 : "Which

we much rather had depart withal," etc. See also B. J., *Every Man out of his Humour*, iv. 7 : " Faith, sir, I can hardly depart with ready money ;" B. and F., *Two Noble Kinsmen*, ii. 1 : " I may depart with little while I live," etc. *Depart* was also often = part, separate ; as in 3 *Hen. VI.* ii. 6. 43 : " life and death's departing." In the English Marriage Service " till death us do part " was originally " till death us depart ;" as in an old play quoted by Nares : " Aye, till death us depart, love." Cf. Spenser, *F. Q.* ii. 10. 14 : " Which Severne now from Logris doth depart."

566. *Rounded.* Whispered ; as in *W. T.* i. 2. 217 : " whispering, rounding," etc. See also *Hen. VIII.* p. 168, foot-note.

568. *Broker.* Go-between. See *Ham.* p. 191. There is a play on the word in *breaks*.

573. *Commodity.* Self-interest. *Tickling* = flattering, cajoling.

574. *Bias.* An allusion to the game of bowls. See *Ham.* p. 200 (note on *Assays of bias*) and *Rich. II.* p. 197 (note on *Rubs*). Henderson quotes *Cupid's Whirligig*, 1607 :

> "Oh, the world is like a byas bowle, and it runs
> All on the rich men's sides."

The *eye* (583) was the hole in which the weight was put to give the bowl its *bias*.

575. *Peized.* Poised, balanced. Cf. *M. of V.* iii. 2. 22 : " to peize the time " (that is, to retard it by hanging weights on it). In *Rich. III.* v. 3. 105, " peize me down " = weigh me down. For *who* = which, see Gr. 264.

579. *Take head from.* Take its own course away from. *Indifferency* = straightforwardness, impartiality. Schmidt makes it = " moderate measure ;" as in the only other instance of the word in S. (2 *Hen. IV.* iv. 3. 23).

584. *Aid.* Coll. adopts Mason's conjecture of " aim ;" but *determined aid* may be = the aid that he had determined to give.

587. *Rail on.* S. uses *on* or *upon* with *rail* much oftener than *at* or *against*.

588. *But for because.* Only because. For *for* (= because) and *for because*, see Gr. 151. Cf. 591 just below.

590. *Angels.* The gold coin so called. Its value was about ten shillings. On one side was a figure of Michael piercing the dragon. The device is said to have been suggested by Pope Gregory's pun on *Angli*

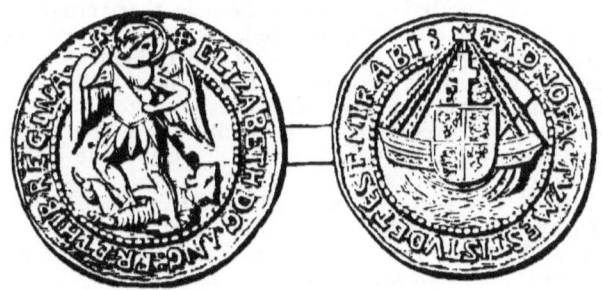

GOLDEN ANGEL OF QUEEN ELIZABETH.

and *Angeli.* For the quibble here, cf. *M. W.* i. 3. 60, *Much Ado*, ii. 3. 35, and 2 *Hen. IV.* i. 2. 187.

591. *Unattempted.* Not tempted. So *attempt*=tempt; as in *M. of V.* iv. 1. 421 : "I must attempt you further," etc.

593. *Whiles.* See on 87 above.

597. *Upon commodity.* That is, when it is for their interest.

ACT III.

SCENE I.—5. *Be well advis'd.* Consider well what you say. Cf. *advised*=considerate, in iv. 2. 214 below.

12. *Capable of.* Susceptible of. Cf. ii. 1. 476 above.

14. *Subject.* Fl. takes this to be the participle, like *waft* in ii. 1. 73 above.

17. *Spirits.* Monosyllabic; as often. Gr. 463. *Take a truce with*= make a truce with, pacify, or quiet ; as in *R. and J.* iii. 1. 162, etc.

19. *Shaking of.* Cf. *J. C.* v. 3. 38 : "saving of thy life," etc. Gr. 178.

22. *Rheum.* Moisture ; often, as here, applied to tears. Cf. *Much Ado*, v. 2. 85, *Rich. II.* i. 4. 8, *Cor.* v. 6. 46, *Ham.* ii. 2. 529, etc. See also iv. 1. 33 and iv. 3. 108 below.

23. *Peering o'er.* "Overpeering" (*M. of V.* i. 1. 12, *Ham.* iv. 5. 99, etc.), rising above.

27. "The way in which Salisbury's character is drawn, refined in speech, gentle in manner, has fitness as well as beauty ; he was son to King Henry II. by Rosamond Clifford, surnamed 'Fair Rosamond'" (Clarke).

33. *Which.* Who (Gr. 265) ; or we may say that the relative refers in a way to both *fury* and *men.*

41. *As.* Cf. 296 below : "So heavy as thou shalt not," etc. Gr. 109.

42. *Be content.* Be calm ; as in *Rich. II.* v. 2. 82, etc.

Clarke remarks here : "The boy's artless appeals to his mother amidst her vehement indignation and passionate lamentation, a compound of maternal ambition and maternal love, should have sufficed to teach her heart the lesson so subtly inculcated by the poet, that ambitious projects indulged for the sake of a being beloved, until they merge affection in violence and absorbing purpose, gradually undermine love in the bosom of the one beloved. It is curious to observe how little of tenderness there is in Arthur towards his mother, as response to all the passionate (but vehemently and even violently passionate) love she lavishes upon him. Thus acutely and truly does Shakespeare indicate his moral lessons " (Clarke).

45. *Sightless.* Unsightly. It means invisible in *Macb.* i. 5. 50 and i. 7. 23. On *blots*, cf. *R. of L.* 537 : "birth-hour's blot."

46. *Swart.* Swarthy, dark ; as in *C. of E.* iii. 2. 104 and 1 *Hen. VI.* i. 2. 84. Cf. *swart-complexioned* in *Sonn.* 28. 11.

Prodigious. Monstrous, unnatural. Cf. *Rich. III.* i. 2. 22 :

> "If ever he have child, abortive be it,
> Prodigious, and untimely brought to light,
> Whose ugly and unnatural aspect
> May fright the hopeful mother at the view," etc.

See also *M. N. D.* p. 190 ; and cf. *prodigiously* in 91 below.

56. *Adulterates.* Commits adultery ; the only instance of the verb in S. Cf. the adjective in *Ham.* i. 5. 42, etc.

65. *Underbear.* Bear, endure ; as in *Rich. II.* i. 4. 29 : "And patient underbearing of his fortune."

69. *Stoop.* That is, stoop to grief (Malone). "Feeling herself bowed down by grief, sinking beneath the load of her sorrows and injuries, she may well say that she will teach them to be proud, to resist the pride of *grief* which makes her *stoop* to its overpowering weight. She feels herself physically giving way under the load of the burden laid upon her ; and with her rich imagination converts the earth to which she is compelled to *stoop* into a *supporter* and *throne*" (Clarke). Some editors adopt Hanmer's "stout" for *stoop*.

73. *Sorrows.* Changed by Pope to "sorrow." Jackson would take the poetry out of the passage by reading "in sorrow."

78. *Plays the alchemist*, etc. Cf. *Sonn.* 33. 1 :

> "Full many a glorious morning have I seen,
> Flatter the mountain-tops with sovereign eye,
> Kissing with golden face the meadows green,
> Gilding pale streams with heavenly alchemy."

Steevens remarks that Milton has borrowed the image in *P. L.* iii. 609 : "The arch-chemic sun," etc.

86. *High tides.* Great days, "high festivals" (1 *Hen. VI.* i. 6. 26). For *tide*=time, see *R. and J.* p. 150, note on *Lammas-tide.*

87. *Nay, rather*, etc. Alluding to *Job*, iii. 3 and v. 6 (Upton).

92. *But.* Except. For *wrack* (the only spelling in the early eds.), see *T. N.* p. 162. This instance of the word is wrongly referred to *Macb.* iii. 1 in Mrs. Clarke's *Concordance.*

99. *Counterfeit.* The word meant a portrait (see *M. of V.* iii. 2. 115 : "Fair Portia's counterfeit," etc.) as well as a false coin ; and perhaps, as Malone and Clarke suggest, the two senses are blended here.

100. *Touch'd and tried.* Alluding to the use of the *touchstone* in testing counterfeit coin.

105. *Painted.* The Coll. MS. has "faint in." Clarke paraphrases the passage thus : "The contentious vigour of appearance and threatening warlike visage with which you came here on our behalf is turned into a lifeless pretence of amity and simulated peace."

107. *Arm, arm*, etc. "This grandly wild appeal of an outraged mother has its sublime parallel in that of the outraged father, Lear ; where he invokes the heavens to make his cause their own, because themselves are old. Shakespeare never repeats himself ; but he has some few of these exceptional similitudes, where Nature herself has them, in the rareness of extreme crises of passion " (Clarke).

110. *Sunset.* Perhaps Fl. is right in reading "sun set," on the ground that S. accents *sunset* on the first syllable. In 3 *Hen. VI.* ii. 2. 116, it is

sunset, but that is "counted out" as not by S. The only other passages in which the noun occurs are *Sonn.* 73. 6 and *R. and J.* iii. 5. 127.

114. *O Lymoges! O Austria!* S. follows the old play in making one personage out of two enemies of Cœur-de-lion. "Leopold, duke of Austria, threw him into prison in a former expedition [in 1193]; but the castle of Chaluz, before which he fell [in 1199], belonged to Vidomar, viscount of Limoges; and the archer who pierced his shoulder with an arrow (of which wound he died) was Bertrand de Gourdon" (Steevens).

119. *Humorous.* Capricious. See *A. Y. L.* p. 146.

121. *Soothest up.* Flatterest. Cf. *Cor.* i. 9. 44: "Made all of false-fac'd soothing," etc.

122. *Ramping.* Rampant. Cf. 1 *Hen. IV.* iii. 1. 153: "a ramping cat;" and 3 *Hen. VI.* v. 2. 13: "a ramping lion."

123. *Party.* See on i. 1. 34 above.

127. *Fall over.* Go over, desert.

129. *A calf's skin.* The folio has "Calues skin," and "Calues-skin" in 131 and 133 below. It is said that the domestic fools used to wear calf-skin, but here the meaning probably is that a *calf-skin* would suit his *recreant limbs* better than a *lion's* (Ritson).

130. *Should.* Changed by Pope to "would," to which it is here equivalent. Cf. Gr. 326.

138. *Of fair Milan cardinal.* Mrs. Clarke's *Concordance* has the curious misprint "fair Milan *cathedral*" in the reference to this passage under *Milan.*

141. *Against.* The only instance of *spurn against* in S. Schmidt compares *Acts,* ix. 5: "kick against the pricks." We find *spurn at* in *V. and A.* 311, *C. of E.* ii. 2. 136, and *Ham.* iv. 5. 6; and *spurn upon* in *Rich. III.* i. 2. 42.

142. *Force perforce.* An emphatic form of *perforce* = by force or violence; used also in 2 *Hen. IV.* iv. 1. 116 and 2 *Hen. VI.* i. 1. 258. In 2 *Hen. IV.* iv. 4. 46, it is = of necessity.

145. *Foresaid.* Not "'foresaid," as often printed.

147. *Earthly.* The folio has "earthie," which is probably a misprint for "earthlie," as Pope and most of the modern editors consider it. The folio has "earthy" in the same sense in *Rich. II.* i. 3. 69, but the quartos have "earthly." The Camb. ed. and Fl. retain "earthy" here.

Interrogatories. Questions asked on oath; as in *M. of V.* v. 1. 298, 300, and *A. IV.* iv. 3. 207. S. uses the word only in these passages and *Cymb.* v. 5. 392. The folio has "intérgatories" in all but the last, and most of the modern eds. give "inter'gatories" there.

148. *Task.* Misprinted "tast" in the 1st and 2d folios (the later ones have "taste"); corrected by Theo.

151. *The pope.* That is, the pope's, or that of the pope. See Gr. 384.

154. *Toll.* Take toll, levy a tax. In *A. IV.* v. 3. 149, it means to *pay* toll.

169. *Revenue.* For the accent, see *M. N. D.* p. 125 or Gr. 490.

173. *Excommunicate.* For the form, cf. 1 *Hen. IV.* v. 1. 72: "These things indeed you have articulate," etc. Gr. 342.

177. *Canonized.* The accent on the second syllable, as elsewhere in S. Cf. iii. 4. 52 below; and see *Ham.* p. 194.

180. *Room with Rome.* This shows that *Rome* was pronounced like *room.* Cf. *J. C.* i. 2. 156: "Now is it Rome indeed and room enough," etc. In *R. of L.* 715, it rhymes to *doom*, and in *Id.* 1644 to *groom.* But it would seem to have had sometimes the modern pronunciation. Cf. 1 *Hen. VI.* iii. 1. 51:

> "*Winchester.* Rome shall remedy this.
> *Warwick.*   Roam thither, then."

201. *Your breeches*, etc. Steevens remarks: "Perhaps there is something proverbial in this sarcasm. Cf. the old play of *King Leir*, 1605:

> 'Well I have a payre of slops for the nonce,
> Will hold all your mocks.'"

For *slops* = breeches, see *Much Ado*, p. 143.

204. *Bethink you.* Consider, reflect; as in *M. for M.* ii. 2. 87, 144, etc.

209. *Untrimmed.* The reading of the folio, which Schmidt makes = "divested of her wedding-gown." Perhaps W. is right in explaining it as "in deshabille; and in some such condition was Blanch on account of her unexpected nuptials and the haste in which they were performed." D. suggested "uptrimmed," comparing *R. and J.* iv. 4. 24: "Go waken Juliet, go and trim her up;" but in this case, as W. remarks, "there was no time to trim Blanch up." He adds: "The obvious allusion, too, to the temptation of Saint Anthony makes it clear that the old text is correct. It is of course not intimated that Blanch was then and there in a condition approaching that in which the temptress of Saint Anthony is generally supposed to have won the victory for the Devil. Constance's epithet has at once a slight taint of womanish spite and a forward look for Lewis." Some see in *untrimmed* an allusion to the fact that brides used to go to church with their hair dishevelled. Cf. Spenser, *Prothalamion*, 22:

> "locks, all loose untyde,
> As each had bene a Bryde;"

and Webster, *White Devil:*

> "Let them dangle loose
> As a bride's hair."

Fl. cites *Tancred and Gismunda*, v. 2:

> "So let thy tresses, flaring in the wind,
> Untrimmed hang about thy bared neck;"

and *Id.* v. 3: "O let me dress up those untrimmed locks." Theo. gave "new and trimmed;" and Richardson conjectures "entrimmed."

212. *Faith.* "Your pledged faith to me" (Fl.).

222. *Bestow yourself.* Behave yourself, conduct yourself, act. Cf. *T. G. of V.* iii. 1. 87:

> "How and which way I may bestow myself,
> To be regarded in her sun-bright eye."

See also *A. Y. L.* iv. 3. 87.

233. *But new before.* Only just before it.

235. *To clap this royal bargain up.* Cf. *T. of S.* ii. 1. 327: "Was ever match clapp'd up so suddenly?" The allusion is to *clapping hands*, or joining hands, in token of mutual pledge of faith. Cf. *Hen. V.* v. 2. 133:

"And so clap hands, and a bargain." See also *W. T.* p. 152, note on *Clap thyself my love.*

238. *Difference.* See on ii. 1. 355 above.

240. *In both.* That is, in both their bloody hostility and their new love.

241. *Regreet.* Greeting, salutation; as in *M. of V.* ii. 9. 89: "sensible regreets." For the verb, see *Rich. II.* p. 162.

242. *Fast and loose.* A cheating game of gypsies and other vagrants. It is thus described by Sir J. Hawkins : "A leathern belt is made up into a number of intricate folds and placed edgewise upon a table. One of the folds is made to represent the middle of the girdle, so that who-ever should thrust a skewer into it would think he held it fast to the table ; whereas, when he has so done, the person with whom he plays may take hold of both ends and draw it away." Cf. *A. and C.* iv. 12. 28 :

> "Like a right gypsy, hath, at fast and loose,
> Beguil'd me to the very heart of loss."

See also *L. L. L.* i. 2. 162 and iii. 1. 104 ; and Drayton, *Mooncalf:*

> "He like a gypsy oftentimes would go ;
> All kinds of gibberish he hath learn'd to know,
> And with a stick, a short string, and a noose,
> Would show the people tricks at fast and loose."

243. *Unconstant.* Inconstant, fickle ; as in *T. of S.* iv. 2. 14 and *Lear,* i. 1. 304. S. more commonly uses *inconstant ;* as in *R. and J.* i. 4. 100, ii. 2. 109, iv. 1. 119, etc. See on *infortunate,* ii. 1. 178 above. Gr. 442.

254. *Opposite.* Opposed, antagonistic. See *Oth.* p. 160 or *T. N.* p. 145.

259. *Chafed.* Theobald's correction of the "cased" of the folios. Pope has "chased" and Coll. "caged." Cf. *Hen. VIII.* iii. 2. 206 : "the chafed lion ;" *T. of S.* i. 2. 203 : "an angry boar chafed with sweat," etc. Fl., who retains "cased" (= "concealed"), says that these passages are not in point, as S. did not write them.

271. *Is not amiss,* etc. "Most," "yet," "but," "done," etc., have been conjectured for *not ;* but the passage was probably intended as a piece of Jesuitical sophistry. *Truly done* is explained by the following *not done:* what you have sworn to do amiss is not amiss if *truly* done ; but the right doing of what is wrong is *not* to do it. Fl. explains it thus : "to do amiss (incompletely) that which thou hast sworn to do, is not amiss when it (your course of proceeding) is truly (honestly) done."

276. *Indirection.* See on *indirectly,* ii. 1. 49 above.

280. *But thou hast sworn,* etc. The passage is pointed thus in the folio :

> "It is religion that doth make vowes kept,
> But thou hast sworne against religion:
> By what thou swear'st against the thing thou swear'st,
> And mak'st an oath the suretie for thy truth,
> Against an oath the truth, thou art vnsure
> To sweare, sweares onely not to be forsworne.
> Else what a mockerie should it be to sweare?"

This is evidently corrupt, at least in the pointing ; but of many attempts to mend it none is quite satisfactory. In 281 we adopt (as Capell, D., and W. do) Johnson's conjecture of *which* for "what." Hanmer's "that" is nearer to the original, and gives the same meaning, but the relative seems better on the whole. Clarke retains "what," explaining the line as including "the double interpretation of 'by swearing to that which is contrary to that which you have sworn,' and 'in swearing by religion against religion.'" *The truth thou art unsure to swear*, etc., is more perplexing. K. explains it thus : "the truth—that is, the *troth*, for which you have made an oath the surety, against thy former oath to heaven— this troth, which it was unsure to swear—which you violate your surety in swearing—has only been sworn—swears only—not to be forsworn ; but it is sworn against a former oath, which is more binding, because it was an oath to religion—to the principle upon which all oaths are made." Clarke makes *thou art unsure to swear* = "thou art hesitating to abide by." He adds : "The difficulty and obscurity in this speech chiefly arise from the expressions *swear* and *swear'st* being equally used for what has been sworn at different times ; or, in other words, 'thy later vows' and 'thy first:' but the very confusion thus produced in the line of argument has characteristic effect." Sr. follows Rowe in changing *swears* in 284 to "swear" (imperative). Schmidt defines *unsure* as "not assured, not certainly knowing." Perhaps the meaning is : the oath you thus swear with no good assurance that you ought to do it. He has just charged the king with giving a pledge inconsistent with his former pledge to the Church ; and this, he implies, could only have been done from imperfect or confused notions as to his duty. *Swears only not to be forsworn* = is sworn only as a matter of form.

Fl. points the passage as follows :

> " But thou hast sworn against religion,
> By what thou swear'st against, the thing thou swear'st ;
> And makest an oath the surety for thy truth,
> Against an oath, the truth ; thou art unsure.
> To swear swears only not to be forsworn ;" etc.

He explains it thus : "But thou hast sworn the thing thou swear'st against religion (thy vow to be the Church's champion) by the religion thou swearest against, and so thou givest, as pledge of thy truth, thy last oath in opposition to thy first one, which was in its own nature truth itself. Thou art untrustworthy, unsafe. Swearing is used only that oaths may be kept." On *unsure*, he compares ii. i. 471 above : "unsur'd assurance." He also quotes *Edward I.* ii. 1 (Shakespeare's part of the play) :

> " Well may I tempt myself to wrong myself,
> When he hath sworn me by the name of God
> To break a vow made in the name of God ;
> What if I swear by this right hand of mine
> To cut this right hand off? The better way
> Were to profane the idol than confound it."

289. *Is.* The subject *vows* is plural, but the verb may be said to agree with the predicate nominative *rebellion*. *To* = towards, against. Cf. *Much Ado*, ii. 1. 244 : "a quarrel to you," etc. Gr. 187.

294. *Vouchsafe them.* Condescend to accept them. Cf. *J. C.* ii. 1. 313 : "Vouchsafe good morrow from a feeble tongue." See also *T. of A.* i. 1. 152 and *Hen. VIII.* ii. 3. 43.

295. *Light.* The plural is to be explained by the intervening *curses.* Gr. 412.

296. *As.* That. Gr. 109.

303. *Churlish drums.* Cf. ii. 1. 76 above, and *V. and A.* 107: "his churlish drum."

304. *Measures.* Marching music. Fl. explains it as "solemn dances" (see *A. Y. L.* p. 197). Cf. the old play:

> "*Blanch.* And will your grace upon your wedding-day
> Forsake your bride, and follow dreadful drums?
> Nay, good my lord, stay you at home with me.
> "*Lewis.* Sweetheart, content thee, and we shall agree.
> "*Philip.* Follow me, lords; Lord Cardinal, lead the way,
> Drums shall be music to this wedding-day."

312. *Forethought.* Ordained, decreed. Elsewhere (in 1 *Hen. IV.* iii. 2. 38 and *Cymb.* iii. 4. 171) the word is = foresee, anticipate.

317. *Muse.* Wonder; as often in S. Cf. *Cor.* iii. 2. 7:

> "I muse my mother
> Does not approve me further," etc.

See also *Macb.* p. 219.

318. *Respects.* Considerations, motives; as in v. 2. 44 and v. 4. 41 below.

320. *Fall from.* Cf. 3 *Hen. VI.* iii. 3. 209: "He's very likely now to fall from him," etc.

337. *Lady, with me, with me,* etc. This is the pointing of the folio. Most of the modern eds. follow Capell in giving "Lady, with me; [that is, go with me] with me," etc. Capell also changed *lies* to "lives." Fl. (who prints "li'es" for *lives* in the next line) says: "*Lives* was often pronounced *lees,* as here; so that *lie* and *live* had the same sound. The letter *v* could be omitted between any two vowels. Thus in *Tancred and Gismunda,* iii. chor., *lo'e* (love) rhymes to *overthrow,* and in *Edward III.* *gi'e* (give) rhymes to *buy;* in *London Prodigal,* ii. 1 *mo'e* (move) rhymes to *too.* Chapman is distinguished from all other dramatists by his frequent adoption of this pronunciation."

339. *Puissance.* Armed force; as in *Hen. V.* prol. 25 and ii. 2. 190, etc. S. makes the word a dissyllable or trisyllable, as suits the measure.

341. *Condition.* Quality; as in *M. of V.* v. 1. 74: "the hot condition of their blood," etc.

SCENE II. — 2. *Airy.* Theo. adopted Warburton's conjecture of "fiery;" but Percy cited in support of *airy* Burton's *Anat. of Melancholy:* "Aeriall spirits or divells are such as keep quarter most part in the aire, cause many tempests, thunder and lightnings, teare oakes, fire steeples," etc. Henderson adds from Nash's *Pierce Pennilesse:* "the spirits of the aire will mixe themselves with thunder and lightning, and so infect the clyme where they raise any tempest, that sodainely great mortalitie shall ensue to the inhabitants."

5. *Hubert.* Pope inserts "There" and Fl. "Good" before *Hubert.* Theo. changes *Philip* to "Richard."

Make up. Hurry on, go along. Cf. 1 *Hen. IV.* v. 4. 5 : "I beseech your majesty, make up ;" *Id.* v. 4. 58 : "Make up to Clifton," etc.

SCENE III.—2. *Cousin.* Used familiarly for almost any kinsman or kinswoman. See *Ham.* p. 179 or *A. Y. L.* p. 147.

8. *Set at liberty,* etc. The folio reads :

> " imprisoned angells
> Set at libertie :" etc.

The transposition was suggested by Walker, and is adopted by W. For *angels* see on ii. 1. 590 above.

10. *Now.* Changed by Theo. to "war," and by Hanmer to "maw."

11. *His.* Changed by Rowe to "its," to which it is equivalent. See Gr. 228.

12. *Bell, book, and candle.* A popular phrase for excommunication, in the ceremonial of which a bell was tolled, a service read from a book, and three candles extinguished in succession. Fl. quotes Marlowe, *Dr. Faustus :*

> " Bell, book, and candle, candle, book, and bell,
> Forward and backward to curse Faustus to hell ;"

and Bale's *Kynge Johan :*

> " For as moch as kyng Johan doth Holy Church so handle,
> Here I do curse hym wyth crosse, boke, bell, and candle," etc.

26. *Time.* Pope's correction of the "tune" of the folios.

28. *What good respect,* etc. How great a regard I have for thee. Cf. iii. 1. 58 above.

29. *Bounden.* Used again in *A. Y. L.* i. 2. 298 : "I rest much bounden to you." Cf. Gr. 344.

36. *Gawds.* Gawdy or garish things. Cf. *M. N. D.* p. 126.

39. *Sound on,* etc. The folio reading. Theo. changed *on* to "one," and "reign," "ear," and "car" have been suggested for *race.* "Ear" is plausible, but no change is absolutely required. "With either reading, *drowsy,* logically, though not grammatically, belongs to *night,* by the usual Shakespearian inversion ; and surely the clock striking twelve may be said to strike on into the course or current of the slow night " (Fl.). Sr. takes it to be a bell tolling at midnight to call recluses to their devotions.

42. *Surly.* Gloomy ; as in *Sonn.* 71. 2 : "the surly sullen bell." Cf. *sullen* in i. 1. 28 above.

43. *Heavy-thick.* Pope's emendation of the "heavy, thick" of the folios. Gr. 2.

44. *Tickling.* The Coll. MS. has "tingling ;" but, as Clarke remarks, the change "deprives the passage of the connection between *tickling* and *laughter* which was evidently meant by the poet."

45. *Keep.* Hold, occupy (Schmidt). Clarke thinks it is also = close, or shut : "laughter dwelling in men's eyes, and causing them to close, or half shut."

48. *If that.* For *that* as a "conjunctional affix," see Gr. 287.

50. *Conceit.* Conception, thought. See *A. Y. L.* pp. 162 and 194.

52. *Brooded.* Brooding; that is, vigilant as a bird on its nest. Pope changed the word to "broad-eyed;" and the Coll. MS. has "the broad." For the active use of passive participles, see Gr. 374.

57. *Adjunct.* Cf. *R. of L.* 133: "Though death be adjunct," etc.

59. *Hubert, Hubert, Hubert.* "How the impression of murderous eagerness and urgency is horribly conveyed by the reiterated name, gasped forth with a mixture of stealth and vehemence—half mean dread, half bloodthirsty incitement!" (Clarke).

65. *Death.* See p. 33 above.

70. *Powers.* The word is used in both numbers to signify an army, as *force* still is. See *J. C.* p. 168, note on *Are levying powers.*

SCENE IV. — 2. *Armado.* Fleet (the Spanish *armada*); as in *C. of E.* iii. 2. 140: "Spain, who sent whole armadoes of caracks," etc. *Convicted* = "defeated, overpowered" (Schmidt). "Collected," "convented," "connected," "convected," "consorted," and "combined" have been proposed as emendations.

8. *England.* That is, the king of England. See *Hen. V.* p. 159 or *Macb.* p. 239.

11. *Advice.* "Deliberate consideration" (Schmidt); as in 2 *Hen. VI.* ii. 2. 68:

> "And that 's not suddenly to be perform'd,
> But with advice and silent secrecy."

12. *So fierce a cause.* So impetuous a proceeding. For *cause* Warb., Hanmer, and some others read "course."

19. *Prison.* Malone compares 3 *Hen. VI.* ii. 1. 74: "Now my soul's palace is become a prison." See also iv. 3. 136 below.

23. *Defy.* Refuse, spurn. Cf. 1 *Hen. IV.* i. 3. 228: "All studies here I solemnly defy," etc.

29. *Detestable.* Regularly accented by S. on the first syllable. See *R. and J.* p. 208, or Gr. 492.

32. *This gap of breath.* This passage of my breath, or my mouth.

35. *Buss.* Changed by Pope to "kiss." The word had not become vulgar in the time of S. Cf. *T. and C.* iv. 5. 220: "Yond towers, whose wanton tops do buss the clouds." The noun occurs in 2 *Hen. IV.* ii. 4. 291: "Thou dost give me flattering busses." Steevens quotes Drayton, *Barons' Wars:* "And we by signs sent many a secret buss." Cf. Spenser, *F. Q.* iii. 10. 46:

> "But every Satyre first did give a busse
> To Hellenore; so busses did abound."

40. *That fell anatomy.* That cruel skeleton, Death. Cf. *C. of E.* v. 1. 238: "A mere anatomy." See also *T. N.* p. 149.

42. *Modern.* Commonplace, trite. Cf. *Macb.* iv. 3. 170:

> "Where violent sorrow seems
> A modern ecstasy," etc.

See also *R. and J.* p. 188 or *A. Y. L.* p. 167. The Coll. MS. gives "widow's" here, and K. adopts Heath's conjecture of "mother's."

44. *Not.* Omitted in the first three folios, but supplied in the 4th. Delius and St. read "unholy."

45. *I am not mad*, etc. See p. 27 above.

52. *Canoniz'd*. Accented on the second syllable, as in iii. 1. 177 above. See Gr. 491.

58. *A babe of clouts*. A rag-baby.

64. *Friends*. The folios have "fiends;" corrected by Rowe.

65. *Sociable*. A quadrisyllable. Gr. 479.

66. *Loves*. Lovers. Cf. 35 above. The Coll. MS. has "lovers" here.

68. *To England, if you will*. Malone supposes this to be addressed to the absent John, and = "Take my son to England." St. takes it to be an apostrophe to her hair. Fl. explains it: "Say this fine speech about faithful love, etc., to England, that is, to John." Perhaps Clarke is right in considering it an answer to what Philip has said in 20 above—"one of those incoherent, but wanderingly-connected speeches which persons in Constance's condition of mind (and even people who are only absent of mind) will frequently make." He adds: "It appears to us that this interpretation of her speech adds another point of characteristic delineation to the many admirable touches with which the poet has drawn a mind bordering on frenzy in this powerfully affecting scene."

73. *Envy at*. Cf. *Hen. VIII*. v. 3. 112:

> " whose honesty the devil
> And his disciples only envy at."

We find *envy against* in *Cor*. iii. 3. 95.

76. *And, father cardinal*, etc. See p. 25 above.

80. *Suspire*. Begin to breathe. Cf. *2 Hen. IV*. iv. 5. 33:

> " By his gates of breath
> There lies a downy feather which stirs not;
> Did he suspire, that light and weightless down
> Perforce must move."

81. *Gracious*. Full of grace, lovely; as in 96 below. Cf. *T. N*. i. 5. 281 : "A gracious person," etc.

82. *Canker-sorrow*. Sorrow, like a canker-worm. See *M. N. D.* p. 150, note on *Cankers*.

90. *You hold too heinous a respect*, etc. You sin in thinking too much of your grief. Cf. *M. of V.* i. 1. 74: "You have too much respect upon the world."

91. *He talks*, etc. Cf. *Macb*. iv. 3. 216: "He has no children."

96. *Remembers me*. Reminds me. Cf. *Temp*. i. 2. 243: "Let me remember thee what thou hast promis'd," etc.

99. *Had you such loss*, etc. "This is a sentiment which great sorrow always dictates. Whoever cannot help himself casts his eyes on others for assistance, and often mistakes their inability for coldness" (Johnson).

101. *This form*. Her head-dress.

106. *Outrage*. Outbreak of rage or madness. Cf. *Rich. III*. ii. 4. 64: "frantic outrage," etc. See also *R. and J.* p. 217.

110. *World's*. Pope's correction of the "words" of the folios. Fl. thinks that "word's" may refer to "the tedious tale of life."

111. *That*. So that; as often. Cf. 151 below. Gr. 283.

115. *Show*. Seem, appear; as in *V. and A*. 1157: "where it shows most toward," etc.

L

125. *Youthful.* Cf. 145 below : "How green you are," etc.

128. *Rub.* Obstacle ; a metaphor taken from the game of bowls. See *Rich. II.* p. 197.

132. *Whiles.* Used by S. interchangeably with *while.* Gr. 137.

133. *Misplac'd.* That is, usurping ; wearing a "crown so foul misplac'd " (*Rich. III.* iii. 2. 44).

135. *Unruly.* Unlawful.

136. *Boisterously.* Violently. See on iv. 1. 95 below.

146. *Lays you plots.* Lays plots for you ; the "dativus ethicus." Gr. 220.

147. *True blood.* "The blood of him that has the *just* claim" (Johnson).

149. *Evilly.* Used again in *T. of A.* iv. 3. 467. For *born* the 1st and 2d folios have "borne," which Clarke thinks may possibly be right (=conducted).

153. *Exhalation.* Meteor. Cf. 1 *Hen. IV.* ii. 4. 352 : "My lord, do you see these meteors? do you behold these exhalations?" See also *Hen. VIII.* iii. 2. 226 and *J. C.* ii. 1. 44.

154. *Scope.* Free play, operation. Pope changed the word to "scape" —"preposterously," according to Schmidt, who explains *no scope of nature* as "no effect produced within the regular limits of nature." K., the Camb. ed., Clarke, Fl., and others retain *scope ;* D., W., and H. adopt "scape." The latter is obviously wrong, as it could refer only to a prodigy or something out of the ordinary course of nature ; while the context enumerates only *common* and *customed* phenomena, which the people *imagine* to be *prodigies and signs.*

155. *Customed.* Not "'customed," as sometimes printed. The word occurs again in 2 *Hen. VI.* v. 1. 188 : "customed right."

158. *Abortives.* Monstrosities ; the only instance of the noun in S.

161. *In his prisonment.* In keeping him in prison.

166. *Unacquainted.* Cf. v. 2. 32 below : "unacquainted colours."

167. *Strong matter of.* Good cause of, powerful reasons for.

169. *Hurly.* Tumult, commotion. Cf. *T. of S.* iv. 1. 206 : "amid this hurly," etc.

174. *Call.* That is, a *bird-call,* the reed or pipe used in catching birds.

176. *As a little snow,* etc. "Bacon, in his *Hist. of Hen. VII.*, speaking of Simnel's march, observes that 'their snow-ball did not gather as it went ' " (Johnson).

179, 180. The folios put commas at the end of both lines. Fl. follows Rowe in putting a period after *discontent,* and a comma after *offence.*

182. *Strong actions.* The reading of the later folios ; the 1st folio has "strange actions," which may be what S. wrote.

ACT IV.

SCENE I.—On the locality of the scene, see on i. 1. 1 above. According to history, Arthur was first confined at Falaise, and afterwards at Rouen, where he died or was murdered.

2. *Within the arras.* That is, between the tapestry hangings and the wall; a common place of concealment. See *M. W.* iii. 3. 97, *Much Ado*, i. 3. 63, *Ham.* ii. 2. 163, iii. 3. 28, iv. 1. 9, etc.

7. *Uncleanly.* Unbecoming.

8. *To say with.* To speak with.

15. *As sad as night,* etc. An allusion to one of the affectations of the day. Steevens quotes Lyly, *Midas,* 1592: "Melancholy! is melancholy a word for a barber's mouth? Thou shouldst say heavy, dull, and doltish; melancholy is the crest of courtiers, and now every base companion, &c. says he is melancholy;" and *The Life and Death of the Lord Cromwell,* 1613:

> "My nobility is wonderful melancholy.—
> Is it not most gentleman-like to be melancholy?"

16. *Christendom.* "Christianity" (Schmidt); "christening or baptism" (Clarke). In *A. W.* i. 1. 188, it is = Christian name, or baptismal name. Halliwell quotes Taylor, *Workes,* 1630:

> "A halfe piece, or a crowne, or such a summe,
> Hath forc'd them falsifie their Christendome."

19. *Doubt.* Suspect, fear; as in iv. 2. 102 and v. 6. 44 below. See also *Ham.* pp. 187, 202.

20. *Practises.* Plots. See *A. Y. L.* p. 140. Cf. the noun in iv. 3. 63 below.

25. *Prate.* Prattle.

33. *Rheum.* Tears. See on iii. 1. 22 above.

34. *Dispiteous.* Pitiless; used by S. only here.

38. *Effect.* Import, meaning. Malone conjectured "a fact."

42. *Handkercher.* The spelling of the folios, as in most other places. See *A. Y. L.* p. 190.

47. *Still and anon.* Ever and anon. For *still* = ever, see Gr. 69.

49. *Love.* Act of love, kindness; as in *Per.* ii. 4. 49: "But if I cannot win you to this love," etc.

50. *Lien.* The folio has "lyen." In *Ham.* v. 1. 190, the quartos have "lien," the folios "lain."

52. *At your sick service.* To attend you when sick.

61. *Heat.* Elsewhere in S. the participle is *heated.* Cf. *waft* in ii. 1. 73 above. Gr. 342. *Heat* is found in *Dan.* iii. 19, in the ed. of 1611.

63. *His.* Capell's emendation of the "this" of the folios. The latter, which Clarke and Fl. retain, may be right after all.

70. The folio reads: "I would not haue beleeu'd him: no tongue but *Huberts.*" Pope gave "believ'd a tongue but Hubert's." K. adopts Steevens's conjecture: "believ'd him: no tongue but Hubert's—" (the sentence being left imperfect). Steevens afterwards suggested "I would not have believ'd no tongue but Hubert's;" which is on the whole the best emendation, if any is needed.

78. *Heaven sake.* Cf. *T. N.* iii. 4. 326: "oath sake;" see our ed. p. 155.

82. *Angerly.* The word occurs also in *T. G. of V.* i. 2. 62 and *Macb.* iii. 5. 1. S. does not use *angrily.*

92. *Mote.* The folios have "moth," which was pronounced *mote.* See *A. Y. L.* p. 179, note on *Goats;* and cf. *Much Ado,* p. 136, note on *Nothing.*

95. *Boisterous.* The word (formerly=intractable, violent) has come to be restricted to "loud weather" (*W. T.* iii. 3. 11) and like noisy demonstrations. We can no longer use it as in *V. and A.* 326 : "his boisterous and unruly beast" (horse) ; or as in *A. Y. L.* ii. 3. 32 : "a base and boisterous sword," etc.

106. *The fire is dead,* etc. "*The fire,* being *created* not to hurt, but to *comfort, is dead with grief for* finding itself *used* in acts of cruelty, which, being innocent, I have *not deserved*" (Johnson). On *extremes.* cf. v. 7. 13 below : "fierce extremes."

117. *Tarre him on.* Set him on, urge him on. See *Ham.* p. 207.

121. *Of note.* Notorious, distinguished.

122. *Eye.* The folio reading ; changed by Steevens to "eyes."

123. *Owes.* Owns. See on ii. 1. 109 above.

125. *This same very iron.* Cf. *Rich. III.* iii. 2. 49 : "this same very day," etc.

130. *Doubtless and secure.* Free from fear and confident. Cf. 1 *Hen. IV.* iii. 2. 20 : "I am doubtless I can purge Myself," etc. On *secure,* cf. *Ham.* p. 196.

133. *Closely.* Secretly ; as in *Ham.* iii. 1. 29, *R. and J.* v. 3. 255, etc. Cf. *close* in iv. 2. 72 below.

SCENE II.—**1.** *Once again crown'd.* This was the *fourth* time that John was crowned. The second coronation was at Canterbury in the year 1201. He was crowned again at the same place, after the murder of his nephew, in April, 1202 ; probably with a view of confirming his title to the throne, his competitor no longer standing in the way (Malone).

4. *Once superfluous.* That is, once too many.

10. *Guard.* Ornament, as with trimmings. Cf. *M. of V.* ii. 2. 164 :

> "Give him a livery
> More guarded than his fellows'; see it done ;"

Hen. VIII. prol. 16 : "In a long motley coat guarded with yellow," etc. See also *Much Ado,* p. 124.

18. *An ancient tale new-told.* Cf. iii. 4. 108 above : "as tedious as a twice-told tale."

21. *Antique.* The regular accent in S. See *A. Y. L.* p. 152 or *Macb.* p. 234.

24. *To fetch about.* To "come about," as the nautical term now is ; to veer round.

29. *Covetousness.* Eagerness. *Confound*=destroy, ruin ; as in v. 7. 58 below.

38. *Since all,* etc. That is, since we make our preferences yield in all cases to your will.

41. *Possess'd you with.* Informed you of. Cf. *M. of V.* i. 3. 65, iv. 1. 35, *Cor.* ii. 1. 145, etc.

42. *When lesser,* etc. The folio has "then lesser," etc. *When* is Tyrwhitt's conjecture, and is adopted by D., K., St., Clarke, Fl., and others. Pope has "the lesser," and W. "than lesser." The Coll. MS. gives "thus lessening my fear." For *more, more strong,* cf. *Cor.* iv. 6. 63 and *Lear,* v. 3. 202.

43. *Indue.* Supply, furnish.

48. *To sound.* To give *sound* or utterance to. Cf. *Rich. II.* iii. 4. 74 : " How dares thy harsh rude tongue sound this unpleasing news ?"

50. *Myself and them.* The grammatical error is probably due in part to the occurrence of the same combination in the preceding line, and in part to the more frequent association of *them* than *they* with *myself.*

55. *In rest.* Either=in possession, as Clarke explains it ; or in repose, in peace, as Schmidt and Fl. give it. Possibly both ideas are combined.

56. *Why then,* etc. Pope transposed *then* and *should,* to give the question the ordinary direct form ; but the question may be considered as indirect, or perhaps as a confusion of the two constructions.

57. *Mew up.* Shut up. See *M. N. D.* p. 126.

64. *Goods.* Abstract nouns are often thus used in the plural. See *Macb.* p. 209 (note on *Loves*), *Rich. II.* p. 206 (on *Sights*), or *W. T.* p. 167 (on *Peaces*).

69. *Should do.* Who was to do. For the ellipsis of the relative, see Gr. 244 ; and for *should*=was to, Gr. 324.

72. *Close aspect.* Reserved, secretive look. For the accent of *aspect,* see on ii. 1. 250 above.

77. *Between his purpose.* That is, showing a conflict in his mind between his *purpose* of killing Arthur and his *conscience.* Cf. 247 below.

78. *Set.* Appointed, posted (Schmidt). Theo. changed the word to "sent." Mr. Arrowsmith would refer *set* to *battles,* but that is hardly admissible.

" It is worthy of notice how in this speech, and in the beautiful one commencing with 9 above, Salisbury maintains that characteristic refinement and poetry of diction which distinguish him in contrast with Pembroke" (Clarke).

89. *Here or hence.* See on v. 4. 29 below.

93. *Foul play.* Fl. joins the words with a hyphen, on account of the accent ; so "fair-play" in v. 1. 67 and v. 2. 118 below. *Apparent*=evident, obvious ; as often. Cf. *M. for M.* iv. 2. 144 :

"*Duke.* It is now apparent?
"*Provost.* Most manifest, and not denied by himself."

See also *Rich. II.* p. 150.

99. *Owed.* Was the right owner of. See on ii. 1. 109 above, and cf. iv. 1. 123.

100. *Foot.* For the plural, cf. *pound* in i. 1. 69 above.

Bad world the while! A bad world nowadays ! Cf. 1 *Hen. IV.* ii. 4. 146 : "God help the while! a bad world, I say ;" and *Rich. III.* iii. 6. 10 : "Here 's a good world the while !"

102. *Doubt.* Suspect, fear ; as in iv. 1. 19 above.

106. *Fearful.* Full of fear ; as in 191 below. Cf. *J. C.* p. 175. On the passage, cf. *Macb.* v. 3. 11, 14.

110. *From France to England.* "The king asks *how all goes in France* ; the messenger catches the word *goes,* and answers that *whatever is in France goes* now *into England*" (Johnson).

116. *O, where,* etc. Cf. *Macb.* i. 7. 35 :

> " Was the hope drunk
> Wherein you dress'd yourself? hath it s'ept since?"

117. *Care.* In the 1st folio the first letter of the word is broken, and may be either an *e* or a *c ;* the later folios have "care." Some editors read "ear" on account of the *ear* in the answer ; but, as Clarke remarks, that word is sufficiently suggested by the king's "*hear* of it," and *care* accords better with the preceding *intelligence.*

118. *Drawn.* Drawn together, levied ; as in v. 2. 113 below.

120. Constance died in 1201 at Nantes (see p. 21 above) ; Elinor in 1204 (Mrs. Jameson and some other authorities say 1203) at Fontevreaux.

124. *Idly.* Incidentally, casually ; explained by the context.

125. *Occasion.* Fortune ; as in *Ham.* i. 3. 54 : "Occasion smiles upon a second leave," etc. The word is a quadrisyllable here ; a metrical license very common in this play. Cf. *preparation* in 111 above, and see 173, 184, 191, and 218 below.

128. *Walks.* Goes. As Schmidt remarks, the verb is "much oftener used in S. than in modern language = to go, move, and even = come."

135. *Afeard.* Used by S. interchangeably with *afraid.* See *M. N. D.* p. 156 or *Macb.* p. 163.

137. *Amaz'd.* Confused, bewildered ; as in ii. 1. 356 above.

139. *Aloft.* The only instance of the prepositional use in S.

141. *Sped.* Fared, succeeded. Cf. *M. W.* ii. 2. 278, iii. 5. 137.

144. *Strangely fantasied.* Filled with strange fancies ; the only instance of *fantasied* in S.

148. *Pomfret.* A town in the West Riding of Yorkshire. See *Rich. II.* p. 208.

In the old play there is a scene between the prophet and the people, and another of the Bastard plundering the abbeys, both of them poor and coarse, and judiciously omitted by S. See pp. 11 and 12 above.

158. *Safety.* Safe keeping, custody ; as in *R. and J.* v. 3. 183 : " Hold him in safety."

This *prophet,* " Peter of Pomfret," although his prediction was fulfilled (see v. 1. 25 below), did not escape the penalty pronounced by the king, but after being dragged through the streets by horses was hanged upon a gibbet (Douce).

165. *Whom.* For the "confusion of construction" (Gr. 410), cf. *Temp.* iii. 3. 92 : " Young Ferdinand whom they suppose is drown'd ;" *Cor.* iv. 2. 2 : " The nobility are vex'd, whom we see have sided," etc.

177. *Sprightful.* Full of spirit. It is used by S. only here, but we have *sprightfully* in a similar sense in *Rich. II.* i. 3. 3.

182. *Five moons.* This phenomenon is mentioned by some of the chroniclers and also in the old play, where the five moons appear visibly and the Bastard says :

> " See, my lord, strange apparitions.
> Glauncing mine eye to see the diadem
> Plac'd by the bishops on your highness head,
> Forth from a gloomy cloud, which, curtain-like,
> Display'd itself, I suddenly espied
> Five moons reflecting, as you see them now," etc.

To-night = last night ; as often. See *R. and J.* p. 155.

185. *Beldams.* Old women, hags ; a curious corruption (or ironical use ?) of the Fr. *belle dame*, fair lady. Cf. *Macb.* iii. 5. 2 : "beldams as you are," etc. Spenser uses the word in its original sense ; as in *F. Q.* iii. 2. 43 : " Beldame, your words doe worke me litle ease," etc.

198. *Contrary feet.* The mutations of fashion are well illustrated by the fact that this passage perplexed the commentators of the last century. Johnson says : " Shakespeare seems to have confounded the man's shoes with his gloves. He that is frighted or hurried may put his hand into the wrong glove, but either shoe will equally admit either foot." Farmer, Steevens, and Malone fill a page of the Var. of 1821 to show that in earlier times shoes were made "rights and lefts." Thus Scot, in his *Discoverie of Witchcraft*, says : " He that receiveth a mischance, will consider, whether he put not on his shirt wrongside outwards, or his left shoe on his right foot," etc. Boswell remarks : " What has called forth the antiquarian knowledge of so many learned commentators is again become the common practice at this day." Cf. *T. G. of V.* ii. 3. 16 : "this left shoe."

Contrary is commonly accented by S. on the first syllable ; but on the second, as here, in *T. of A.* iv. 3. 144 and *Ham.* iii. 2. 221. Cf. *W. T.* p. 208.

199. *A many.* Cf. *Hen. V.* iii. 7. 79 : "you bear a many superfluously ;" and see our ed. p. 170.

200. *Embattailed.* Embattled ; the spelling of the early eds., to be preserved here, as the word is a quadrisyllable. Cf. *Hen. V.* iv. ii. 14 : " The English are embattled, you French peers," etc.

207. *No had.* Changed by Rowe to " Had none," and by K. to " None had ;" but the idiom is found elsewhere. Arrowsmith (*N. and Q.* i. 7. p. 521) cites Dekker, *Fortunatus:* " No does?" Foxe, *Martyrs:* " No did ?" etc. Fl. adds Lodge, *Marius and Sylla*, iv. 1 : " No relent ?" and St. gives an example of *No had* from a letter of Sir Thomas More.

214. *More upon humour*, etc. More on account of mere caprice than from deliberate consideration. For *upon* cf. ii. 1. 597 above : "upon commodity ;" and see Gr. 191. For *advised*, see *M. of V.* p. 130 or *Rich. II.* p. 165 ; and for *respect*, on iii. 4. 90 above.

220. *Make deeds ill done.* Capell transposed *deeds* and *ill*, and is followed by K., Clarke, and some other editors. Theo. changed *make* to " makes ;" but the plural is to be explained by the proximity of *deeds.* Cf. iii. 1. 295 above. Gr. 412.

Hadst is apparently a dissyllable here. Capell prints " Hadest ;" Pope has " for hadst."

222. *Quoted.* Noted, set down ; as in *A. W.* v. 3. 205 ; " He 's quoted for a most perfidious slave," etc.

224. *Aspect.* For the accent, see on 72 above.

226. *Liable.* Suitable, fit ; as in *L. L. L.* v. 1. 97 : " The posterior of the day, most generous sir, is liable, congruent, and measurable for the afternoon : the word is well culled," etc.

227. *Broke with thee.* Cf. *Much Ado*, i. 1. 311 : " I will break with her " (see also 328) ; *Id.* i. 2. 16 : " break with you of it," etc. In *Id.* ii. 1. 162 and iii. 2. 76, we find " break with him *about*," etc.

229. *Made it no conscience.* Had no scruples. Cf. *Hen. VIII.* v. 3. 67:

> "That I shall clear myself,
> Lay all the weight ye can upon my patience,
> I make as little doubt as you do conscience
> In doing daily wrongs."

231. *Hadst thou,* etc. Johnson observes: "There are many touches of nature in this conference of John with Hubert. A man engaged in wickedness would keep the profit to himself, and transfer the guilt to his accomplice. These reproaches, vented against Hubert, are not the words of art or policy, but the eruptions of a mind swelling with consciousness of a crime, and desirous of discharging its misery on another. This account of the timidity of guilt is drawn *ab ipsis recessibus mentis,* from the intimate knowledge of mankind, particularly that line in which he says that *to have bid him tell his tale in express words* would have *struck him dumb;* nothing is more certain than that bad men use all the arts of fallacy upon themselves, palliate their actions to their own minds by gentle terms, and hide themselves from their own detection in ambiguities and subterfuges."

234. *As bid.* That is, as if to bid or prompt. Pope changed *As* to "Or," and Malone to "And." Cf. Gr. 107.

245. *Fleshly.* Corporeal; used by S. only here. On the passage, cf. *J. C.* ii. 1. 68:

> "the state of man,
> Like to a little kingdom, suffers then
> The nature of an insurrection;"

and see also 2 *Hen. IV.* iv. 3. 118, *T. and C.* ii. 3. 185, and *Macb.* i. 3. 140.

255. *Motion.* Impulse; as in *J. C.* ii. 1. 64:

> "Between the acting of a dreadful thing
> And the first motion," etc.

See also i. 1. 212 above.

264. *Feature.* For the singular, cf. ii. 1. 126 above.

265. *Foul imaginary eyes of blood.* "The sanguinary eyes of my imagination" (Schmidt).

268. *Expedient.* Expeditious, swift; as in ii. 1. 60, 223 above.

269. *Conjure.* S. accents the word on either syllable without regard to the meaning. See *M. N. D.* p. 164.

The old play is divided into two parts, the first of which ends with the king's sending Hubert on this errand; the second begins with "*Enter Arthur,*" etc., as in the next scene.

SCENE III.—3. *There's.* Cf. *Cymb.* iv. 2. 371: "There is no more such masters," etc. Gr. 335.

10. *Heaven take my soul,* etc. S. here follows the old play. The fate of Arthur is not certainly known. Matthew Paris, relating the event, uses the word *evanuit* (he disappeared); and the business was doubtless managed with great secrecy. The French historians say that John, coming in a boat at night to the castle of Rouen, where Arthur was confined, ordered him to be brought forth, and having stabbed him, fastened a stone to the dead body and threw it into the Seine, in order to give some-

colour to the report, which he afterwards caused to be spread, that the prince, attempting to escape by a window, fell into the river and was drowned (Malone).

11. *Saint Edmundsbury.* See on v. 4. 18 below.

16. *Private with me.* That is, private or personal communication to me. For *with me* the Coll. MS. gives " missive," and Spedding conjectures " witness."

20. *Or ere.* A reduplication, the *or* being=before. Cf. v. 6. 44 below, and see *Temp.* p. 112.

21. *Distemper'd.* Disaffected. See *Ham.* p. 229.

24. *Thin.* The Coll. MS. gives "sin ;" but, as Clarke remarks, *thin* "exactly agrees with the metaphor implied in *line.*"

29. *Griefs.* Grievances; as in *J. C.* i. 3. 118, iv. 2. 42, etc. *Reason*= speak ; as in *M. of V.* ii. 8. 27 : " I reason'd with a Frenchman yesterday," etc.

34. *What is he lies here?* That is, *who* is he *that* lies here? For *what* =who. cf. ii. 1. 134 above ; and for the ellipsis, Gr. 244.

41. *Have you,* etc. The 1st and 2d folios have " You have," which Fl. retains.

44. *That.* Changed by Pope to " What."

48. *Savagery.* Atrocity. In *Hen. V.* v. 2. 47 (" deracinate such savagery") it is=wild growth.

49. *Wall-eyed.* " Fierce-eyed " (Schmidt) ; perhaps simply=with perverted or unnatural vision. See Wb. s. v.

50. *Remorse.* Pity ; as in 110 below and ii. 1. 478 above.

54. *Sin of times.* That is, of the times, of the age. Some editors adopt Pope's "sins of time."

56. *Exampled by.* Cf. *T. and C.* 1. 3. 132 :

> " so every step,
> Exampled by the first pace," etc.

63. *Practice.* Plotting. See on iv. 1. 20 above, or *A. Y. L.* p. 156.

64. *Whose.* Of whom ; the " objective genitive."

71. *Head.* Farmer's emendation of the " hand " of the folios. Fl. retains " hand," because in the early Christian iconography a hand was sometimes surrounded by a nimbus. Clarke thinks that "the vow to dedicate his own *hand* to the service of winning *glory* by attaining vengeance, and giving it the honour or *worship* of having fulfilled a so-esteemed sacred duty, is perfectly consistent with one of the practices of chivalrous times ;" but this explanation seems a little forced.

Giving it the worship of revenge=" ennobling it by revenge " (Schmidt).

79. *Your sword is bright,* etc. Cf. *Oth.* i. 2. 59 : " Keep up your bright swords, for the dew will rust them." Here, as there, the expression is contemptuous.

84. *True.* Rightful, just.

87. *Dunghill.* For the personal use, cf. *Lear,* iv. 6. 249 : " Out, dunghill !"

91. *Yet.* As yet, up to this time. For its use before a negative, see *R. and J.* p. 165, or Gr. 76.

94. *Stand by.* Stand back; as in *Much Ado*, iv. 1. 24, *T. of S.* i. 2. 143, etc.

95. *Thou wert better.* It were better for thee. So "you were best;" as in *M. of V.* ii. 8. 33, etc. See Gr. 352.

97. *Spleen.* See on ii. 1. 68 above.

99. *Toasting-iron.* Contemptuous for sword. Cf. *Hen. V.* ii. 1. 9: "I will wink and hold out mine iron: . . . it will toast cheese," etc. Steevens cites Fletcher, *Woman's Prize:* "dart ladles, toasting-irons," etc.

104. *Hour.* A dissyllable, as often. Gr. 480.

108. *Rheum.* See on iii. 1. 22 above.

109. *Traded.* "Professional" (Schmidt). *Traded in it*=expert in it, as if it were his *trade.* Cf. *T. and C.* ii. 2. 64: "Two traded pilots," etc.

110. *Remorse.* See on 50 above.

116. *Here's a good world!* Ironical=*bad world the while!* in iv. 2. 100 above.

121. *Damn'd as black.* St. remarks: "S. had here probably in his mind the old religious plays of Coventry, some of which in his boyhood he might have seen, wherein the damned souls had their faces blackened." Sharp, in his account of these performances, says that there were uniformly three *white* and three *black* souls. He quotes the following ancient bill in this connection :

> "Itm̄ payd to iij whyte sollys   vs
> Itm̄ payd to iij blake sollys   vs
> Itm̄ for makyng and mendynge of the blakke soules hose   vjd
> p'd for blakyng the sollys fassys   —"

126. *Do but despair.* Do nothing but despair, only despair.

133. *Up.* Used intensively, as often by S. See *A. Y. L.* p. 155.

137. *Embounded.* Bounded, enclosed; used by S. only here. For the prefix *en-*, see Gr. 440.

140. *Amaz'd.* See on iv. 2. 137 above.

142. *Easy.* Easily; as very often. Cf. *Sonn.* 109. 3, *M. N. D.* v. 1. 22, *Macb.* ii. 3. 143, v. 8. 9, etc.

146. *Scamble.* Scramble, struggle. See *Hen. V.* p. 144 or *Much Ado*, p. 164.

147. *Unowed.* Unowned, or without rightful owner. Cf. *owe* in ii. 1. 109 above. "In this hour of ripened moral perception, the speaker suffers himself to confess that the only rightful possessor of England is gone, and that John is but possessor by tenure of usurpation and wrong; nevertheless, Philip's sense of fidelity and personal gratitude to the present occupier of the throne will not let him abandon him or his cause, especially now that they are in jeopardy and peril" (Clarke).

151. *From home.* Away from home, abroad.

152. *Waits.* Clarke says that the *on* of the next line is "understood" with *waits;* but this is not absolutely necessary. The verb may be transitive (as in *L. L. L.* v. 2. 63, etc.), and the *on* may be inserted for the measure or on account of the omission of the verb.

On the passage, cf. *J. C.* v. 1. 85 fol.

154. *Wrested.* Wrested from its rightful owner, usurped. Schmidt

thinks it may be a misprint for "wretched;" and the Camb. ed. gives the anonymous conjecture "wasted."

155. *Cincture.* Girdle; Pope's correction of the "center" of the folios. Clarke suggests that the latter may have been in familiar use as a corruption of the Fr. *ceinture.*

158. *Businesses.* S. uses the plural no less than six times. Cf. *A. W.* i. 1. 220, iii. 7. 5, iv. 3. 98, *W. T.* iv. 2. 15, and *Lear*, ii. 1. 129.

Are brief in hand = "must be speedily dispatched" (Schmidt).

ACT V.

SCENE I.—2. *Circle.* Diadem; as in *A. and C.* iii. 12. 18: "The circle of the Ptolemies." Cf. *round* in *Macb.* i. 2. 59 and iv. 1. 88.

Take again. Take it again. Some make *greatness and authority* the object, inserting a comma after *pope.*

6. *And from his holiness,* etc. And use all your power from his holiness. Cf. Gr. 419*a.*

7. *Inflam'd.* Burned up, destroyed.

8. *Counties.* Some take the word to be = counts, nobles (see *Much Ado,* p. 131); but it may have its ordinary sense, as Schmidt explains it.

12. *Mistemper'd.* Distempered (see on iv. 3. 21 above), disaffected. See *R. and J.* p. 142.

13. *Qualified.* Moderated, abated; as in *R. of L.* 424, *Ham.* iv. 7. 114, etc.

14. *The present time 's so sick,* etc. For the metaphor, cf. *Macb.* v. 2. 27. See also v. 2. 20 below.

19. *Convertite.* Convert or penitent; as in *R. of L.* 743 and *A. Y. L.* v. 4. 190.

25. *Is this Ascension-day?* See on p. 34 above.

27. *Give off.* Give up; the only instance of the expression in S.

31. *Dover Castle.* Hubert de Burgh with a hundred and forty soldiers defended it for four months (French).

35. *Amazement.* Confusion, bewilderment. Cf. the verb in iv. 2. 137 and iv. 3. 140 above.

54. *Glister.* Glisten (not used by S.). Cf. *M. of V.* ii. 7. 65: "All that glisters is not gold," etc.

55. *Become.* Adorn; as in ii. 1. 141 above.

59. *Forage.* Go forth in search of prey. Cf. *Hen. V.* i. 2. 110:

> "Whiles his most mighty father on a hill
> Stood smiling to behold his lion's whelp
> Forage in blood of French nobility."

See also the noun in *L. L. L.* iv. 1. 93: "And he [the lion] from forage will incline to play." Fl. quotes *Edward III.* ii. 1 (Shakespeare's part):

> "The lion doth become his bloody jaws,
> And grace his foragement by being wild,
> When vassals fear his trembling at their feet;"

and Chapman, *Bussy's Revenge:* "Lions foraging for prey."

60. *Displeasure.* Often used by S. in a stronger sense than now ; as in *Much Ado,* i. 3. 68, ii. 2. 6, *Cor.* iv. 5. 78, *Lear,* i. 1. 202, iii. 3. 5, etc.

66. *Upon the footing of our land.* Standing upon our own land.

67. *Orders.* Sr. adopts the "offers" of the Coll. MS. But *orders,* from meaning orderings, arrangements, may come to be=stipulations, conditions. Cf. v. 2. 4 below.

69. *Invasive.* Invading ; used by S. only here.

70. *Cocker'd.* Pampered ; used by S. nowhere else. For the masculine use of *wanton,* cf. *Rich. II.* v. 3. 10 and *Ham.* v. 2. 310.

71. *Flesh his spirit.* "Taste blood for the first time" (Fl.). Cf. 1 *Hen. IV.* v. 4. 133 :

> "Come, brother John ; full bravely hast thou flesh'd
> Thy maiden sword ;"

1 *Hen. VI.* iv. 7. 36 : "Did flesh his puny sword in Frenchmen's blood," etc. See also *Hen. V.* p. 160 (note on *Hath been flesh'd*) or *T. N.* p. 157 (note on *Well fleshed*).

72. *Mocking the air,* etc. Cf. *Macb.* i. 2. 49 :

> "Where the Norweyan banners flout the sky,
> And fan our people cold."

Malone remarks : "From these two passages Mr. Gray seems to have formed the first stanza of his celebrated Ode :

> 'Ruin seize thee, ruthless king!
> Confusion on thy banners wait!
> Though fann'd by conquest's crimson wing,
> They mock the air with idle state.'"

SCENE II.—2. *Remembrance.* A quadrisyllable ; as in *W. T.* iv. 4. 76 : "Grace and remembrance be to you both." Gr. 477.

3. *Precedent.* Original copy, first draught ; as in *Rich. III.* iii. 6. 7 : "The precedent was full as long a-doing."

4. *Order.* Arrangement, agreement. See on v. 1. 67 above.

6. *Sacrament.* Oath ; as in *Rich. II.* iv. 1. 328, v. 2. 97, etc.

13. *Plaster.* For the metaphor, cf. *Temp.* ii. 1. 139 :

> "you rub the sore
> When you should bring the plaster."

16. *Metal.* See on ii. 1. 401 above.

26. *Were.* The reading of the later folios ; the 1st has "Was."

27. *Stranger march.* The folios have "Stranger, march," which Clarke retains. Theo. made the correction. For *stranger*=foreign, cf. v. 1. 11 above.

30. *Spot.* The Coll. MS. has "thought," which W. adopts. "Spur" and "spite" have also been suggested. *Spot*=stain, disgrace (Schmidt) ; as in v. 7. 107 below. *Upon*=on account of ; as in iv. 2. 214 and v. 1. 18 above. *Enforced*=involuntary ; as in *M. of V.* v. 1. 240, *Rich. II.* i. 3. 264, etc.

34. *Clippeth.* Embraceth. Cf. 1 *Hen. IV.* iii. 1. 44 : "clipp'd in with the sea," etc. See also *Oth.* p. 192.

36. *Grapple.* Pope's correction of the "cripple" of the folios. Fl. adopts Steevens's conjecture of "gripple," which means the same.

39. *To spend.* Clarke and Fl. adopt Steevens's conjecture of "to-spend," in which the *to* is intensive ; but it seems to be merely an instance of the insertion of *to* with a second infinitive after its omission with the first. Cf. i. 1. 134 above : "hadst thou rather be . . . and to enjoy." See Gr. 350. There is no clear example of this archaic intensive *to* in S.

42. *Doth.* Changed by Hanmer to "Do ;" but it may be the old 3d person plural in *-th*. See *R. and J.* p. 140, and cf. Gr. 334.

44. "*Compulsion* is here used in reference to what Salisbury has just before called *this enforced cause ;* that is, the cause to which he felt himself compelled by *the infection of the time. Brave respect* is used for *noble consideration, patriotic regard*" (Clarke). Cf. iii. 1. 58 above.

45. *Dew.* For the application to tears, cf. *R. of L.* 1829, *L. L. L.* iv. 3. 29, *W. T.* ii. 1. 109, and *Rich. II.* v. 1. 9.

46. *Silverly.* Silver-like ; used by S. only here. The same is true of the verb *progress.*

50. *This shower,* etc. Malone compares *R. of L.* 1788 :

> "This windy tempest. till it blow up rain,
> Held back his sorrow's tide, to make it more."

59. *Full of warm blood.* The folios have "Full warm of blood," which may be right, though it does not suit the rest of the line so well as the transposition in the text. The latter is due to Heath, and is adopted by D. and the Camb. editors.

64. *An angel spake.* Fl. says : "This phrase was proverbial, and usually involved a quibble ; as in *Two Angry Women of Abington :*

> "*Coomes.* There speaks an angel. Is it good?
> "*Mrs. Gourney.* Ay.
> "*Coomes.* Then I can 't do amiss ; the good angel goes with me ;"

and in *Eastward Ho,* ii. 1 :

> "*Quicksilver.* Security will smell out ready money for you instantly.
> "*Petronel.* There spake an angel."

Here there may be a similar play upon the expression, referring to the *purse* just mentioned and to the *holy legate* whom he sees approaching. For the coin called an *angel,* cf. ii. 1. 590 and iii. 3. 8 above.

79. *Propertied.* Made a property of, treated as a mere tool or instrument. Cf. *T. N.* iv. 2. 99 : "they have here propertied me." Note also the use of the noun in *J. C.* iv. 1. 40 :

> "do not talk of him
> But as a property."

89. *Interest to.* Claim to, interest in ; as in 1 *Hen. IV.* iii. 2. 98 :

> "He hath more worthy interest to the state
> Than thou the shadow of succession."

99. *Underprop.* Support, uphold. Cf. *R. of L.* 53 : "Which of them both should underprop her fame ;" and *Rich. II.* ii. 2. 82 : "Here am I left to underprop his land," etc.

100. *Charge.* Expense ; as in i. 1. 49 above.

101. *Liable.* Allied, associated. Cf. its use = subject, in ii. 1. 490 above.

104. *Bank'd.* The most natural meaning would be "thrown up in-

trenchments before " (Steevens), but the corresponding passage in the
old play favours the interpretation "sailed along the banks of." Schmidt
thinks the word is probably=the Fr. *aborder*, to land on the banks of.
St. suggests that it is a term in card-playing=put into a bank or rest, won.

105. *Cards.*   S. here anticipates the invention of playing-cards by about
a century and a half.   See on i. i. 24 above.

107. *Set.*   Game, match ; as in *L. L. L.* v. 2. 29, *Hen. V.* i. 2. 262, etc.

113. *Drew this gallant head.*   Levied this gallant army.   For *drew*,
see on iv. 2. 118 above ; and on *head* cf. 1 *Hen. IV.* i. 3. 284 : "To save
our heads by raising of a head ;" *Id.* iv. 4. 25 : "a head Of gallant warriors," etc.

115. *Outlook.*   Outface (cf. v. 1. 49 above) ; the only instance of the
word in S.

124. *Wilful-opposite.*   Obstinately contrary ; not hyphened in the early
eds.   Cf. iii. 1. 254 above.

125. *Temporize.*   Come to terms ; as in *T. and C.* iv. 4. 6, *Cor.* iv. 6.
17, etc.

130. *And reason,* etc.   And there is reason, etc.   Cf. *W. T.* iv. 4. 417 :

" reason my son
Should choose himself a wife," etc.

132. *Unadvised.*   Inconsiderate, rash.   Cf. ii. 1. 45, 191 above.   *Harness'd*=wearing *harness*, or armour ; as in *T. and C.* i. 2. 8.

133. *Unhair'd.*   The folios have "vn-heard" or "unheard ;" corrected by Theo.   *Unhaired*=beardless.   Cf. v. 1. 69 above.   *Hair* was often
spelt *hear* or *heare.*   Schmidt prefers *unheard* (=unprecedented) ; and
the Coll. MS. has "unheard sauciness of."

138. *Take the hatch.*   Leap over the hatch.   See on i. 1. 170 above.

139. *Concealed wells.*   That is, wells in out-of-the-way places.   The
expression has troubled certain of the commentators.

144. *The crying of your nation's crow.*   "The sound of your nation's
crow ;" alluding to the crowing of the cock, which is the national bird of
France, and to the boastful crowing natural to Frenchmen, to which S.
has another allusion in *Hen. V.* iii. 6. 160 (Clarke).   Schmidt takes *crow*
to be a contemptuous name for the French cock.   Rowe changed *your*
to "our ;" and the Coll. MS. has "cock" for *crow.*

145. *His.*   The folios have "this ;" corrected by Rowe.

146. *Feebled.*   The verb occurs again in *Cor.* i. 1. 199.

149. *Aery.*   Brood.   See *Ham.* p. 207.   *Tower* was a term in falconry
for the spiral upward flight of the bird ; as *souse* was for its pouncing
upon its prey.   Cf. ii. 1. 350 above ; and see *Macb.* p. 203.

151. *Ingrate.*   "Ingrateful" (v. 7. 43 below), or ungrateful ; as in *T. N.*
v. 1. 116, *Cor.* v. 2. 92, etc.   *Revolts*=deserters ; as in v. 4. 7 below, and
in *Cymb.* iv. 4. 6.

154. *Pale-visag'd.*   Cf. "maid-pale" in *Rich. II.* iii. 3. 98.

157. *Needles.*   The 1st and 2d folios have "Needl's," indicating the
metrical contraction of the word.   Some editors give "neelds ;" as in *R.
of L.* 319, *M. N. D.* iii. 2. 204, and *Per.* iv. prol. 23.   See *M. N. D.* p. 165.

159. *Brave.*   Bravado.   Cf. 1 *Hen. VI.* iii. 2. 123 : "Now where 's the
Bastard's braves, and Charles his gleeks ?"

162. *Brabbler.* Brawler. It is the name of a dog in *T. and C.* v. 1.
99. Cf. *brabble*=brawl, in *T. N.* v. 1. 68, and see our ed. p. 162.

176. *And in his forehead sits,* etc. Cf. *Rich. II.* iii. 2. 160 :

" for within the hollow crown
That rounds the mortal temples of a king
Keeps Death his court, and there the antic sits," etc.

SCENE III.—8. *Swinstead.* Halliwell reads "Swineshead," which is
unquestionably correct; but S. copied the mistake from the old play.
Swineshead is in Lincolnshire, about seven miles southwest of Boston.
It is now a rural town, but was then a seaport. The abbey, about half a
mile east of the town, was founded by Robert de Greslei in 1134. It was
a large and magnificent structure, but nothing is now left of it. The
mansion known as Swineshead Abbey stands near the site, and was built
with materials from the ancient abbey (Timbs).

9. *Supply.* Reinforcements; as in v. 5. 12 below. See also 1 *Hen.
IV.* iv. 3. 3, 2 *Hen. IV.* i. 3. 28, etc.

11. *Are.* Changed by Capell to "Was ;" but *supply* is used as a col-
lective noun (cf. v. 5. 12). The relative in the intervening line takes a
singular verb, but this is not uncommon. See Gr. 247. For *wrack'd*
(=wrecked ; the only spelling in the early eds.), see *T. N.* p. 162.

The *Goodwin Sands* or "the Goodwins" (*M. of V.* iii. 1. 4) are danger-
ous shoals off the eastern coast of Kent, not far from the mouth of the
Thames. Tradition says that they were once an island belonging to Earl
Godwin, which was swallowed up by the sea about A.D. 1100.

THE GOODWIN SANDS, DURING A STORM.

12. *Richard.* The messenger here uses the Christian name given to
the knight, though he has just called him *Faulconbridge.* " It is as if the

poet wished to show that the renownedly brave man was known familiarly by both titles " (Clarke).

13. *Retire themselves.* Retreat. For the reflexive use, cf. *Temp.* v. 1.
310, *W. T.* iv. 4. 663, *Oth.* ii. 3. 386, etc.

SCENE IV.—1. *Stor'd with.* Well supplied with. Cf. *Hen. V.* iii. 5.
31 : " To new store France with bastard warriors," etc.

5. *In spite of spite.* " Come the worst that may " (Schmidt). Cf. 3
Hen. VI. ii. 3. 5 : " And, spite of spite, needs must I rest awhile."

7. *Revolts.* See on v. 2. 151 above.

10. *Bought and sold.* Betrayed. Cf. *C. of E.* iii. 1. 72 : " It would
make a man mad as a buck, to be so bought and sold." See also *Rich.
III.* v. 3. 305, *T. and C.* ii. 1. 51, etc.

11. *Unthread the rude eye.* Changed by Theo. to " Untread the rude
way," and in the Coll. MS. to " Untread the road-way." Johnson says
that " the metaphor is certainly harsh," but he does not think the passage corrupted. Malone compares *Lear*, ii. 1. 121 : " threading dark-
eyed night ;" and *Cor.* iii. 1. 127 : " They would not thread the gates."
See also *Rich. II.* v. 5. 17 :

> " It is as hard to come, as for a camel,
> To thread the postern of a needle's eye."

Clarke says : " The metaphor has the more propriety because to thread
the eye of a needle is a process of some difficulty [cf. the paraphrase from
the Bible in the passage just quoted], while to unthread a needle's eye is,
on the contrary, one of the most easy of tasks : therefore the proposal to
unthread the rude eye of rebellion appropriately metaphorizes the intricate
course they have taken in forsaking the English side and revolting to the
French, and also the facile one they would take in withdrawing themselves from it and returning to their natural allegiance." Schmidt under
Eye suggests that the word here may be a misprint for " tye " (*tie*) ; but
under *Unthread* he says : " The constant combination of the words *thread*
and *eye* in all these passages [the present one and those quoted above
from *Rich. II.* and *Lear*] is sufficient to refute the different emendations
proposed by the commentators, not excepting that attempted in this lexicon sub *Eye*." For the homely character of the metaphor, Halliwell
compares iv. 3. 148 above : " the bare-pick'd bone of majesty," etc.

14. *Lords.* The Camb. editors conjecture " lord," which is favoured by
the *he* in the next line. Cf. *Hen. V.* iv. 4. 80 : " The French might have
a good prey of us if *he* knew of it ;" and 30 below : " I say *again*, if Lewis
do win the day," where *Lewis* must be *the French* of the present passage.

This loud day. " By the one little monosyllable *loud* here, how finely
does the poet set before our imagination the uproar of battle—the drums,
and tramplings, and trumpetings, and shoutings, and groanings of an en-
gagement !" (Clarke).

17. *Moe.* More. See *A. Y. L.* p. 176.

18. *Saint Edmundsbury.* The ancient town of Bury St. Edmund's in
Suffolk, about 60 miles northeast of London. Portions of the abbey, in
which this famous meeting of the nobles took place, still remain. The
illustration of the altar on p. 111 (from Knight's *Pictorial Shakspere*) is

copied from Lydgate's *Life of St. Edmund* (Harl. MS. 2278) ; the manner of taking the oath, from an illumination in the *Metrical Hist. of Rich. II.* (Harl. MS. 1319), representing the Earl of Northumberland at Conway Castle, swearing on the gospels to secure safe conduct to Richard on his journey to London ; and the costumes, from the effigies of Salisbury (in Salisbury Cathedral), Pembroke (in the Temple Church, London), and other contemporary monuments.

23. *Quantity.* A *small* portion ; as in *T. of S.* iv. 3. 112 : "Away, thou rag, thou quantity, thou remnant ;" 2 *Hen. IV.* v. 1. 70 : "If I were sawed into quantities, I should make four dozen of such bearded hermit's staves," etc.

25. *Resolveth.* Dissolveth ; as in *Ham.* i. 2. 130 : "Thaw and resolve itself into a dew," etc.

27. *Use.* Utility, advantage.

29. *Hence.* In another world ; antithetical to *here*=this world, as in iv. 2. 89 above. Cf. *Ham.* iii. 2. 232 : "Both here and hence pursue me lasting strife," etc.

37. *Rated.* Appraised. "It were easy to change *rated* to *hated*, for an easier meaning, but *rated* suits better with *fine*. The Dauphin has *rated* your treachery, and set upon it a *fine*, which your lives must pay" (Johnson).

41. *Respect.* Consideration. Cf. iii. 1. 318 above.

42. *For that.* Because that. Gr. 151 and 287. The line is taken from the old play.

44. *In lieu whereof.* In return for which ; the only meaning of the phrase in S. See *A. Y. L.* p. 157.

45. *Rumour.* Confused sounds ; as in *J. C.* ii. 4. 18 : "I heard a bustling rumour, like a fray."

49. *Beshrew.* A mild form of imprecation. Cf. v. 5. 14 below.

50. *Favour.* Aspect, look. Cf. *Sonn.* 125. 5 : "dwellers on form and favour," etc.

52. *Untread.* Retrace. Cf. *V. and A.* 908 : "She treads the path that she untreads again." See also *M. of V.* ii. 6. 10.

53. *Bated and retired.* Abating and receding. Cf. *M. of V.* iv. 1. 72 : "And bid the main flood bate his usual height." On *retired*, cf. Gr. 374.

54. *Rankness.* Exuberance, excess, overflowing.

55. *O'erlook'd.* Schmidt make this=slighted, despised ; but it may be =risen so high as to look over. Cf. *overpeering* in *Ham.* iv. 5. 99 : "The ocean overpeering of his list." See also iii. 1. 23 above : "Like a proud river peering o'er his bounds."

60. *Right.* "In a manner deserving the name" (Schmidt) ; as in iii. 1. 183 above. Hanmer changed the word to "pight" (placed) and Capell to "fight." The Coll. MS. has "bright."

61. *Happy newness*, etc. "Happy innovation that purposes the restoration of the ancient rightful government" (Johnson).

SCENE V.—3. *English measure.* The folio reading, changed to "th' English measur'd" by Pope and some modern editors. As Fl. remarks, "the meaning is general, *at English measuring*, not specific."

M

4. *Retire.* See on ii. 1. 326 above.

7. *Tottering.* "Waving" (Fl.). Cf. *The Spanish Tragedy:*

> "A man hanging and tottering and tottering,
> As you know the wind will wave a man."

Schmidt makes it=hanging in rags, tattered. Cf. *tottered*=tattered, in 1 *Hen. IV.* iv. 2. 37 (1st folio): "a hundred and fiftie totter'd Prodigalls." The 1st and 2d quartos have "tottered" in *Rich. II.* iii. 3. 52: "this castle's totter'd battlements" ("tatter'd" in folios). If *tottering*= *tottered* here, it is an instance of the active participle used for the passive. See Gr. 372. The Coll. MS. has "totter'd."

Clearly is either=quite, completely (cf. iii. 4. 122 above), as Fl. explains it; or=stainlessly, as Schmidt gives it. The Coll. MS. has "closely," and the Camb. editors conjecture "cleanly."

13. *Are.* See on v. 3. 11 above.

14. *Shrewd.* Bad, evil. See *J. C.* p. 145 or *Hen. VIII.* p. 202.

18. *The stumbling night.* That is, in which one is liable to stumble. Cf. v. 6. 12 below: "eyeless night" (that is, in which one cannot see).

20. *Keep good quarter.* "Keep your posts or watches in good order" (Fl.). Cf. 1 *Hen. VI.* ii. 1. 63: "Had all your quarters been as safely kept."

22. *Adventure.* Hazard, chance. Cf. *C. of E.* ii. 2. 218: "At all adventures" (=at all hazards), etc.

SCENE VI.—6. *Perfect.* Right, correct; as in 2 *Hen. IV.* iii. 1. 88: "a perfect guess," etc.

12. *Eyeless.* See on v. 5. 18 above. Fl. thinks it is=starless, "the stars being the night's eyes, as the sun is the day's." The 1st folio has "endles," the later folios "endlesse" or "endless;" corrected by Theo. Schmidt explains "endless" as "infinite, excessive, that is, extremely dark."

15. *Scape.* Not "'scape," as usually printed. See *Ham.* p. 188 or Wb. s. v.

16. *Sans.* Without. See *A. Y. L.* p. 163.

17. *Brow of night.* "As we say, in the face of day" (Fl.).

22. *Swoon.* Spelt "swound" in the first three folios. Cf. *R. of L.* 1486, where it rhymes with *wounds.* Elsewhere in the early eds. we find "swoond," "swoon," "swoun," "swown," and "sound."

24. *Broke out.* Forced my way (Schmidt).

26. *The better arm you,* etc. "The better prepare yourself to encounter the sudden change that will take place in affairs after the king's death" (Clarke).

27. *At leisure.* That is, less promptly, or at other people's leisure.

28. *Taste.* It was the custom for kings to have their food tasted before it was served, as a precaution against poison. See *Rich. II.* p. 220, note on *Taste of it first.* Halliwell quotes Deloney, *Strange Histories*, 1607:

> "For why, the monke the taste before him tooke,
> Nor saw the king how ill it made him looke;
> And therefore he a hearty draught did take,
> Which of his royal life dispatch did make."

29. *Resolved.* Resolute, determined. Cf. *Rich. III.* i. 3. 340: "How now, my hardy, stout, resolved mates?"

Malone remarks: "Not one of the historians who wrote within sixty years after the death of King John mentions this very improbable story. The tale is, that a monk, to revenge himself on the king for a saying at which he took offence, poisoned a cup of ale, and having brought it to his majesty, drank some of it himself to induce the king to taste it, and soon afterwards expired. Thomas Wykes is the first who relates it, in his *Chronicle*, as a *report*."

32. *Who.* For *whom*, as often. Gr. 274.

39. *Power.* Force. See on iii. 3. 70 above.

40. *Taken by the tide.* On the 14th of October, 1216, as the king was attempting to ford the Wash at low water, and had already got across himself, with the greater part of his army, the return of the tide suddenly swept away the carriages and horses that conveyed all his baggage and treasures; and the spot is still known as "King's Corner." It was on the same night that the king arrived at the Cistercian monastery at Swineshead, and was taken with the fever of which he died.

44. *Doubt.* Fear. See on iv. 1. 19 above; and for *or ere*, on iv. 3. 20.

SCENE VII.—1. *Prince Henry.* The prince was only nine years old when his father died.

2. *Corruptibly.* So as to be corrupted; used by S. only here. For *pure* W. reads "poor," but the folio has "pure," not "pore" as he assumes. Halliwell cites Deloney's account of John's death in his *Strange Histories:* "Distempering then the pure unspotted braine."

10. *Orchard.* Garden. See *J. C.* p. 142.

John did not die at Swineshead (or *Swinstead*), as here represented. On the day after he arrived there (see on v. 6. 40 above), though very ill, he was conveyed in a litter to the Castle of Sleaford, and thence on the 16th of October to the Castle of Newark, where he expired on the 18th, in the 49th year of his age and the 17th of his reign.

16. *Insensible.* The folio has "inuisible," which is retained by K., the Camb. editors, and Fl. K. explains it as "unlooked-at, disregarded." Fl. puts a comma before it, and says that death "is visibly acting while preying on the body, but invisible when he attacks the mind." Neither of these interpretations seems to us satisfactory, and we have little hesitation in adopting Hanmer's emendation, as do D., St., Sr., W., H., and Clarke. Steevens suggested "invincible," and the Coll. MS. has "unvisited."

22. *Who chants*, etc. For the allusion to the poetic idea of the dying song of the swan, see *R. of L.* 1611 :

> "And now this pale swan in her watery nest
> Begins the sad dirge of her certain ending;"

Phœnix and Turtle, 15 : "the death-divining swan;" *Oth.* v. 2. 247 :

> "I will play the swan,
> And die in music;"

and *M. of V.* iii. 2. 44 :

> "Then if he lose, he makes a swan-like end,
>   Fading in music."

26. *Indigest.* Indigested or shapeless mass, chaos ; the only instance of the noun in S. The adjective (=chaotic, formless) occurs in *Sonn.* 114. 5 : "monsters and things indigest." Ovid (*Met.* i.) describes Chaos as " rudis indigestaque moles."

32. *I am a scribbled form*, etc. See p. 35 above.

35. *Fare.* Metrically a dissyllable (Gr. 480). Fl. reads "ill-faring," and Daniel suggests " ill-fated."

37. *To thrust his icy fingers*, etc. Steevens quotes Dekker, *Gul's Horn-book*, 1609 : "the morning waxing cold, thrust his frosty fingers into thy bosome ;" and *The Great Frost*, etc., 1608 : " The cold hand of winter is thrust into our bosoms." The corresponding passage in the old play reads thus :

> " Philip, some drink. O, for the frozen Alps
>   To tumble on, and cool this inward heat,
>   That rageth as a furnace seven-fold hot."

42. *Cold comfort.* There is a play upon the phrase, which was ironi- cally used, as it still is, in the sense of small comfort. Cf. *T. of S.* iv. 1. 33 : "or shall I complain of thee to our mistress, whose hand, she being now at hand, thou shalt soon feel, to thy cold comfort, for being slow in thy hot office?" For the quibbling on a death-bed, cf. *Rich. II.* ii. 1. 73 fol., and see our ed. p. 172.

Strait. Niggardly, parsimonious.

43. *Ingrateful.* Used by S. interchangeably with *ungrateful.* So *in- certain* and *uncertain, infortunate* (ii. 1. 178 above) and *unfortunate*, etc.

50. *Spleen.* Eagerness, impetuosity. See on ii. 1. 68 above.

51. *Set.* That is, close.

52. *Tackle.* For the metaphor, cf. *Cor.* iv. 5. 67 :

> "Thou hast a grim appearance, and thy face
> Bears a command in 't ; though thy tackle 's torn,
> Thou show'st a noble vessel."

58. *Module.* The spelling of the folio here and in *A. IV.* iv. 3. 114: "this counterfeit module." Elsewhere it is *model*, which Hanmer and others substitute here. The word is=image ; as in *Rich. II.* i. 2. 28 :

> " In that thou seest thy wretched brother die,
> Who was the model of thy father's life ;"

Hen. VIII. iv. 2. 132 : " The model of our chaste loves, his young daugh- ter," etc.

Confounded=ruined ; the most common meaning in S. See *Macb.* p. 189, and cf. iv. 2. 29 above.

59. *Preparing hitherward.* For the ellipsis, cf. *Rich. II.* v. 1. 37: "pre- pare thee hence for France ;" and *Cor.* iv. 5. 140 : " Who am prepar'd against your territories."

60. *Heaven.* Walker conjectures "God." Very likely that was the original word, changed by the editors of the folio on account of the statute of James against the use of the divine name on the stage. Cf. iii. 1. 156 above; and see *Oth.* p. 11.

62. *Upon.* On account of, for the sake of. Cf. ii. 1. 597, iv. 2. 214, and v. 1. 18 above. Gr. 191.

63. *Were in the Washes,* etc.   This accident really happened to John himself.   See on v. 6. 40 above.

66. *But now a king, now thus.*   V. remarks : " The tragic poet has here brought the death of John into immediate contact with his most atrocious crime, as the natural sequence and just retribution of his guilt towards young Arthur.   The matter-of-fact commentators complain, with Mr. Courtenay (*Commentaries on Shakespeare's Historical Plays*), that here is a long interval leaped over at once in which 'foreign and cruel wars had raged with varied success, and *one* event had happened of which, although it is that by which we now chiefly remember King John, no notice is taken whatever.   This is no other than the signature of *Magna Charta.*'   The plain answer to this is, that the poet's design was not to turn the chronicle of John's reign into dramatic dialogue, but to produce from the materials an historical tragedy ; for which purpose Constance, Arthur, and the half-fictitious Faulconbridge afforded more suitable materials for his imagination than *Magna Charta,* and the political rights of Englishmen acquired under it.   By the selection he made he was naturally led to the exhibition of female character as intense, as passionate, and as overflowing with feeling, and with the most eloquent expression, as his own Juliet, but with the same all-absorbing affection transferred from the lover to an only child.   On the other hand, had he chosen the great political question for the turning-point of interest in his drama—and if touched on at all it must have been made the main and central point of the action—it would have required all the poet's skill to have avoided the too literal but unpoetical truth which Canning has so drolly ridiculed in his mock-German play, when one of the exiled Barons informs the other that—

> 'The charter of our liberties receiv'd
> The royal signature at five o'clock,
> When messengers were instantly dispatch'd
> To cardinal Pandulph, and their Majesties,
> After partaking of a cold collation,
> Return'd to Windsor.'

" Mr. Knight's remarks on this point are exceeedingly just and eloquent :—' The interval of fourteen years, between the death of Arthur and the death of John, is annihilated.   Causes and consequences, separated in the proper history by long digressions and tedious episodes, are brought together.   The attributed murder of Arthur lost John all the inheritances of the house of Anjou, and allowed the house of Capet to triumph in his overthrow.   Out of this grew a larger ambition, and England was invaded.   The death of Arthur, and the events which marked the last days of John, were separated in their cause and effect by time only, over which the poet leaps.   It is said that a man who was on the point of drowning saw, in an instant, all the events of his life in connection with his approaching end.   So sees the poet.   It is his to bring the beginnings and the ends of events into that real union and dependence, which even the philosophical historian may overlook, in tracing their course.   It is the poet's office to preserve a unity of action ; it is the historian's to show a consistency of progress.   In the chroniclers we have manifold changes of fortune in the life of John, after Arthur of

Brittany has fallen. In Shakespeare, Arthur of Brittany is at once revenged. The heart-broken mother and her boy are not the only sufferers from double courses. The spirit of Constance is appeased by the fall of John. The Niobe of a Gothic age, who vainly sought to shield her child from as stern a destiny as that with which Apollo and Artemis pursued the daughter of Tantalus, may rest in peace !' "

74. *Now, now, you stars*, etc. Addressed to the revolted nobles who had returned to their allegiance.

86. *Presently to leave.* Immediately to give up. For *presently*, cf. ii. 1. 538 above.

99. *At Worcester.* John died at Newark (see on 10 above), commending his body and soul to God and to St. Wulfstan, the last great English saint who had been canonized. His body, arrayed in royal apparel, was accordingly conveyed to Worcester, where it was interred in the Cathedral, the great church begun by Wulfstan in 1084 and dedicated to his honour in 1218.* The tomb on which the king's effigy rests (see cut on p. 131 above) is a work of the 16th century, but the effigy itself is said to be the original cover of the stone coffin in which the remains of John were discovered under the pavement of the choir in 1797. It is the earliest sculptured representation of an English monarch that remains in the country.

108. *Give you thanks.* Rowe's correction of the "give thanks" of the folios. The Camb. editors conjecture "fain give thanks."

110. *O, let us pay*, etc. "As previously we have found sufficient cause for lamentation, let us not waste the present time in superfluous sorrow" (Steevens). Clarke paraphrases the passage thus: "Let us pay but the due amount of lamentation to that woe which is past ; since time now promises to put a period to our griefs by better unity among ourselves."

116. *Come the three corners*, etc. That is, let the rest of the world come against us, and we shall withstand them. Cf. *Temp.* i. 2. 491 : "all corners else o' the earth;" and *Cymb.* iii. 4. 39 : "All corners of the world."

118. *If England to itself do rest but true.* Cf. the ending of the old play:

> "Let England live but true within itself,
> And all the world can never wrong her state.
>
> *   *   *   *   *
>
> If England's peers and people join in one,
> Nor pope, nor Fraunce, nor Spain, can do them wrong."

See also 3 *Hen. VI.* iv. 1. 40 :

> "Why, knows not Montague that of itself
> England is safe, if true within itself?"

Steevens cites Churchyard, *Discourse of Rebellion*, 1570 :

---

* In 1207 John visited Worcester, and after praying at the tomb of Wulfstan gave three hundred marks for the repair of the Cathedral.

According to Holinshed, the king was buried at Croxton Abbey in Staffordshire ; but Matthew Paris states that it was at Worcester. He says: "Et his ita gestis, sciscitatus est ab eo Abbas de Croestuna si ipsum mori contingeret, ubi vellet eligere sepulturam. Cui Rex respondens dixit, Deo et Sancto Wlstano corpus et animam meam commendo. Qui postea in nocte quae diem Sancti Lucae Evangelistae proxime sequuta est, ex hac vita migravit. Cujus corpus regio schemate ornatum ad Wigorniam delatum est ; et in ecclesia Cathedrali ab Episcopo loci honorifice tumulatum."

"O Britayne bloud, marke this at my desire:
If that you sticke together as you ought
This lyttle yle may set the world at nought."

Reed traces the sentiment back to Andrew Borde (who died in 1549),
Introd. of Knowledge: "for if they [the English] were true wythin themselves they nede not to feare although al nacions were set against them."

ADDENDA.

MRS. SIDDONS ON CONSTANCE.—Mrs. Siddons left behind her in manuscript her own analysis of the character of Constance, and we extract
from Campbell's *Life of Siddons* this commentary of a great actress on
the poet :

"My idea of Constance is that of a lofty and proud spirit, associated
with the most exquisite feelings of maternal tenderness, which is, in
truth, the predominant feature of this interesting personage. The sentiments which she expresses, in the dialogue between herself, the King of
France, and the Duke of Austria, at the commencement of the second
act of this tragedy, very strongly evince the amiable traits of a humane
disposition and of a grateful heart.

*   *   *   *   *   *   *   *   *

"The ideas one naturally adopts of her qualities and appearance are,
that she is noble in mind, and commanding in person and demeanour ;
that her countenance was capable of all the varieties of grand and tender expression, often agonized, though never distorted by the vehemence
of her agitations. Her voice, too, must have been 'propertied like the
tuned spheres,' obedient to all the softest inflections of maternal love, to
all the pathos of the most exquisite sensibility, to the sudden burst of
heart - rending sorrow, and to the terrifying imprecations of indignant
majesty, when writhing under the miseries inflicted on her by her das-
tardly oppressors and treacherous allies. The actress whose lot it is to
personate this great character should be richly endowed by nature for its
various requirements ; yet, even when thus fortunately gifted, much,
very much, remains to be effected by herself ; for in the performance of
the part of Constance great difficulties, both mental and physical, present themselves. And perhaps the greatest of the former class is that
of imperiously holding the mind reined in to the immediate perception
of those calamitous circumstances which take place during the course of
her sadly eventful history. The necessity for this severe abstraction will
sufficiently appear, when we remember that all those calamitous events
occur while she herself is absent from the stage ; so that this power is
indispensable for that reason alone, were there no other to be assigned
for it. Because, if the representative of Constance shall ever forget,
even behind the scenes, those disastrous events which impel her to break
forth into the overwhelming effusions of wounded friendship, disappointed
ambition, and maternal tenderness, upon the first moment of her appearance in the third act, when, stunned with terrible surprise, she exclaims—

'Gone to be married—gone to swear a peace!
False blood to false blood join'd—gone to be friends!'—

if, I say, the mind of the actress for one moment wanders from these distressing events, she must inevitably fall short of that high and glorious
colouring which is indispensable to the painting of this magnificent portrait.

"The quality of abstraction has always appeared to me so necessary
in the art of acting that I shall probably, in the course of these remarks,
be thought too frequently and pertinaciously to advert to it. I am now,
however, going to give a proof of its usefulness in the character under
our consideration; and I wish my opinion were of sufficient weight to
impress the importance of this power on the minds of all candidates for
dramatic fame. Here, then, is one example among many others which I
could adduce. Whenever I was called upon to personate the character
of Constance, I never, from the beginning of the play to the end of my
part in it, once suffered my dressing-room door to be closed, in order
that my attention might be constantly fixed on those distressing events
which, by this means, I could plainly hear going on upon the stage, the
terrible effects of which progress were to be represented by me. More-
over, I never omitted to place myself, with Arthur in my hand, to hear
the march, when, upon the reconciliation of England and France, they
enter the gates of Angiers to ratify the contract of marriage between the
Dauphin and the Lady Blanch; because the sickening sounds of that
march would usually cause the bitter tears of rage, disappointment, betrayed confidence, baffled ambition, and, above all, the agonizing feelings
of maternal affection, to gush into my eyes. In short, the spirit of the
whole drama took possession of my mind and frame, by my attention being incessantly riveted to the passing scenes. Thus did I avail myself
of every possible assistance, for there was need of all in this most ardu-
ous effort; and I have no doubt that the observance of such circumstances, however irrelevant they may appear upon a cursory view, was
powerfully aidant in the representations of those expressions of passion
in the remainder of this scene, which have been only in part considered,
and to the conclusion of which I now proceed.

"Goaded and stung by the treachery of her faithless friends, and almost maddened by the injuries they have heaped upon her, she becomes
desperate and ferocious as a hunted tigress in defence of her young, and
it seems that existence itself must nearly issue forth with the utterance
of that frantic and appalling exclamation—

'A wicked day, and not a holy day,
What hath this day deserv'd? what hath it done,' etc.

"When King Philip says to her—

'By heaven, lady, you shall have no cause
To curse the fair proceedings of this day.
Have I not pawn'd to you my majesty?'—

what countenance, what voice, what gesture, shall realize the scorn and
indignation of her reply to the heartless King of France? And then the
awful, trembling solemnity, the utter helplessness of that soul-subduing,
scriptural, and prophetic invocation—

'Arm, arm, you heavens, against these perjur'd kings!
A widow cries: be husband to me, heavens!
Let not the hours of this ungodly day
Wear out the day in peace ; but, ere sunset,
Set armed discord 'twixt these perjur d kings '

" If it ever were, or ever shall be, portrayed with its appropriate and solemn energy, it must be then, and then only, when the power I have so much insisted on, co-operating also with a high degree of enthusiasm, shall have transfused the mind of the actress into the person and situation of the august and afflicted Constance.   The difficulty, too, of representing, with tempered rage and dignified contempt, the biting sarcasm of the speeches to Austria (iii. 1) may be more easily imagined than explained.

" But, in truth, to beget, in these whirlwinds of the soul, such temperance as, according to the lesson of our inspired master, shall give them smoothness, is a difficulty which those only can appreciate who have made the effort.

" I cannot, indeed, conceive, in the whole range of dramatic character, greater difficulty than that of representing this grand creature.   Brought before the audience in the plenitude of her afflictions ; oppression and falsehood having effected their destructive mark ; the full storm of adversity, in short, having fallen upon her in the interval of their absence from her sight, the effort of pouring properly forth so much passion as past events have excited in her, without any visible previous progress towards her climax of desperation, seems almost to exceed the power of imitation.   Hers is an affliction of so ' sudden, floodgate, and o'erbearing nature ' that art despairs of realizing it, and the effort is almost life-exhausting.   Therefore, whether the majestic, the passionate, the tender Constance has ever yet been, or ever will be, personated to the entire satisfaction of sound judgment and fine taste, I believe to be doubtful ; for I believe it to be nearly impossible.

" I now come to the concluding scene ; and I believe I shall not be thought singular when I assert that, though she has been designated the ambitious Constance, she has been ambitious only for her son.   It was for him, and him alone, that she aspired to, and struggled for, hereditary sovereignty.   For example, you find that, from that fatal moment when he is separated from her, not one regret for lost regal power or splendour ever escapes from her lips ; no, not one idea does she from that instant utter which does not unanswerably prove that all other considerations are annihilated in the grievous recollections of motherly love. That scene (iii. 4), I think, must determine that maternal tenderness is the predominant feature of her character.

" Her gorgeous affliction. if such an expression is allowable, is of so sublime and so intense a character that the personation of its grandeur, with the utterance of its rapid and astonishing eloquence, almost overwhelms the mind that meditates its realization, and utterly exhausts the frame which endeavours to express its agitations."

THE "TIME-ANALYSIS" OF THE PLAY.—This is summed up by Mr. P. A. Daniel (*Trans. of New Shaks. Soc.* 1877–79, p. 263) as follows :
"Time of this play seven days ; with intervals, comprising in all not more than three or four months.

Day 1. Act I. sc. i.
　　　　Interval. Return of French Ambassador, and arrival of John in France.
"　2. Act II. sc. i., Act III. sc. i. to iii.
　　　　*Interval.**
"　3. Act III. sc. iv.
　　　　Interval.†
"　4. Act IV. sc. i. to iii.
　　　　Interval.‡
"　5. Act V. sc. i.
　　　　Interval.§
"　6. Act V. sc. ii. to v.
"　7. Act V. sc. vi. and vii.

Historical time : A.D. 1199–1216 ; the whole of King John's reign."

THE ILLUSTRATIONS.—Most of these are from Knight's *Pictorial Shakspere*, and are meant to be "illustrations" in the strict sense of the term. The figures of historical characters are from their monumental effigies and other contemporaneous representations. For the cut on page 111, which will give a general idea of the military and priestly costume of the period, see p. 176, note on *Saint Edmundsbury*. The "Room of State" on p. 41 is an ideal sketch, but is in keeping with the architecture of John's time. The view of Angiers (p. 51) is from an old print.

---

* " Some little time must be supposed to have elapsed since the battle ; for the French know that John has fortified the places he has won, and has returned to England ; from whence also they have intelligence that the Bastard is ransacking the Church."
† "During this interval, the deaths of Constance and Elinor (28th March and 1st April) must take place (see Act IV. sc. ii.)."
‡ "The arrival of Ascension Day, the presence of Pandulph, the news of the Dauphin's successes, imperatively demand an interval between this scene and the preceding Act ; on the other hand, we find that the Bastard has only now returned from his mission to the nobles, and that the King now hears for the first time of Arthur's actual death : these facts are incompatible with any interval ; they connect this scene with the scenes of Act IV., as part of Day 4. The main plot, however, is impossible without a supposed interval, and we must force the play to allow it."
§ "Including at least Pandulph's return journey to the Dauphin, the Bastard's preparation for defence, and his and King John's journey with their army to Edmundsbury."

INDEX OF WORDS AND PHRASES EXPLAINED.

Ay, marry, now my soul hath elbow-room (v. 7. 28).

SHAKESPEARE.

WITH NOTES BY WM. J. ROLFE, A.M.

The Merchant of Venice.
The Tempest.
Julius Cæsar.
Hamlet.
As You Like it.
Henry the Fifth.
Macbeth.
Henry the Eighth.
A Midsummer-Night's Dream.
Richard the Second.
Richard the Third.
Much Ado About Nothing.
Antony and Cleopatra.
Romeo and Juliet.
Othello.
Twelfth Night.
The Winter's Tale.
King John.
Henry IV. Part I.
Henry IV. Part II.

King Lear.
The Taming of the Shrew.
All 's Well That Ends Well.
Coriolanus.
Comedy of Errors.
Cymbeline.
Merry Wives of Windsor.
Measure for Measure.
Two Gentlemen of Verona.
Love's Labour 's Lost.
Timon of Athens.
Henry VI. Part I.
Henry VI. Part II.
Henry VI. Part III.
Troilus and Cressida.
Pericles, Prince of Tyre.
The Two Noble Kinsmen.
Poems.
Sonnets.
Titus Andronicus.

Illustrated. 16mo, Cloth, 56 cents per vol.; Paper, 40 cents per vol.

FRIENDLY EDITION, complete in 20 vols., 16mo, Cloth, $30 00; Half Calf, $60 00. (*Sold only in Sets.*)

In the preparation of this edition of the English Classics it has been the aim to adapt them for school and home reading, in essentially the same way as Greek and Latin Classics are edited for educational purposes. The chief requisites are a pure text (expurgated, if necessary), and the notes needed for its thorough explanation and illustration.

Each of Shakespeare's plays is complete in one volume, and is preceded by an Introduction containing the "History of the Play," the "Sources of the Plot," and "Critical Comments on the Play."

From HORACE HOWARD FURNESS, Ph.D., LL.D., *Editor of the "New Variorum Shakespeare."*

No one can examine these volumes and fail to be impressed with the conscientious accuracy and scholarly completeness with which they are edited. The educational purposes for which the notes are written Mr. Rolfe never loses sight of, but like "a well-experienced archer hits the mark his eye doth level at."

From F. J. FURNIVALL, *Director of the New Shakspere Society, London.*

The merit I see in Mr. Rolfe's school editions of Shakspere's Plays over those most widely used in England is that Mr. Rolfe edits the plays as works of a poet, and not only as productions in Tudor English. Some editors think that all they have to do with a play is to state its source and explain its hard words and allusions ; they treat it as they would a charter or a catalogue of household furniture, and then rest satisfied. But Mr. Rolfe, while clearing up all verbal difficulties as carefully as any Dryasdust, always adds the choicest extracts he can find, on the spirit and special "note" of each play, and on the leading characteristics of its chief personages. He does *not* leave the student without help in getting at Shakspere's chief attributes, his characterization and poetic power. And every practical teacher knows that while every boy can look out hard words in a lexicon for himself, not one in a score can, unhelped, catch points of and realize character, and feel and express the distinctive individuality of each play as a poetic creation.

From Prof. EDWARD DOWDEN, LL.D., *of the University of Dublin, Author of "Shakspere : His Mind and Art."*

I incline to think that no edition is likely to be so useful for school and home reading as yours. Your notes contain so much accurate instruction, with so little that is superfluous ; you do not neglect the æsthetic study of the play ; and in externals, paper, type, binding, etc., you make a book "pleasant to the eye" (as well as "to be desired to make one wise")—no small matter, I think, with young readers and with old.

From EDWIN A. ABBOTT, M.A., *Author of "Shakespearian Grammar."*

I have not seen any edition that compresses so much necessary information into so small a space, nor any that so completely avoids the common faults of commentaries on Shakespeare—needless repetition, superfluous explanation, and unscholar-like ignoring of difficulties.

From HIRAM CORSON, M.A., *Professor of Anglo-Saxon and English Literature, Cornell University, Ithaca, N.Y.*

In the way of annotated editions of separate plays of Shakespeare, for educational purposes, I know of none quite up to Rolfe's.